UPHEAVAL!

Ogre's Assistant

Book Two

DJ Martin

Chapter 1

"We need to talk," Cassandra said as she made my morning latte.

"About your wedding plans? Then you've set a date?" I eagerly replied. Cassandra was my BFF and the owner of the deli downstairs from my office. She was engaged to one of the guys who worked for her. After a few hiccups, she and Tommy had finally decided to make it a permanent arrangement.

"No. Well, yes, we need to talk about that, too. But I was referring to testing your magical abilities."

Shit. It had only been a couple of weeks since we'd banished a matchmaking demon who was making my life hell and I was enjoying having a normal life. Well, as normal as it could be given that my boss, Evander, was a smelly ogre who threw temper tantrums on a daily basis.

"I know what your dad said at the winter ceremony but honestly, I don't think I'm a witch. I never do anything magical like you and Tommy."

Did I forget to mention my best friend was also a witch? Normal is a relative term for me.

Cassandra sighed. "Just because you don't go cooking up potions on a regular basis doesn't mean you don't have any magical abilities. I've been seeing signs. You *do* need to find out so if you are, you can be trained to handle your powers."

I sighed right back. "I don't have time to be a witch. And even if I did, I don't want to be one. I like my life just the way it is. Can we just forget about it?"

"We can't *forget* about it but we can table the discussion for a little while. Amy, I'm not kidding when I say if you have magical abilities, you need to learn about them. Bad things, *disastrous* things can happen to someone who doesn't know how to control their own abilities. I'll let it slide for now but I'm not going to let up on you for long.

"In the meantime, we do need to talk about the handfasting. Can you come over for dinner tonight?"

For one of her meals, I was almost always available. Having a chef for a friend when one hated to cook was a definite benefit. But not this night. My side job as a paranormal romance author took precedence over my stomach. "Sorry, can't. I have an editing deadline looming and it's going to be nose to the grindstone for the next several nights. What do we need to talk about?"

"Tommy and I have almost everything set including the date, which is the Spring Equinox. I was going to tell you what we have planned and then sometime real soon, you and I need to go dress shopping."

I had to think a moment. My calendar consisted of my boss' parties and writing deadlines. "The Spring Equinox? That's mid-March, right? How are you going to pull everything together in less than two months?"

"You're right on the date. This year it's March twenty-first. Pulling it together was actually fairly easy. We just made a couple of phone calls to people we know for catering and the disc jockey. Tommy's dad knows someone on the Parks and Recreation Board and arranged the site. My only problem is getting Mom to pare down her part of the guest list. She seems to think this is going to be the biggest magical gathering of the year and I'll be damned if I'm going to feed some of those jackasses."

I laughed at that one. Both sets of their parents were pretty high up in the magical community but thus far, neither child had shown a lick of interest in that type of politicking. Then again, they were fairly young for a witch and wizard. "I'm assuming you told her family and close friends only."

"Naturally. But all those high muckety-mucks are *close friends* in her mind. She's going to have to cut her list by more than half and she's not happy."

"I have faith. I should have everything to my editor by Friday so how about either Sunday or Monday after work for shopping?"

She thought a bit. Sunday was the only day off we had in common – I worked Monday through Friday and the deli was open Tuesday through Saturday. "How about next Sunday? We have things to do this weekend."

I promised to write it on my calendar and then headed upstairs to begin my day. While my pot of coffee perked and the computer whirred its way to functionality, I thought about the wedding – handfasting. (I was going to have to wrap my head around the new vocabulary.) I knew she wanted something simple and outdoors but an outdoor wedding – handfasting – in March? In Minneapolis? The weather was awfully iffy at that time of year. I'd have to ask about alternate plans when we went dress shopping.

Mondays are never fun at my office. The aforementioned ogre owned the largest personal security firm in the Upper Midwest, specializing in providing non-human bodyguards. Although everyone had Ev's cell number for emergencies at night and on weekends, there were always a boatload of non-emergency daily reports to read immediately just in case there was a situation warranting fast attention, plus my normal load of email about the business end of the things.

I'd just finished slogging through the emails when a horrible aroma permeated my office. I knew my reading had taken far more time than I'd anticipated because when I looked at the clock down in the corner of my computer screen, it read nearly eleven o'clock. Without looking up from my notepad I said, "Good morning, Ev. How was your weekend?"

"It was *wonderful*," Ev gushed. That caused me to look up. Ev didn't usually gush. But the look on his face said it all. Ev was in love. Again. He fell in lust on a regular basis and if the lusty get-togethers lasted for more than a month or two, he thought he was in love. He and another ogre, Marianna, had been seeing each other regularly for about three months, so it was time. I raised an eyebrow.

"Marianna and I spent the most wonderful weekend. Parties both Friday and Saturday nights punctuated by some of the best sex I've ever had."

I lowered my eyebrows and wrinkled my nose. Eeew. Ogre sex. Not something I wanted to think about on a Monday morning. I told him as much.

He shrugged his shoulders. "What time is Sally getting here? I'm taking Marianna on vacation in a couple of months and I want to get all the arrangements made. Just the two of us in a woodland cabin for a whole week. I can't wait." (Sally was *my* assistant and part of her job involved handling the travel arrangements.)

I guffawed. "You? Vacation for a whole week? Five bucks says you can't stay off the phone for more than two days. And as you well know, Sally comes in about one. Write everything down and put it on her desk." I tore a sheet off my notepad. "Here's your list of phone calls to make. Oh, and the Petrolino contract is up next month. Decide if you want to renew it as is or make changes. It's been in your inbox for the last two weeks."

"This time will be different. I really want to spend the time alone with Marianna, away from work concerns. You won't hear a peep out of me the whole time."

I snorted as Ev turned to leave my office. My boss couldn't stay away from work or the glitzy parties that long. I knew that whenever the vacation was, I'd be five dollars richer. I turned back to the paperwork on my desk.

Sally came in promptly at one, looking as always like a chic Valkyrie. I was continually amazed that a society matron wanted to work. But there she was in her designer suit and understated-yet-expensive jewelry, with her perfectly-coiffed blonde hair and ice-blue eyes, picking up Ev's note and laughing. She came into my office.

"Did you know Ev wants to go on vacation?"

"Yep," I chuckled. "I bet him five bucks he wouldn't stay away from work more than two days. I forgot to ask him. When?"

"Last week in March. And a cabin? Away from the city and all the parties? I'll go halfsies on the bet with you. There's no way he'll last!"

We both laughed again and went back to work. At the appointed hour – four o'clock, I shut down my computer and walked the three blocks home, anticipating my afternoon nap. Starting work at seven-ish gave me the perk of leaving early and getting a nice, long afternoon nap in before changing hats from administrative assistant to author.

I shared my dinner salad with a tuna garnish with my spoiled cat, Fudge, and sat down to do my least-favorite authorial task: editing. Oh yes, I had an excellent professional editor but all the changes she made were only suggestions. I still had to go through every single one, decide if they were changes I wanted to make and then do some rewriting to make it all flow. I'd much prefer if I could just write the stories and have them come out perfect the first time.

Normally, Fudge just curled up next to the keyboard and supervised when I wrote. Tonight, however, he wasn't content to just sleepily oversee. Every time I positioned my hands over the keys, he batted them away. Twice, he knocked my cell phone to the floor and each time I picked it up, it was ready to dial Cassandra.

I sighed with exasperation, glared at him and put him on the floor. "I don't know what's wrong with you but I really have to work. I know you like Cassandra but she can't come over to play tonight. Give it a rest, will you?"

Although I spoke to Fudge as if he understood English, he was just a cat. But this night, I swore he understood me. After glaring back at me, he heaved a sigh and, padding over to the couch and curling up on it, began to give himself what was probably his hundredth bath of the day. I finally could get down to – ick, editing.

Chapter 2

March had come in like a lion with a lot of snow. But only two weeks into the month, it finally felt like spring was arriving. The snow melted and dried up quickly. Early flowers started poking their stalks above the ground. The population started emerging onto the sidewalks and paths around the lakes like people waking from a season-long sleep. The morning of the vernal equinox dawned sunny and unusually warm.

I would normally have bemoaned sitting in an office all day but not this particular Tuesday. Instead of sitting at my desk, plowing through piles of paperwork, I was running around like a chicken with its head cut off. It was the day of Cassandra and Tommy's handfasting.

As the maid of honor, I had to dress and prepare not only myself but the blushing bride as well. In the preceding two months, I'd found out a witch/wizard wedding was pretty much like every other. Invitations, flowers, reception … the whole nine. About the only difference was what they said to each other. They even had to do the blood tests and courthouse thing to make it legal, which we'd taken care of on Monday.

I didn't need to be at Cassandra's until eleven but naturally, I was awake at my usual early hour, thanks to the fact that I couldn't have room-darkening drapes. Fudge shredded anything decent. Being up that early gave me plenty of time to bemoan the fact that I wouldn't be able to take my afternoon nap.

After checking the pile on the couch about a hundred times, still feeling like I was missing something, it was finally time to leave. I grabbed my dress, accessories and makeup and with loaded arms, walked the three blocks to her house.

It was already bedlam there. Gert, Cassandra's cousin, childhood buddy and the other attendant, was in tears, sobbing how she'd never thought Cassandra would get married and that she and

Tommy were so perfect for each other. Celeste, Cassandra's mother, was on the phone, harassing the caterer. Cassandra was trying to calm them down. Tommy and his soon-to-be father-in-law, Marcus, had wisely left and were doing whatever guys do the morning of the wedding at Tommy's father's house.

"Hey," I yelled. "We still have three hours. That's plenty of time to get everyone ready, everything together and get over to the park. Cassandra, is there any coffee left?" Gert's crying subsided to a sniffle, Celeste hung up the phone and both just looked at me.

"Everything is on schedule and unless one of us is going to require more time in the bathroom than I anticipate, why don't we all take a breath, huh?" I said a little more quietly.

"I just made a fresh pot. Help yourself." Cassandra came over, took my things and gave me a hug, quietly saying, "Thanks for that. Mom and Gert are giving me a headache. I've told Mom things are under control but she doesn't believe me, and Gert won't stop blubbering."

Just as I finished pouring my coffee, the doorbell rang. It was the florist's delivery guy with our part of the floral arrangements. I took delivery of two boxes and three centerpiece arrangements. After confirming he was on his way to drop off the rest of it at Tommy's dad's, I opened the boxes to sort through, oohing and aahing to myself. The centerpieces were mostly white carnations and daisies with a scattering of deep yellow roses. Everything for the ceremony itself was white roses and rosemary. Although I'd never pictured using herbs in a bouquet before, I couldn't help but be impressed with the beauty, not to mention the fragrance.

"Wow. They did a wonderful job with what to them was an unusual request," Cassandra said as she came up behind me.

"I'll admit it's unusual to me," I countered. "The white roses I get, but rosemary?"

"You know the roses signify purity. Rosemary is traditional in our handfastings. It means fidelity. The guy's boutonnieres are the same."

We moved the centerpieces to the dining room table and laid the bouquets and Celeste's corsage on the hall table next to the door so we wouldn't forget them.

Just then the doorbell rang again. Cassandra greeted Mark, the friend who was catering the reception, with a hug and, "You know your way around. I don't think we'll need the tent, do you? The centerpieces are on the dining room table." Mark nodded and went back outside. I heard shuffling of feet down the sidewalk that led to the back gate and subsequently saw Mark and three others begin to transform the yard into an outdoor reception hall.

"Mom and Gert, it's probably time you started dressing," Cassandra told them. "I'll want my bathroom in about twenty minutes and I'm sure Amy needs a mirror, too." As the women headed upstairs, Cassandra plopped down on the couch with a sigh.

"We should have eloped or something. I knew it was going to be like this. They've only been here since yesterday and I'm already at wits' end. Gert's acting like once we're married, I won't be the same person. Mom still seems to think this is a full-on gathering of every magical person in the country. Even though she knows we can't change the calendar or the way the solar system works, it's inconvenient to hold the ceremony in the middle of the week. And she's still pissed that we're not going anywhere for a honeymoon so won't let any of the family stay here."

I commiserated with her. "It's like that at every other wedding I've attended – including my own. It's that 'special day' aura that descends on everyone in attendance except the bride and groom, I think. I don't know about you but I'm going to enjoy my coffee while I watch Mark and his people set up. Once your Mom is out of your bathroom, we can go commandeer your bedroom and shut them out until it's almost time to leave. Gregory should be here shortly after one. Ev said he was going to be dropped off at the park and just hang out people watching until the party started."

I mused at that last statement. Ev hanging out in a park people watching? More like people would be watching him. At over seven feet tall with puce skin, he didn't blend well.

We both stood quietly at the windows of her workroom sipping coffee and watching the crew set up the tables, chairs, and makeshift dance floor. Mark came in to get Cassandra's keys to the deli. "The refrigerators over there are a lot bigger, as is the prep table. Since it's right next door, I'm using it instead of trying to cram everything in here," he told me when I raised my eyebrows.

Celeste and Gert finally came downstairs. "It's all yours, sweetheart," Celeste said as she smoothed the sides of her gown. "Are you sure I can't help with anything?" She was almost pleading.

"Mom, all I'm going to do is put on my makeup and dress," Cassandra answered with a big sigh. "Amy can help zip me up which, I think, is all the help I'm going to need. Have a snack. You know you get headaches if you don't eat regularly. And for goodness' sake, stay out of Mark's hair. He really does know what he's doing. We'll be down in a bit."

She grabbed my hand and hauled me up the stairs. "Do your makeup first, while I'm laying everything out. I'm sure I'll also have to convince Merlin not to cover my dress with his fur."

I'd totally forgotten the cat. "Where is he?"

"Under the bed. He headed there as soon as Gert started her sniveling. Tears bother him for some reason. Go, huh?"

I followed instructions, put on my makeup and emerged to find her hugging Merlin to her chest. He was only making a show of disliking his position. He was a snuggler at heart. "Mine doesn't seem to be a problem but he won't stay off *your* dress. I didn't want his claws pulling threads or anything. Get dressed so I can put him down, will you?"

I pulled on the dress we'd picked out and she took Merlin into the bathroom with her. As soon as she put him down, he headed back under the bed. At least he wouldn't claw the dresses for which I was glad. I liked my dress. I'd be able to wear it later on to one of Ev's fancy-dress parties: a close-fitting, long-sleeved gown in forest green silk with gold trim. I had two sets of shoes to match: a pair of gold heels so I wouldn't look like a shrimp in all the photos and a pair of flats for when the reception started swinging.

I knew Cassandra didn't like makeup but I swore she should wear it more often. A little contouring with eye shadow and blush and she looked like a Celtic goddess or something just as exotic. I helped her into her dress which was just as simple as mine, only white. She'd left her hair loose and I pulled one side back, clipping a single white tea rose just above her ear. After stepping into her shoes, she did a slow pirouette. "Well, how do I look?"

"Like a bride. But you should blush some to make the look more authentic."

"Why in blazes would I blush? It's not like I'm a virgin or anything. C'mon. Mom's going to want to gush and Gert will probably start tearing up. I hope she doesn't smear her makeup before all the pictures are done."

I went downstairs first, so Cassandra could make an entrance. She was right. Celeste cried "my baby" and Gert just cried. Celeste started fussing with Cassandra's dress and hair.

I went over to Gert. "Hey, girl. You've got to stop the waterworks. You'll smear your makeup before we get pictures taken."

"I always do this at handfastings. I even cry at happy endings in books and films. I can't help myself," she told me. "But my makeup is no problem. Watch." She passed her hand over her face once. The tear tracks disappeared, the redness in her eyes was gone and she looked like she'd just got up from a makeup artist's chair.

"Mom taught me that spell a long time ago," she grinned. "We figured it was easier than trying to stop me crying. I just wish I could snap my fingers and have makeup appear rather than just fixing it. So don't worry, I won't ruin the photographs."

Just a minute later, the doorbell rang again. "Your chariot awaits, m'lady." Gregory made a low bow to Cassandra.

"Go on with you," Cassandra shot back. "By the way, thanks for playing chauffeur for us today. We really appreciate it."

"My favorite sandwich-maker is getting married. I was the one who talked Ev into letting you two use his limo so I could drive you around. But we had better leave. There isn't usually a lot of traffic around the lake this time of year but today's weather is bringing all the crazies out. You don't want to be late for your handfasting!"

I checked my clutch one more time for Tommy's ring and the four of us headed out to the limo. Several of Cassandra's regulars were waiting outside the deli (which had a sign that read, "Closed on Account of Matrimony!") and they clapped as we made our way down the front walk.

"Give him hell, Cassandra," one of them yelled.

"No worries, Gus, he's already there!" she hollered back just before Gregory helped her to her seat.

Celeste was fidgety on the ride over. Cassandra was getting irritated. "Mom, will you calm down? You're not the bride here."

"Have you checked with the park? Is everything ready?"

"I'm sure everything is okay. Rhys was going to check on it this morning."

Thankfully it was only a fifteen-minute drive, otherwise I think Celeste would have rubbed a hole in the seat area of her dress with all her wiggling around.

Don't ask me how he got permission, or even if he did, but Gregory pulled off the road and right onto the walkway to let us out. I retrieved Tommy's ring from my clutch, put it on my thumb and left the purse in one of the limo's hidden compartments. We'd be riding back to the house in the same vehicle.

The men were resplendent in their formal robes. Each man gave his hand to his partner to help her out: Marcus to Celeste;

Charlie to Gert; Jamie, Tommy's brother and best man, to me and finally, Tommy to Cassandra. Tommy's eyes were glowing. "You look gorgeous, Dra. You ready?"

"You betcha. What about you? After yesterday, you could've gotten out of it. After today, no way, buddy." She grinned at him. He answered by planting a kiss on her neck.

I finally had a chance to look at the setting. If you've never been there, you need to visit the Lyndale Park Peace Garden. I won't give you the scoop here but you can certainly look it up online. It's gorgeous. Anyways, the park had roped off the central area and arranged chairs for the guests. Rhys, in full wizard regalia, was waiting for us in front of the sculpture. The flowering shrubs were just starting to put on some color and provided a beautiful backdrop.

The photographer insisted on a couple of "before" shots. The guests were already seated but all turned in their chairs to watch. I felt like an animal in the zoo with everyone looking on and the sound of the camera's shutter clicking every few seconds. Once the posing was finally done, Rhys went to stand in front of the main sculpture and we took our places in front of him. Cassandra handed her bouquet to me and turned to face Tommy. Her expression was radiant.

Rhys began, "Loved ones, we gather here today to witness the binding in love of Cassandra and Tommy, now and forever. Love flourishes and blooms in the light and in the dark, laying down no ultimatums, making no demands at all. It is a gift we give to ourselves, and an honor we give to others from the bottom of our hearts and souls. When two people come together and give one another this gift, it is certain the universe is sitting back and smiling upon us, laughing and showering us with every possible blessing."

I heard a cell phone ring. Rhys paused long enough to glare at Ev, who shrugged his shoulders and reached into his pocket, silencing it. Rhys continued.

"I may preside here but more importantly as the father of the groom, it is my pleasure to offer these blessings to the couple: may you be gifted with the light of the rising sun each day; the heat of passion; a warm, loving home; a commitment as deep as the ocean; and the knowledge that holding one another each night is a solid foundation.

"Cassandra and Tommy, your journey together begins today. Help each other along the path and without doubt, you will find the ability to weather any adverse conditions you may encounter.

"Now, I ask you to look into one another's eyes and hearts. Tommy, please place the ring on Cassandra's finger. Do you promise to show Cassandra your honor and fidelity, to share her laughter and joy, to support and stand by her in times of difficulty, to dream and hope together with her, and to spend each day loving her more than the day before?"

Tommy smiled at Cassandra. "I do, sir."

Rhys continued. "Cassandra, please place Tommy's ring on his finger. Do you, Cassandra, promise to show Tommy your honor and fidelity, to share his hopes and dreams, to laugh with him and share endless days of joy, to stand side by side with him in times of trouble, and to spend each day loving him more than the day before?"

Cassandra's reply was so quiet, I barely heard, "I do so promise."

"The vows of love have been spoken. Now, please cross your wrists over each other and take one another's hands." They did as Rhys asked and he wrapped a piece of golden cord around their hands, tying a knot as he finished.

"Tommy and Cassandra, this cord symbolizes your life, your love, and the eternal connection the two of you have found with one another. The ties of this handfasting are not formed by this cord. They are formed instead by your vows, by your pledge, your souls, and your two hearts, now bound together as one forever.

"By Earth, Air, Fire and Water, I say it is done. Tommy and Cassandra, please kiss to seal your vows."

As they kissed, the cord that was twined around their hands shimmered and disappeared. I heard Gert sniffle into the handkerchief she'd carried along with her bouquet.

That was probably the most innocent kiss I've ever seen at a wedding. More like a quick, embarrassed peck than a kiss. At that point, I felt a slight pressure in my ears and had to swallow hard a couple of times to clear them, which was much more polite than yawning with my mouth wide open to make my ears pop.

Rhys finished with, "Please turn to face your loved ones. Ladies and gentlemen, I present to you Mr. and Mrs. Tommy Llewellyn!"

Not only the invited guests but several onlookers out on the walking path broke into applause as the newlyweds turned around. I handed the bouquet back to Cassandra and they started walking down what passed for an aisle, showered with rose petals by the guests as they went.

Just as everyone was rising to leave, Rhys yelled, "If I could have your attention for a moment, please." They paused and turned back to face him. "Naturally, the photographer wants a few minutes with the parties involved. You all know your way to the house. If you'll make your way out back, the caterer has some light refreshments to tide you over until supper. We'll be along shortly and then you can wrinkle their clothing with your hugs to your heart's content."

They all laughed and dispersed back to their vehicles. Ev got into the limo and Gregory pulled quickly into traffic. I knew he'd be back in record time to retrieve us.

The photographer certainly knew his business. His assistant quickly figured out who was who and thirty minutes later, we were all done posing and smiling for the camera. "I'll follow you over to the house to get some candid shots and then whatever other photos your family may want," he said to Tommy just as Gregory pulled back onto the walking path.

Everyone headed for their cars. Tommy, Cassandra, Jamie and I rode in the limo.

"Gorgeous ceremony, you two," Gregory said over his shoulder. "I've never met your dad, Tommy, but he sure cuts a fine figure in his official robes."

Tommy chuckled. "Tell him yourself. When Mom was alive, she had to cajole him into wearing them when it's necessary. He'd rather wear jeans and flannel shirts all the time."

In no time, we were back at the house and had to form the reception line. I doubted I'd ever see most of the family members again but I smiled while trying to remember names and relationships at least for one day. The few "pompous asses" I also smiled at, promptly forgetting their names and positions. I knew almost all of the other guests by virtue of always running into them at the deli or in Cork's pub over the years.

Mark did a stellar job. Finger food and champagne kept everyone busy with toasts for an hour or more while the photographer kept snapping away at one group or another, always with Tommy and Cassandra in the middle. Just as the sun was setting they lit all the patio heaters then brought out trays of real food. All of a sudden, it got very quiet as people stuffed themselves. The DJ arrived about half way through dinner and played instrumental music on low to help with digestion.

Once the cake was cut and demolished, the DJ cranked up the music, Mark opened the bar and the party got started. I found out Jamie was just as bad a dancer as me. We spent three and a half minutes trying not to step on each other's toes, laughing the whole time. The obligatory song ended and I was about to suggest we go sit down to give our toes a rest when a familiar figure tapped Jamie on the shoulder and then looking at me, said, "May I have the next dance?" Jamie looked at me and seeing that I was quite alright with the stranger, let go my hand and disappeared into the crowd.

"No. I need to give my toes a break. But you can have the next slow one," I said very quietly to Tony, my boyfriend who just happened to get furry once a month when the moon was full. "I thought you were in some high-level meetings in LA."

"I am but I canceled today and got on a plane. I'll need to go back on the red-eye. I may have missed the handfasting but I can at least give Cassandra and Tommy my best on the day. Not to mention it was a perfect excuse to see you." He bent down and kissed me.

We walked over to where the happy couple was sitting. Both of them were shocked. "I thought you were stuck in LA," Tommy said. Tony gave them the same explanation he had given me before leaning down and kissing Cassandra's cheek.

"Glad you could make it. Enjoy your few hours with Amy," Cassandra told him.

"Oh, I plan to," Tony replied with a grin. I sat next to Cassandra while Tony made his way over to the bar, returning with a glass of wine for both of us. The music was too loud to really have a conversation so I enjoyed the wine and the feeling of Tony sitting next to me.

I looked up to see Ev heading our way. About halfway over, he stopped and, pulling his cell out of his pocket, answered a call. It was too loud for me to hear what he was saying but the expression on his face wasn't good. When he completed his conversation, he finished walking over toward us. He shook Tony's hand and, looking down at me said, "I need to go and won't be in the office tomorrow. I'll call you in the afternoon sometime and let you know when I'll be back." Before I could even open my mouth to reply, he said goodbye to Cassandra and Tommy, grabbed Gregory and they rushed out the gate.

"I wonder what that's all about," I mused.

"It's Ev. Why would you even try to think of what was bothering him?" Tony asked. "Enjoy your evening and worry about it tomorrow."

I knew he was right but… "I know what you're saying but it seems whenever he gets that look on his face, it means he's either pissed someone off or is about to. At the very least, it will mean I'll have yet another mess to untangle."

"Whatever it is, you won't find out anything tonight. Therefore, I suggest you forget him and concentrate on me."

I let out a little sigh. It sounded like good advice so I took it. We sipped our wine, danced a couple of slow songs with Tony easily avoiding my feet and just generally hung out, listening to all the different conversations around us.

Although people had left in dribs and drabs, the party officially came to an end around nine when the DJ announced it was time to go and leave the happy couple to their wedding night.

"Go home," Cassandra told me. "I'll bring your makeup case and clothes to work with me tomorrow. Thanks for everything." She kissed one cheek; Tommy kissed the other. I took that as a dismissal.

"Come on," I said to Tony. "If I've only got a few hours, I want to make the most of them."

He grabbed his briefcase from where he'd set it next to the fence and we walked in companionable silence back to my apartment. Fudge greeted us at the door, even rubbing up against Tony's leg. I put down the cat food, set up the coffeepot for the next morning and made my way into the bedroom.

Tony helped me out of my dress and even hung it in the closet. "We have until four, which is when the cab will arrive. Let's make the most of it." We did.

Chapter 3

My best friend's handfasting was over, my sometimes boyfriend was on a plane back to LA and I was in my office, trying to make sense of the mounds of paperwork on my desk. It was a Wednesday but having had Tuesday off to be the maid of honor/witness, my sense of the week was all screwed up. I'd had very little sleep the night before and wasn't able to go back to sleep after Tony left in his taxi at four in the morning. It was a pot-and-a-half of coffee kind of day.

The entire office had been closed the day before to attend the handfasting so in addition to paper, there were voice mail and email messages to catch up on. It had taken me the better part of the morning to get through all those and I had a long list of things to talk to my boss about when he called in.

Sally walked in about noon. "How do you manage to always look so put together?" I whined.

"Leaving the reception early and getting a good night's sleep with my husband of fifteen years instead of making love until two in the morning with a long-distance boyfriend has a lot to do with it," she grinned back. "I take it you enjoyed Tony's company but didn't get a lot of sleep last night."

"You're right on that one. I'll catch up tonight, I guess."

Sally sniffed the air. "Where's Ev? He's got to be out. It smells too good in here."

"Hell if I know. He left the reception in a hurry last night, didn't say where he was going and now isn't answering his phone. I'm waiting on him to call me to answer a shit pot full of questions, not the least of which is where is he and when is he coming back."

"At least I'm here to answer the phones now so you can get some paperwork done. Anything else I can do to help?"

I gave her one of the credit card statements to reconcile and turned back to the one I was working on. The numbers swam before my eyes even as I took a swig of my eighth (twelfth?) cup of coffee. I slogged on.

Ev finally phoned in just as I was about to call it a day.

"Where are you?" I asked. "I have a pile of things to talk to you about."

"I'm in Atlanta," he answered. "Something's come up and I need to be here for a few days. What's up?"

Heaving a sigh and delaying my nap, I spent the next half hour going over two days' business with him. As we finished the conversation he said, "I may be in and out of cell phone range for the next few days. Can you hold the fort for me, maybe even through the weekend? I know we have an agreement about you not working overtime but I can't be sure I'll get all the calls as they're coming in."

I sighed yet again. "Okay. Forward your cell to the office. I'll forward the office phone to mine. But I get a day off when you return. Deal?"

Ev may be a bit of a pain in the backside but he was very fair when it came to my going above and beyond a forty hour week. He easily acquiesced and although I wasn't looking forward to fielding phone calls for three or more days and nights, I consoled myself with the thought of a long weekend sometime in the not-too-distant future. We disconnected, I cleaned off my desk and on the way out the door, told Sally to forward the phone to mine when she left for the day. She had a questioning look on her face but agreed to do so. Thankfully, my phone stayed quiet and I was able to get a good night's sleep.

It was much earlier than my normal quitting time the next day but I was cleaning off my desk in preparation for a long meeting with the back of my eyelids when, with a 'poof', a piece of paper appeared on my desk. I yelled, "What the hell?" and Sally came rushing into my office.

The paper had the look and feel of parchment, complete with the deckle edge. I gingerly picked it up and read the calligraphic handwriting aloud:

> *Miss McCollum,*
> *Your employer, Evander Angelich, is our guest. While he would prefer to be conducting his business in the comfort of his office, we are enjoying his company. If you would like him to be returned to work, perhaps even in one piece, bring $500,000 in unmarked, untraceable $100 bills with you*

This had to be some sort of joke. Who would kidnap Ev? And how does one go about subduing an ogre, anyways? They're larger than most other species that walk on two legs and magical spells bounce off them.

"You think it's real?" Sally asked.

"Can't be," I replied. "It's nearly impossible to capture an ogre if he or she isn't willing. This must be one of his friends playing a joke." So, I wrote:

They weren't lying. The parchment disappeared from underneath my pen with the last "M". I picked up my purse and lunch dishes to drop off downstairs, and followed Sally out to the reception area, on my way out the door to that appointment. A second 'poof' and another piece of parchment appeared on Sally's desk. Ev's signet ring landed next to it with a clatter.

Sally and I looked at each other with wide eyes. It wasn't a joke. Ev's bracelet-sized ring was proof positive.

I grabbed the phone off Sally's desk and dialed Gregory's number with shaking hands. He sounded upset when he answered the phone with, "Ev, where the hell have you been?"

"Gregory, it's Amy. We have a problem. Please come to the office *now*."

"Amy! I thought it was Ev finally contacting me. Is there a problem?"

"I'll explain it when you get here. Just come, OK?" My voice was trembling.

"I'm en route. I should arrive in about twenty minutes."

I wasn't the only anxious one. Sally's voice shook as she asked, "How are you going to get that money?"

"There's enough in the corporate and Ev's personal accounts to cover it, I think. If not, I can make up the difference from my personal savings. How to convert it to cash without drawing any attention? I haven't the slightest idea. But I'm going to wait for Gregory to get here before doing anything. I just don't know how to handle this."

Sally made another pot of coffee while I paced. The thought of sleep was long gone. Television shows about kidnappings don't even come close to portraying the terror I was feeling. On TV, the parents (or whoever) always contacted the police and everything turned out okay in the end.

However, I was obviously dealing with magical beings who could keep tabs on me and would know if I called anyone in a position of authority. The second note had appeared on Sally's desk, not mine. I didn't have the first one to prove anything to the authorities, anyways. I continued pacing. Sally sat at her desk, wringing her hands.

Two cups of coffee later, Gregory strode into the office. "I'm here. What's the problem?"

I pointed to the piece of parchment still lying where it had appeared on Sally's desk. "This is what I got when I didn't believe the first one."

He scanned it, taking note of the ring next to it. "Where's the first one?"

"It went 'poof' when I signed my reply."

Gregory's eyes went blank for a moment. "Shit. Someone knows their business. They've masked my tracking spell and there's no magical signature on this note. What did the first one say?"

I related the first one to him as best I could. "What are we going to do?"

He seemed so calm. He thought for a moment. "Call Martin and have him get the money together. Kidnappings in the paranormal world aren't that unusual and I would wager this won't be the first one he's had to deal with. I will use the telephone in Ev's office to make our travel arrangements. Sally, can you work full time until we get Ev back? It goes without saying that Ev and Amy are just out of the office and you will be taking messages."

"Sure thing. Will it be okay if I tell Jack what's going on? We don't normally keep secrets and he'll want to know why I'll be working so much."

"I don't see why not, as long as he doesn't tell anyone else. Let's keep it in the family." Gregory went into Ev's office and one of the telephone line lights blinked on.

I teetered back into my office on unsteady legs, picked up the phone and called our investment manager. Thankfully, he was still in the office rather than out golfing. He harrumphed when I explained the situation.

"Ev? Who would want a smelly ogre? It's not a problem, Amy. I'll have the cash for you by noon tomorrow. Stop by my office on your way to the airport."

So it *was* a fairly normal occurrence. It still didn't make me feel any better. I met Gregory back in the reception area.

"Come with me to Ev's house," he said. "I want to go through his things to see if we can determine who would want to do this."

"Okay." I looked at Sally. "Call me if something comes up you can't handle or delay. Otherwise, I'm leaving this whole shebang in your hands until we get Ev back."

She nodded. "No worries. I promise the building will still be standing when you get back."

Gregory and I climbed into a Humvee rather than Ev's limo.

"A Hummer?" I asked.

"It drives somewhat like the limo and even when we have a foot of snow, I can still get around. I haven't driven it this week and cars like to be driven."

That made sense. Minneapolis gets a *lot* of snow and knowing Ev, unplowed streets wouldn't deter him if he wanted to go somewhere. We rumbled west to the fancy suburb Ev called home, Gregory maneuvering the huge machine through traffic as easily as if he were driving a VW Bug.

Arriving at Ev's house, Gregory let us in the back door. "You do his office. Go through his desk drawers, the wastepaper basket and if you can log onto his computer, read his recent emails. I'm going upstairs to his bedroom."

"What am I looking for?" I asked.

"Anything out of the ordinary. You know him and his temper so normal arguments aren't going to worry us. We're looking for things that aren't usual, or appear threatening. Call me if you find something."

I turned, not toward Ev's home office but toward the kitchen. "First, I need more coffee. You want some?"

He started heading the same direction. "Please. Anything he has that's caffeinated will be fine."

Ev had one of those new cup-at-a-time coffeemakers with a box of almost every kind of coffee available so it was easy to brew a hazelnut coffee for me and a French Roast for Gregory. We took our mugs and parted company at the stairs.

What I found in Ev's office made me cringe. Oh, the top of the desk looked normal enough. The usual accoutrements, a photo of him and Marianna near a lake and his laptop. But in the lower drawer were photos of Ev and ladies *not* Marianna in various stages of undress. I *so* did not need to have my ogre boss' undressed body or his perversions burned into my brain!

Logging onto his laptop was just as bad. (That was easy. His password for everything was "1Evander!" What an ego.) Reading through his emails for the last couple of months was a lesson in writing erotica. He would be so dead if Marianna read any of these…not a single one was from her and let me tell you, female ogres' tempers are just as bad as their male counterparts.

I'd just finished gagging through the emails from January when Gregory came bounding in, a triumphant look on his face. "Did you know Ev's father is still alive?" he asked.

"No. He's never spoken a word about either of his parents so I just assumed they were dead. Even his grandfather never said anything."

"The man who was here a couple of months ago? That's his maternal grandfather. I knew his mother and father went their separate ways when Ev was a child but that's not surprising. The tempers, you know. His mother died about twenty years ago but he's never said anything about his father except for mentioning the breakup.

"*However*, I found this letter buried under a collection of ladies' underwear in one of his drawers. It's from his father. Here, read it." He handed me a piece of airmail paper.

In childish handwriting, someone named Aeneas addressed Ev as "son", said he had read about Ev's successful company, was proud of him and could Ev see his way to lending him about five thousand dollars to see him through a rough patch? It was dated the previous September and postmarked in Athens – Greece, not Georgia.

My jaw dropped. "Wow. What cheek. Don't see your kid for over a hundred years and then out of the blue, ask him for money? I wonder if Ev replied. There was no check made out to anyone by this name but given how much spending cash he takes out of the bank on a regular basis, he could've sent a money order or something."

"I doubt it," Gregory said. "Ev is generous but only to those who give him something in return, like loyalty, friendship, or a business favor. We may have our first lead on his kidnapper. Did you find anything?"

"Just a bunch of porn," I grimaced.

Gregory grinned. "That's our boy. Come on. Let's get some dinner and I will take you home. We have some difficult days ahead of us."

We stopped at an Applebee's for dinner and if not for the roar of the oversized tires on the road, I would have fallen asleep on the drive home. It had been a very long day.

"I will pick you up at the office at eleven tomorrow. Try to get some sleep," Gregory said as he walked me to the door.

It was only nine o'clock but I wasn't going to quibble with the clock and a perceived bedtime. I fed Fudge, changed into my jammies and crawled into bed. As always, he joined me, kneading my hair into an appropriate nest before proceeding with his post-dinner bath. I was so tired, falling asleep wasn't a problem.

Chapter 4

I only thought I was tired enough to sleep like the dead but I woke up in a cold sweat about three in the morning with Fudge staring at me.

The dream was terrifying. I saw Ev in what looked like a cave. He was surrounded by rough-hewn stone walls that seeped. I could hear the "plink, plink" of water dripping somewhere close by and the air was dank. I shivered from the chill. The only light came from a lantern a few feet away from where Ev sat in a chair.

That wasn't the worst of it. Ev looked like he'd been severely beaten. His eyes were nearly swollen shut; his lips were split with his green blood drying on them. The rest of his face was a mass of dark green on a puce background. He was bruised beyond belief. I could hear him snuffling with each breath he took and an occasional moan escaped as he shifted where he sat.

Ev wasn't just sitting in the chair, he was tied to it. His hands were behind his back, suggesting those were tied, too. The ropes securing his chest to the chair and the ones around his ankles glowed a sickly green. Each time he shifted, the glow intensified then died back.

"Ev!" I screamed, and then woke myself up. As I usually do when I have a bad dream, I sat up and turned on the light. That dispels any residual feelings from a nightmare. This time, however, nothing faded from my memory. I could still see, hear and smell every detail as if I were still dreaming.

Fudge crawled in my lap, reached up and caressed my face with his paw. He'd never done that before and to my sleepy eyes, he appeared to have a look of concern on his face.

"It's just a bad dream caused by the kidnapping. Let's go back to sleep," I told him. I turned the light out and snuggled back down. Fudge returned to his usual place in my hair and I fell back to a restless sleep.

When the alarm went off, I could tell it was going to be "same shit different day." I was as groggy from lack of sleep as I had been two mornings previous, only this time I hadn't been making love until two in the morning. I fervently wished for something stronger than caffeine but had to settle for coffee. While blearily stuffing some clothes and toiletries into an overnight case, I was reliving my dream and scaring myself. I'd never had a dream stay with me that long.

I stopped into the deli for my usual morning latte and while Cassandra set the machine to hissing and gurgling, I told her of Ev's kidnapping, Gregory and Martin's seemingly calm response to it all, and related my dream. It was just as vivid as it had been in the dark of the early morning. She stopped in the middle of steaming the milk and stared at me.

"You had a true dream."

"A what?"

"It's what I call a vision you have while you're asleep. What you saw is real."

"Huh? How do you know it's real? You're scaring me."

She sighed. "I don't mean to scare you but the details of true dreams stay with you, rather than fading like regular dreams. Ev is being held wherever you saw and is in just as bad shape as you saw."

I started shaking. "Why now? I've never had anything like this happen to me before."

"You've been exhibiting signs of witchiness for the last few months. I warned you, remember? Although you don't need to be a witch to have visions, I think it's all part and parcel of your magic waking up. Sometimes it takes a really stressful situation to manifest a gift. Your experience with that matchmaking demon and now Ev's trouble is probably what tipped you over the edge."

She grinned. "We *will* talk when all this is over. But stay calm. Gregory is right: kidnappings in the paranormal community happen all the time, probably because we have a longer lifespan to amass savings. Go get your boss. Tell Gregory about your dream. He may be able to use some of the details."

Just then, Sally walked in the door. "Morning, you two! You look awfully serious for this early in the morning. What's up besides the kidnapping?"

Cassandra answered her. "I think Amy's a witch. I'll let her tell you the details. What's your morning poison?"

As Cassandra poured a cup of plain ol' coffee for Sally, other customers started trickling in. That was our cue to start work. We tromped upstairs, turned on the lights and coffeepot, and started to work, trying to pretend it was a normal day.

After checking voice mail, Sally brought me a fresh cup of coffee. "What's this with you being a witch?"

I sighed and told her about the dream and what Cassandra had said.

"I'm jealous. I've always wanted to be able to do magic," she pouted. "I'm about as plain-vanilla human as you get. So, did you find anything at Ev's and what's the timetable for today?"

"There are a few decisions I'm going to have to make. They won't wait for Ev's return tomorrow or the next day so I have some phone calls to make. Gregory is picking me up here at eleven, we'll stop by Martin's to get the cash and then head for Atlanta. Beyond that, I have no idea. Thankfully, it's not quite the end of the month so there shouldn't be a lot of paperwork piling up. If you could pull the contracts that are up for renewal in June and compile the notes on those while I'm gone, that will help."

Sally went back to her desk and I picked up the phone. As much as I hated making these sorts of decisions in Ev's absence, we had clients waiting for bodyguards that weren't on payroll, yet. I decided on three wizards Ev had interviewed and called to make job offers. When Gregory strolled in shortly before eleven, I had just laid the contracts on Sally's desk for her to type up.

"Are you ready?" Gregory asked me.

"As ready as I'm ever going to be. We need to stop by Martin's on the way to the airport."

"I know. I spoke with him a few minutes ago. He has the money ready."

Gregory had been with Ev for over ten years. It stood to reason he'd know almost as much about the business as I did but it still took me by surprise that he knew who the investment manager was. I told him as much.

"It's all in the family," he grinned. "Martin takes care of my investments, as well. Come. We have a plane to catch."

I told Sally to call my cell if anything came up and she told me she expected updates when I could give them to her. Gregory grabbed my bag and as we passed the stairwell door to the deli, I heard a quiet, "Good luck." Cassandra had poked her head out the door.

I climbed into the front of the limo with Gregory. Today, I didn't feel like being all alone in the back seat. I'd just fastened my seatbelt when a thought hit me.

"Oh shit. Fudge," I cried, reaching into my purse for my cell phone. "How could I forget my cat?"

A quick call to let the upstairs neighbor, Elinda, know I was going to be out of town on business for an unknown number of days and I felt much better. She and Marge would ensure Fudge was fed and his litter box kept scrupulously clean.

"You've never been under this kind of stress before, have you?" Gregory asked.

"Hell, no. I thought that damned matchmaking demon was bad but wondering if my boss is alive is tearing me apart."

"He's alive. No one pays for a body," came the practical answer.

"Yeah, but he's been beaten up pretty bad. What if it gets worse?"

Gregory's hands clenched the steering wheel as we pulled into the parking garage for Martin's building. "What do you mean he's been beaten? How do you know?"

"I had a dream and Cassandra tells me it's true. She said I should tell you and I just now remembered I'm supposed to. I'll tell you the whole thing after we've seen Martin."

Ten minutes later, Gregory was towing an overnight-sized suitcase on wheels. He put it in the trunk with our bags and we started for the airport. You're thinking Minneapolis-St. Paul International Airport, right? Wrong. Gregory headed southwest to Flying Cloud Airport in Eden Prairie. That's where the corporate jet service Ev used was based. It would be my first time in a small jet and I was a nervous flyer in the big boys the commercial airlines used. I wasn't looking forward to the experience.

"Tell me about your dream," Gregory commanded.

I took a huge breath, tried to put the idea of flying out of my mind and made myself even more nervous as I once again related the dream. It didn't get easier with every retelling.

"Interesting," Gregory said as he pulled into a parking spot. "We need to talk about this but hold everything until we're at the hotel in Atlanta. We're sharing this flight and there is no need to let strangers in on our worries."

Security, while just as thorough as at the main airport, was quick. I'm not sure how all the bills showed up on the x-ray but no one said a word when Gregory hefted that suitcase off the conveyor belt. A quick walk across the tarmac and we were seated in luxury even commercial first class couldn't match. The seats were as comfortable as a recliner and swiveled around so you could actually look at the person you were talking with.

The flight was uneventful. Our four traveling companions seemed nice but after brief introductions, involved themselves in conversation about a corporate takeover. The flight attendant served a pork tenderloin lunch along with my favorite gin and tonic – extra limes. It appeared Gregory had thought of everything.

Two and a half hours later, we landed at a small airfield outside Atlanta and were whisked downtown by a limo that was waiting for us on the tarmac. Gregory checked us into the Marriott Marquis using my name and a bellhop ushered us into a suite on the forty-sixth floor. While I knew Ev lived high on the hog, I was truly impressed with the accommodations. From the window, I could see the rise of the Appalachian Mountains to the north. If I hadn't been so uptight, I would have felt like some sort of celebrity.

"You take that bedroom," Gregory said as he pointed to his right. "I will take the other. Fix yourself a drink if you want one. I want to talk to you about your dream while we wait for the phone call."

I usually don't drink during the day but between the small airplane and the circumstances, I felt justified in having a second gin and tonic before five. After dumping my overnight bag and purse in my bedroom, I found all the appropriate ingredients at the bar, including a freshly cut lime in the refrigerator.

Gregory grabbed a Heineken from the fridge and plopped down on one of the couches. "How long have you been having true dreams?"

I knew Gregory was trying to distract me from staring at the telephone, willing it to ring.

"If what Cassandra tells me is right, that the details of true dreams stay with you where others fade, then this is the first. Sure, I sometimes remember things when I wake up but not in such vivid detail or for more than an hour or so."

"She is correct. And that concerns me. If Ev is in as bad shape as you saw, this isn't your garden variety kidnapping-for-ransom. It's a lot more personal. I have put out feelers to try to find Ev's father. I have a suspicion he's behind this from the wording in that letter we found. So far, nothing.

"If you have another vision, either waking or sleeping, I want you to tell me immediately. Not just for Ev's sake but so I can help you understand what you're seeing and what to do with it. Do you want to watch television while we wait?"

I felt like such a child. Whatever was going on with me the adults, meaning Cassandra and Gregory, wanted to stick their noses in. And ugh. Daytime TV. Not my cup of tea. Thankfully, my cell phone rang as Gregory channel-surfed, settling on some news channel. Seeing who it was via Caller ID, I went into my bedroom to answer.

"Hi Doll. I'm sorry I didn't get a chance to call last night but things got crazy around here and I didn't get free until well after your bedtime. Why aren't you in the office?"

As much as I hated to tell the story yet again, I told my boyfriend about the previous forty-eight hours.

"You're having true dreams? About Ev? Where are you? I'm on my way."

I sighed. "There's no need for you to come, Tony. I'm with Gregory who apparently not only knows how to handle the situation but is a wizard who knows about these things, too."

"I don't care." Tony was adamant. "If something's upsetting you, I'm coming. I don't want Gregory or anyone else comforting you if you're scared. Besides, my nose might come in handy and I'm better with my fists than any wizard."

I told Tony where we were.

"I'm in Nashville and will be there in about four or five hours. Tell Gregory I'm coming – he'll have to tell the concierge service to give me a pass to your floor." He hung up and I sat there a moment, trying to formulate a good way to tell Gregory we were going to have company, wanted or not.

Gregory just nodded when I told him. "I assumed he'd find out and the way he looks at you when you're together tells me he would want to be wherever you are. It's okay. I imagine he knows how to handle himself in tetchy situations, given his nature.

"If you can, I suggest you try to nap for an hour or so then we will order dinner. I have a feeling it's going to be a late night." He headed into his bedroom.

Even though I didn't think I'd sleep, I lay down on my bed and closed my eyes. I was actually just about to drop off when I felt something land on my chest with a thump. I grunted with the sudden weight, my eyes flew open and "What the hell?" was about to come out of my mouth when I saw Fudge staring down at me at close range. He was batting at a scroll tucked into his collar. I took it off him and as I unrolled the note, he made himself comfortable next to me and started his usual bath.

> *Darlin',*
> *You sounded mighty upset when you called and you've never gone out of town without giving me plenty of advance warning. Something's up. Whatever it is, Fudge wouldn't let me near him and just kept yowling. I figure he needs to be with you wherever you are so am sending him on. He knows where you are but I don't – all I did was give him a push, as it were. You need to call me to tell me where you are so I can send his food and litter box.*
>
> *E*

Holy shit. Witches can teleport animals? And now I had not only a kidnapped boss and an overprotective boyfriend to contend with but a cat that wouldn't stay home.

(Witches can only send *familiars* through the ether. We know where we are at all times. Stupid pets would get lost and die. That fat witch knew what I was from the beginning but stayed silent. My human will learn these things. In the meantime, she has dreams I need to help with and I cannot do that from a thousand miles away. F.)

I resolved to get at least a few minutes' view of the back of my eyelids before calling Elinda. I must admit, I felt better with Fudge's warmth curled next to me. I drifted off …

And found myself back in that damned cave, staring at Ev. He didn't look any worse but didn't look any better, either. No sounds came from him this time and after a slightly panicked moment, I saw his chest rise and fall. Although I thought I was alone, a voice said, "Turn around. Notice your surroundings."

I started at the voice but turning in a complete circle, I saw Ev and no one else. If I was going to hear voices in my head, at least it was only in a dream. I hoped it didn't start happening when I was awake. Since what I dreamed was supposedly real, it wouldn't hurt to have a look around.

Ev was definitely in a cave but man had been here. There were floor-to-ceiling beams visible in places. An old mine, maybe? The lantern light showed a tunnel behind me, just a little higher than I was tall, and I'm short for a human. Whoever brought Ev in here would have to be strong, to haul a 500-pound ogre while stooped over. I walked down the tunnel, feeling my way along the wall, conscious of the fact that I was in bare feet. The tunnel floor was cold and the rocks made me wince with almost every step.

About fifty steps along, the tunnel widened and I was lucky I was walking slowly. I came upon the mouth of the cave abruptly and although there wasn't a drop-off, the ground sloped steeply away from me. I would have stumbled and probably fallen flat on my face if I'd been walking any quicker.

The moon was at a quarter and with clear skies, gave off just enough light for me to see I was in a forest. As a matter of fact, about all I could see were trees. There wasn't even much of a clearing before the woods started, maybe twenty feet. I took a couple steps out of the cave and looked around.

I was on the side of a mountain. Or at least that's what I thought since the ground continued up from where I was. Somewhere in the distance off to my left, I could see a light twinkling from another hill. But that was all I could see. There wasn't any noise to speak of, just a gentle soughing of the breeze in trees that were starting to leaf out.

"Wake up, now," said the voice. "You need to tell the wizard what you have seen."

I felt myself wake and although upset, I didn't feel nearly as rattled as I had twelve hours earlier, after the first true dream. I opened my eyes to a view of nothing but chocolate brown fur. Fudge had draped himself over my head. His fur was long enough that it tickled my nose and my sneeze effectively dislodged him. He took the ungracious movement in stride and after licking my nose once, started cleaning the part of his stomach I had sneezed into.

My cat was acting very strange. He'd never slept on my head before. In my hair, always, but sprawled across my face? Never. I heaved a sigh. Gregory had said to tell him immediately if I had another dream and the voice had said the same thing so I'd better do as I was told.

First, though, I had to comb the snarls out of my hair and splash some cold water on my face. The clock said it was shortly before 7:00 p.m. My stomach said it was getting to be dinner time.

When I walked into the living room, Gregory was lounging on the couch, watching the evening news. He looked up when I cleared my throat. "I take it you slept a bit. Are you ready for dinner?"

"Yes, I'm hungry," I replied. "Gregory, I had another dream about Ev."

"First, let's order room service. While we wait for the delivery, you can tell me about it."

Although my stomach said I was hungry, my brain didn't want a lot of solid food. I ordered a salad and some broccoli cheese soup. Gregory ordered a steak. How could he be so calm in such a crisis? Men!

"About your dream," Gregory prompted.

"Hang on. I have to call Elinda. Fudge just appeared on my chest with a note from her."

"Your cat is here? You didn't tell me you were a witch, just that you were having true dreams!"

I slumped in my chair. "I didn't know! All this stuff is new to me, too. Cassandra said something about it and so did her dad but I've never cast a spell in my life."

"If your cat was able to make his way here, he's a familiar, Amy, not just a pet. That makes you a witch. Did you hear any disembodied voices in your dream?"

"Erm. Yes." I told him what I'd seen and what the voice had said, both at the beginning and just before I woke up.

"The place doesn't sound familiar but then again, I am a stranger to these parts. Some people I know might have a better idea and if I need to, I will call them.

"The voice you heard was Fudge, guiding you. Wait until Ev finds out he has a witch for an assistant. He's going to have a conniption fit!" Gregory was almost bouncing in his seat with glee.

"Fudge can talk?" I asked.

"Not in the conventional sense, no. You will hear him in your dreams and as you become more comfortable with who you are, you will sense what he's doing or thinking when you're working magic. It's difficult to describe to someone who's not accustomed to it. I think you will have to find out for yourself how things work in that regard.

"As far as Fudge's accoutrements are concerned, you may be able to bring them here yourself."

"Me? How would I do that?" This was all too much to handle.

Gregory frowned but then the corners of his mouth turned up a bit. "You're a witch, Amy. You can do things mundane humans cannot, and that *might* include being able to teleport objects. You don't know what your strengths are, except for having true dreams. If you like, I can help you try or I can just get them for you."

It didn't take me but a second to make up my mind. I was too riled about Ev, the dreams and having my life turned upside down yet again to process anything more. "I can't handle this at the moment. You do it."

"Not a problem. I've been in your apartment and know his litter box is in the bathroom but where do you keep his food?"

I told Gregory which kitchen cupboard held Fudge's food. He closed his eyes and just a few seconds later, Fudge's litter box and food container landed on the floor in front of me with a 'plop' that was hard enough to scatter some litter around.

"Sorry for the mess. I usually only transport closed containers. Call Elinda and tell her you're with a wizard who got Fudge's things for you, but no more details."

I dutifully made the call and Elinda was really good about not asking for any details of what was bothering me. All she said was, *Be careful, darlin'* before disconnecting. I took Fudge's things into my room, surprised to find his dish inside the food container. Gregory was thorough.

While we ate dinner, I admonished Gregory not to say anything to anyone, especially Ev, about these new-found abilities of mine. "I have no idea how I feel about it all. I don't need him nosing in my private business any more than he already does."

He acquiesced but I could tell he was disappointed. I had no idea why Ev would freak out about me being a witch. Gregory, however, did and wanted to watch the show when Ev was told.

"When do you suppose we'll hear from the kidnappers?" I asked, trying to get back to the most important subject.

"I'm rather surprised we haven't heard anything by now. Based on what you told me happened in your office, they're able to keep tabs on you and I would have thought you'd get a phone call or note shortly after we checked in."

He shoveled another piece of steak into his mouth and around it, continued, "But I wouldn't worry. They're probably trying to keep you off balance for some perverted reason. As long as your dream says Ev is in the same place and not in any worse condition, I won't get concerned until tomorrow."

We finished eating and while Gregory put the cart back into the hallway, I grabbed the remote and started looking for something to watch on television. I'd brought my tablet but knew I wouldn't be able to concentrate enough to read. A James Bond movie was on and I thought that was mindless enough to watch while stressed. Fudge came out from the bedroom, curled up in my lap and went back to sleep.

"I love James Bond," Gregory said as he sat back on the couch he'd claimed for his own. "Have you ever noticed how he always has exactly the proper equipment he needs for whatever situation he's in, and it's always such an amazing gadget?"

I remarked that I had, and added that the car chases were always fun, too, and wondered how much the British government had to pay for all the destruction. We watched in companionable silence until there was a knock on the door around 9:30 p.m.

Gregory motioned me to stay seated and I could see some sparkles in the hand he held behind his back as he opened the door with the other. The sparkles immediately disappeared as soon as he saw who it was.

"Hello. I see you had no difficulties getting onto this floor," he told Tony, opening the door wide.

"Nope. All I had to do was show the concierge my ID and he gave me a room key. I thought it safer to knock, though, knowing what was happening. Hi, Doll."

Tony crossed the room in three strides, sat on the couch next to me and enveloped both me and Fudge in a big hug. After kissing the top of my head, he held me back and, looking sternly at me, asked, "Are you holding up okay and why did you bring your cat?"

Fudge extricated himself from the embrace and moved farther down the couch. He tolerated the werewolf but wasn't overly fond of being so close to a dog, human form or not. I answered with, "As best I can, I guess. I didn't bring Fudge. He brought himself a couple of hours ago, apparently with Elinda's help. Everyone's telling me I'm a witch as well as having these damned dreams."

"When did you find this out and why didn't you tell me?"

"Cassandra's dad mentioned it a few months ago but it sort of came to a head when I told her about the dream. I would've told you eventually but it's not something you say on the phone, y'know?"

"Wow." Tony looked at me as if I had a huge zit on my nose. "Not that it changes anything but this is rather unexpected."

"Would you two like me to go into my room so you can continue your conversation in private?" Gregory interjected.

"No, because there's really nothing more to discuss." I was starting to get peeved. "Whatever I am, it's an 'is' and I'll deal with it when Ev is home, safe and sound. Until then, the commercials are over and I'd like to watch the movie."

After looking at Gregory for direction, Tony put his overnight bag in my bedroom, stopped at the bar to fix drinks for both of us and sat down next to me. Both men appeared to be totally relaxed. I felt like a jack-in-the-box, ready to pop with the next turn of the crank.

When the movie finished at 11:00 p.m., Gregory yawned and stretched. "I'm going to call it a night. It's rare I get to go to bed this early and I'm going to take advantage of it. I doubt we will hear anything before morning so I suggest you get a good night's sleep, too, if you can." He nodded at us and went into his bedroom, closing the door behind him.

Tony nodded, too. "Go to bed, Doll. My body is still on west coast time and I don't need that much sleep anyway, so I'm going to get caught up on some emails. I'll be in to bed in awhile." He gave me a kiss and a little shove.

I knew I needed the sleep after two very short nights, so headed into bed, Fudge following. Despite all the tension, I dropped off quickly and barely felt Tony crawl into the other side of the bed some time later.

Chapter 5

It was still dark when I woke but Tony was already out of bed. I pulled on the robe so graciously provided by the hotel and stumbled into the living room to find him and Gregory sipping coffee and sharing the morning paper.

"Good morning," Gregory greeted me. "I ordered enough coffee for ten, knowing how you like your caffeine jolt."

I mumbled "Morning" back and after pouring myself a cup from the urn, slumped on the couch. Tony wordlessly handed me his laptop, knowing I wake up by checking social networking.

I also remembered to check my email for the first time in over a day. Shit. With all the turmoil, I'd forgotten I was supposed to have submitted a draft of my next paranormal romance book to my editor the day before. I thought it was done but always like to have one more read-through before sending a manuscript off.

Although I could have accessed my documents stored in the Cloud, read it and fired it off, I knew a couple of things. First, I wasn't in the right frame of mind nor did I think I had the time to read it all the way through or make any changes. Second, even though Tony knew what I did in secret in my spare time, neither Ev nor Gregory did. I wasn't ready to entrust Gregory with yet another secret he had to keep from Ev. I replied with a very terse, "Sorry. Something's come up. Will get it to you within the week." I'd never been late with a submission before so hoped I'd be forgiven.

Two cups of coffee later, I felt awake enough to turn on the news. It was only 8:00 a.m., yet the first station I found was already on a national program. Flipping channels, I finally found one that would give me the local weather. A quirk of mine: I like to know what it's going to be like outside no matter where I am – even in an office. It was supposed to be a wonderful spring day with highs in the 70's. What a change from Minnesota! The anchor had just started a story about an accident on the freeway, commenting that it was a good thing it was Saturday or it would tie up rush hour traffic when, with another 'poof', a piece of parchment appeared on the coffee table. Before I could reach for it, Gregory snatched it and read it aloud:

Welcome to Atlanta. We hope you are enjoying your luxurious accommodations and slept well last night. Transfer our money from your suitcase to a large ladies' carryall. This afternoon, you will attend the 2:00 p.m. tour of the Cyclorama in Grant Park. There is no assigned seating so be early enough to ensure you sit in the second-from-the-front row, third seat in from the right. Enjoy the docent's commentary and be sure to leave the bag under your seat as you leave. We'll be in touch.

"Whoever is doing this is good. They're leaving no magical signature at all for me to read," Gregory said.

Tony reached his hand out. "May I see it?"

Gregory handed him the parchment and Tony, just like the dog he was, took a good, long smell.

"Whoever wrote this is a werewolf. And it's been near pine trees. Oak and maple, too, if I don't miss my guess, and another tree or shrub I'm not familiar with. They're in the woods."

"That ties with Amy's dreams," Gregory answered. "A were, you say? Then we have at least one witch or wizard and probably two or three male weres in on this. It would take that amount of strength to subdue and then carry Ev. Do you know the local clan leader?"

"Not personally, but I know who it is and can call him. I'll work on that angle. I presume you have magical contacts here you can call."

"Of course." Gregory turned to me. "Amy, there are shops down in the Atrium that sell ladies accessories and I believe there is a luggage shop, too. You will need to buy something that fits the description.

"They're probably not open yet so enjoy your coffee. I'm going to take a shower and by the time I'm done, it should be a decent enough hour to call people." He headed into his bedroom and closed the door. Shortly, we heard the sound of the shower running.

Knowing I had at least a couple hours to kill, I poured myself another cup, and turning my attention back to the computer, looked up "Cyclorama". Interesting. A diorama depicting a battle from the

Civil War. What caught my eye, though, was it was right next to the Atlanta Zoo and they had pandas!

"I know it's a non sequitur to all this but since they specified two o'clock, do you suppose we could kill some time and go early enough to see the pandas?" I asked. "I've never seen one in person before and they're so cute in pictures."

"I don't see why not but let's find out what Gregory has in mind. If there isn't time, I promise to bring you back here just so we can go see the pandas, okay?" Tony nuzzled my hair. "I'm going to go shower and then I'd like you to take yours right away so the sound isn't in the background while I'm on the phone."

That left me and the television. And Fudge. As soon as Tony went into the bedroom, the cat came out and curled up in the just-vacated spot. It was almost like a Saturday at home except I was a thousand miles away and probably about to get myself into a world of trouble.

As soon as I finished drying my hair, Tony came into the bathroom and cleaned my brush. "What are you doing?" I asked.

"When you buy your bag, be sure it has an unzippered outside pocket. I want to put your hair in it so I can track the bag."

"You can do that?" I knew weres had keen noses but…

"If the scent is *really* familiar, as yours is to me, yes. I can find you within fifty miles or so. Other aromas within maybe ten, if I have a good enough sample first. It also depends on air quality. Smog, like in Los Angeles, severely limits the range."

Wow. I was finding out all sorts of new things. Creepy things, too. I'm not sure I liked the fact that my scent was almost as good as a GPS to him and his kind. There was nothing I could do about it at the moment, so I finished dressing and, grabbing my purse, went shopping.

Finding a ladies' bag the size of a small suitcase wasn't a problem. While I favored as small a purse as I could get away with, a lot of women like being able to carry the kitchen sink. I cringed as I handed over my credit card for a leather Etienne Aigner, priced almost twice what I'd pay at a regular shopping mall. "It'll go on the expense report," I told myself.

I walked back in the room to find Tony watching a muted television and Gregory just completing a phone call. They both approved of my purchase. Gregory transferred the money from the suitcase, zipped it shut and handed it to Tony, who stuffed a few strands of my hair down into the outer compartment presumably designed to hold a cell phone.

"Tony told me you want to go see the pandas. As much as I would like to indulge you, I'd feel better if we weren't carrying around a half million dollars in a crowded zoo on a Saturday," Gregory told me. To be honest, I hadn't thought about it that way but he was right.

Noon saw more room service for lunch. I may like being indulged on occasion but I was getting tired of the hotel room, suite or not. Finally about one, Gregory stood. "Amy, give your wallet to Tony and put your mobile phone down in the pocket over your hair so it will smell like the hair just drifted down there. You need to look like you're only carrying the one handbag."

I retrieved the items from my purse and handed my wallet to Tony, who put it in an inside pocket in his jacket. I grabbed my coat, slung the bag over my shoulder (it was *heavy*), and we trooped down to a waiting limo. I teased Gregory about being able to sit in the back seat.

"It does feel strange not to drive. Even when I go on vacation, I rent a car," he grimaced. "But I don't know the city so…"

Within minutes, we pulled up to the gates of Grant Park. Gregory reminded the driver that he should wait for us and that we expected to be a little over an hour, then he led the way to the building that housed the Cyclorama. I could easily have spent hours wandering around the neighborhood, looking at the Victorian architecture but time was short, so we got in line, purchased our tickets and sat through a quick film about the history of the painting before we were escorted up into the room housing the painting itself.

My luck was running true to form. We weren't quick enough and someone took the designated seat. It appeared to be a family because a small child was sitting where I was supposed to leave the bag. Gregory heaved a quiet sigh and went to speak with the man who was probably the father. It took some doing but after four people in the front row were paid off and moved a few rows back, the family moved down one row and we took our seats. I placed the bag between my feet. I'm certain everyone thought we were crazy because all eight of them took time to stare at us before relocating.

"What did you tell them?" I asked in a low voice.

Gregory grinned. "That the two of you were on your honeymoon and you wanted to sit in the same seats you had when

Tony proposed. I also suggested you might be someone famous to explain my presence. Hence the stares."

The lights dimmed and if I hadn't been so nervous, I would have been fascinated by the presentation and viewing of the world's largest oil painting. Twenty-some minutes later, the guide had answered the last question from the audience and everyone was leaving. I grabbed my cell phone and shoved the bag under the seat with my foot as I stood, looking around to see if anyone was watching.

"Do you see anyone suspicious?" I whispered to Tony.

"No, nor do I smell the person who wrote it, although a crowd of about a hundred people can easily disguise individual scents, especially when some of them reek of baby vomit."

Eew. I was glad I couldn't smell *that*.

"Let's get a funnel cake," Gregory said over his shoulder on the way out. "I haven't had one of those in a long time."

In as leisurely a manner as we could, we bought funnel cakes and coffees, found a bench with a view of the entrance to the Cyclorama and sat down to eat. Neither man paid a lot of attention to what he was doing – they both had powdered sugar down the front of their jackets. That was to be expected when eyes weren't on the flimsy paper plate but on the crowd. And me without my regular purse and wet naps!

Just as I finished the last bite, Tony very quietly said, "There. The woman in the blue coat has the bag and she's with the guy in the distressed brown leather jacket." He took a long breath with his mouth open.

I looked toward the entrance to see the couple Tony had indicated and she was most definitely hauling the bag I'd purchased that morning. She was a few inches taller than me, brunette and built like an athlete. He looked something like a blond version of Tony…around six feet tall and also athletically built, but then again, most weres were. They didn't look unusual, just a middle-class couple out enjoying the spring day. If I didn't know better, I'd say they were talking about what they'd just seen at the Cyclorama. For all I knew, they were. They would have had to sit through the presentation, wouldn't they?

"I see them," Gregory said just as quietly. "Let them go. As long as you can track Amy's hair, we don't want to attract attention and jeopardize getting Ev back. But now we know at least one of the perpetrators is a woman. We'll wait a few minutes to let them think they're safe, then go back to the hotel and put the next phase into operation."

"Phase?" I asked.

"Yes. Getting not only Ev but the money back. *And* finding out who's behind it all."

Gregory called the driver from his cell and by the time we'd wended our way through the crowd and out to the street, he was waiting with the car door open. Tony paused to take a sniff before getting into the back seat.

Once we were seated with me in the middle and the privacy glass up, I turned to Gregory. "What do you mean 'getting the money back'? I don't give a shit about that, I just want Ev in one piece."

Gregory shifted in his seat to face me. "First, no one, not even the mundane police, would *not* try to get the money back. The kidnappers know this and expect it. Second, to ensure at least this one person doesn't try it again, we need to know who's behind it and deal with him or her."

Tony put his hand on my arm. "Most kidnappings don't come with nasty beatings, Doll. Gregory and I both agree this is something personal. If we let whoever it is get away with it, they'll probably just do it again."

He leaned forward so he could talk to Gregory around me. "The woman carrying the bag is your note author. The guy is also a were. But I don't think she's strong enough to have had a hand in capturing Ev. So there are more."

Gregory nodded. We were silent for the rest of the drive back to the hotel.

Back in the room, Tony made a phone call. "They're headed north. Do you know anyone north of the city?"

He listened for a moment. "Hmm. I'll need some help. Two or three of your guys ought to do it. How much?"

More listening. "Have them on standby. I'll call you when I know more." He hung up.

"What was that all about?" I asked.

"The local clan leader. Their territory extends up to the Tennessee and North Carolina state lines so the city folks have room to run when they need it. But he tells me there are plenty of rogues in the mountains with lots of places for them to stay out of the clan's way. I just hired some muscle if we need it."

"Thank you," Gregory said. "North, eh?" He pulled a map out of the desk drawer. "Look. There are a lot of woods and hills once you get out of Atlanta and its suburbs. What do you think?"

Tony looked over Gregory's shoulder. "Got a car reserved?" Gregory nodded. "Okay, I suggest we head up this highway, get out of the city and then let me take another sniff. Say about here," he pointed. "If I do it there, we'll know whether we need to head west, east or continue northbound."

"Sounds like a plan," Gregory said. "We will stay here until the next note arrives and then leave. Amy, does Fudge travel well without a carrier or do I need to get one?"

"He's fine without one, why?"

"I don't know when or if we will be back here so I certainly want to bring him with us. I can magically get his things from here if need be."

"No problem. He'll sit quietly in my arms. At least he usually does when I take him up north with me."

At the sound of his name, Fudge strolled out of the bedroom, bumped my leg and meowed for further attention. Of course, I obeyed, picked him up and scratched between his ears.

"Nothing to do now but wait. I'm going to take a nap. Call me if anything happens." Gregory went into his room.

"I have some work to do and I'll use the desk in the bedroom," Tony said. That left me and Fudge to watch television, curled up together on the couch.

I'd just turned on a soccer match when another note poofed its way onto the coffee table. "Hey guys," I yelled. "The next note is here."

Both men strolled out of their respective rooms and coming to stand behind me, read over my shoulder.

> *Trying to keep tabs on us and the money with a were and hair wasn't part of our agreement. Mr. Wellington is well known to some of us, as is his relationship with you, Miss McCollum. Therefore, if you want Evander back in nearly one piece, an additional $500,000 will be required. You have two days to make those arrangements without leaving Atlanta. We will be in touch.*

"What the fuck do we do now?" I was so angry I could spit nails. "Another half mil is going to break the bank."

"Now even I'm upset," Gregory said. "Normally, kidnappings are just a game. This is going beyond that."

"And how the hell do they know me?" Tony was befuddled. "I don't have any business in Atlanta, didn't know the weres we saw at the park and didn't smell anyone familiar around."

My fists clenched, I started crying and then started shaking. So did the building.

"Bloody hell. Amy. You're an Earth witch. Calm yourself, girl!" Gregory's eyes were wide open and it seemed he couldn't close his mouth, either.

"What the hell are you talking about?" I was so upset I was almost screaming. Fudge rose from his spot on the other side of the couch, draped himself on my chest, nuzzled my shoulder and purred very loudly.

"Doll, please try to calm yourself," Tony said as he sat next to me and put his hand on my shoulder.

"Amy, please, take deep breaths and calm down. You're radiating so much energy you're causing an earthquake. I promise I will explain but you need to pull yourself together *right now*." Gregory stood in front of me with a very concerned look on his face.

I took several gulps of air and my tears subsided to sniffles. The building stilled. "What the hell?" I asked.

"Tony, fix her a drink, would you? She needs one." Gregory sat down on the coffee table in front of me.

"Amy, according to what you told me and what I've seen over the past two days, your powers are starting to manifest. I know you think you're too old but you're just a late bloomer. Unfortunately, they're manifesting in a big way. Although any witch or wizard can work with any element, we usually have an affinity for one. I work most easily with Air. That's why transporting Fudge's things here wasn't difficult for me. Cassandra works best with Earth. That's why her garden is so lush and she's such a good cook."

He took the drink from Tony and handed it to me. "Take a swig of this."

I did as I was told and the burn of the gin going down my throat felt good. "Go on," I said, still dripping a tear here and there.

"When people have strong emotions, even mundane people, they radiate energy. When magical people experience the same feelings, they need to control that energy or unfortunate things can happen. That's why, in the years you've interacted with magical people, you've never seen one lose his or her temper. Although we may seethe inside, we need to keep control of our emotions.

"You're an untrained Earth witch and the energy you radiated when you lost your temper was strong enough to cause a minor earthquake."

"Very minor," Tony said from the chair where he was sitting with his laptop open. "3.4 on the Richter Scale and centered on this very building. It's all over the Internet because earthquakes don't normally happen south of the mountains. No damage reported except some broken dishes."

"I caused an earthquake?" This was too much to take in. I took another gulp of my drink.

(Yes, my lovely human, you did. Your strength is far above what the Familiar Council anticipated. We are going to have such fun when you are trained!)

"Yes," Gregory replied. "From now on, you need to keep a tight rein on your emotions, especially anger. I know it won't be easy given our current situation but I will be right here to help, as will Fudge. Once we're back in Minneapolis, Cassandra can work with you. You have about twenty years of catch-up learning since you're manifesting at this age."

"About the new note," I said, trying very hard to be just irritated instead of pissed.

"I can't begin to tell you what I will do to whoever this is once we find him," Gregory answered. "Call Martin at home. I'm sure he can make arrangements for us to pick up the money down here on Monday."

"In the meantime, I suggest we take that drive up north tomorrow," Tony interjected. "They may have found Amy's hair but her scent is still on that bag. I'd like to see if I can get a better idea of where they are so once we have the money and the next set of instructions, we can have a battle plan in place."

"Good idea," Gregory agreed. "According to the concierge, there's a most excellent restaurant within walking distance so I had him make reservations for an hour from now. I suggest we stroll over there and enjoy something other than room service before turning in early tonight."

I called Martin at home, who uttered a string of expletives that would make a sailor blush before telling me he'd make the arrangements and call me Monday morning with a name and address. "There's not that much cash available in Ev's accounts," he said. "I'll have to arrange a loan and it won't be at the local bank."

"I understand," I groaned. That sort of loan was going to cost. "I really don't care what you have to do, Martin. I'll deal with the fallout after this is all over."

"Understood. I'll call you about nine o'clock your time on Monday. Try to relax, okay? It'll all work out somehow."

I hung up from the call and nodded to Gregory. After changing out of jeans into a business casual outfit, we walked a couple of blocks over to the Westin Peachtree Hotel and took the elevator up to the top where the Sun Dial Restaurant had the most marvelous 360° view. (I could have done without the view from the glassed-in elevator, though.) I'd never been to a restaurant that rotated before and was fascinated with not only the sights but how the whole thing worked. I even managed to bump into a few tables as I watched the floor move rather than paying attention to where the maître d' was leading us.

Over dinner, Gregory and Tony plotted in low voices while I stared out the window watching the scenery as the sun set, remembering to take a bite of food every now and again. When our table had a northern view, I could see the mountains and that, inevitably, brought Ev and our circumstances back to mind.

When my apartment had been trashed by a crazy, lovesick vampire, Ev had stepped in to help, insisting that we were like family. I'd never really felt anything other than a close working relationship until now. I'm not sure what *sort* of family an ogre would be, maybe a sixth cousin twice removed or something. However, I knew I was as worried about him as I would be about Cassandra, and she was like a sister to me.

The more I mused about the situation, the more convinced I became that the "someone close" probably wasn't Ev's father but someone who had worked for Angelich Security at some point. The first note mentioned me possibly losing my cushy job. What the writer apparently didn't know is that I didn't *need* my job. I made a very comfortable living off my novels. My job with Ev was not only a source for characters but something I actually enjoyed doing. I made a big decision. I was going to let Gregory in on my secret life.

I took a big swig of my gin and tonic. "Gregory, I don't think our kidnapper is Ev's father."

"Why would you say that?"

With a sidelong glance at Tony, I told Gregory about my secret life as a paranormal romance author and my conclusions based on that and the first note.

"I'm only telling you this because it might affect how you guys approach things. You are sworn to secrecy, Gregory. No one, especially Ev, is to *ever* learn about my writing, got it?"

"You are just full of surprises, aren't you? I swear by Air, Earth, Fire and Water to never reveal what you just told me." I felt my ears pop. Gregory had just sworn a binding oath so I knew my secret was safe.

"You knew about this, I presume," Gregory looked at Tony.

Tony grinned back with pride. "She finally told me a few months ago. The first book is based on me."

"This changes things, but not a lot. It doesn't change the fact that we need to get Ev and the money back but Ev has only fired a handful of guards over the last ten years, so it narrows our suspects down. When we get back to the hotel, I want you to access the personnel files on the office computer. Let's see who would hold that sort of grudge."

We finished dinner in silence, each probably thinking about who would do such a thing. The walk back to the Marriott was quiet, too.

When we got back to the suite, I put the grilled shrimp I'd ordered for Fudge in his bowl and fired up Tony's laptop. A few keystrokes later, I was looking at a screen that duplicated the one in my office. Technology is a wonderful thing, isn't it?

A few more keystrokes got me into the non-current personnel files. Gregory sat next to me and we looked over the eight profiles together.

"There," Gregory pointed to a name at almost the same time as my finger went to that spot on the screen. "David Johnson. He got into an altercation with the authorities on his last assignment and Ev fired him as soon as he made bail."

"I remember," I said. "He claimed it was racial bias, that the police officer didn't like dwarves and the officer took the first swing. Security footage said otherwise and David's blood alcohol level was twice that needed for a DUI conviction. He did a year for that, didn't he?"

"Two years. And here in Atlanta, if I'm not mistaken. He would have been released about a year ago. He had some friends among the other guards and if he's stayed in contact with them, news of you and Tony would have percolated back through the rumor mill."

"So now what?" I asked.

"In a way, a dwarf makes sense. Four or five of them are strong enough together to bring down an ogre. Dwarves are a very tight-knit community and he could easily have obtained assistance from unsavory friends. I have no contacts I can call there. However, he's obviously allied himself with at least one witch or wizard and two weres. That probably came from his time in jail. I can try working that angle."

"Fortunately or unfortunately, weres are in and out of jail a lot," Tony added. "Just like ogres, our tempers can easily get us into trouble if we don't control ourselves. Jarvis, the local clan leader, can probably help in that regard. I'll call him in the morning."

After that, I actually felt a little better. Yes, I was still upset about the entire situation but having a possible focus for my anger helped to keep me calm. I remembered that little creep. He always dressed and spoke properly, but underneath the suave exterior, you could tell there was a scumbag. The few times I saw him in the office, he leered at me and made some very inappropriate comments when Ev was out of earshot. I ignored the comments because I thought he was doing a good job for our client and didn't want to upset the applecart. I hadn't thought he was smart enough to pull off something like this but maybe he had a few somewhat-intelligent friends.

Chapter 6

Sleep that night eluded me. Despite Tony's amorous advances (which I fended off) and Fudge's attempts to calm me by snuggling at my side, I couldn't help but think of Ev in his predicament and how badly I wanted to hurt David, if he was indeed the "brains" behind the kidnapping. So Tony could sleep, I finally got out of bed about two a.m., went into the living room and turned the television on low. Fudge followed and we snuggled on the couch, watching late-night sitcom reruns. Even that couldn't lull me completely to sleep.

A couple of hours later, I was dozing when Gregory came out of his room and sat on the couch next to me.

"Couldn't sleep?" he asked.

"Not really, no. I was tossing and turning so much I finally decided to come out here to let Tony sleep. I couldn't shut my brain off."

"It will catch up with you, you know," he nudged my shoulder. "I can help you to sleep, if you like. Air wizards are good with that."

Crap. More magic mumbo-jumbo worming its way into my life. "If it becomes an issue, I'll ask. I've gone on short rest on more than one occasion and been okay."

"Just making the offer. Want some coffee?"

"Room service doesn't open for an hour. How are you going to get coffee? Magic it here?"

"I could but I'd probably end up burning both of us with the hot liquid. Not to mention that some wait person at whatever restaurant I got it from might lose control of their bladder when both coffee and cups disappeared. No, I had the concierge get us a coffee pot yesterday."

The man thought of everything. While he puttered around at the wet bar, starting the coffee, I took a closer look at him. Although he'd been a peripheral part of my life since I'd started working with

Ev, I really only knew what I saw: a little under six feet tall, obviously in shape but not a body builder, looked in his mid-forties with salt-and-pepper black hair and chocolate brown eyes that were always roving, checking out his surroundings. Like most bodyguards, he was close-mouthed. I decided it was time to find out more about Ev's shadow.

"Gregory, we've known each other since I started working for Ev, yet I don't know a lot about you. Are you married? What do you do with whatever free time you have? And why, as intelligent as you seem, are you content to be a limo driver?"

He chuckled. "In order. Never married. I like my independence too much. To stave off the next question, I'm not seeing anyone at the moment. As to my free time, I actually have quite a bit, just not in any really large blocks. I have a garden next to my cottage where I grow herbs, I spend a lot of time on that and putting potions together for other people. When I'm not driving, gardening or making magic, I read. A lot.

"My job? As you well know, Ev pays me a princely sum in addition to giving me the cottage behind the house to live in. It's almost always an easy paycheck but when it's not, I find myself in a situation that requires problem-solving and ingenuity, like now. I enjoy these sorts of challenges and they're not something you'd find in a normal job.

"What surprises me is Ev hasn't told you how we got together."

I made a face. "I try very hard not to ask Ev about his past. I don't want to know anything more than necessary so I don't get dragged into his personal life. But okay. Do tell."

More quiet laughter. "Ev and I were working at the same club before he got his job as a guard for that vampire agent's client. As you know, he was a bouncer. I was a bartender. He got into trouble once by making a play for a mundane customer's girl. You know how he is about women. In any case, I stepped in and smoothed the customer's ruffled feathers with a little magic. I managed to keep Ev from getting fired over it and he told me some day he'd pay me back."

The coffeepot gurgled. "When he started his business, he knew he'd have to project a certain image if he wanted the type of clients he has now. He somehow found me and asked if I'd play driver for him, offering to split the first contract with me. I wasn't doing anything exciting so said yes."

A gurgle and a hiss later, the coffee was done and Gregory handed me a cup. "It turned into a good relationship. Yes, he's a little odd but he's loyal to a fault, I make a good living and have the occasional odd problem to solve. Does that answer?"

"It gave me something other than our current situation to think about, yes." I took a sip of the coffee. It was some of the smoothest I'd ever tasted. "Wow. You were a bartender. Have you also been a barista? This is good!"

"No, but I lived in Italy for a few years and learned my way around a coffeepot. I'm a coffee snob, actually."

"I love Cassandra's coffee but this is better than even hers. What's your secret?"

Gregory smiled. "I get my coffee from a friend in Italy who roasts his own. He sends me five pounds every month. I always pack some when I travel, just in case I get somewhere that has a pot."

"You should turn her on to your friend. I'm serious. This is really good."

Another smile. "I tried several years ago. She says it's too expensive and she'd have to raise her prices too high."

That made sense. Cassandra liked coffee, too, but would sacrifice a little to keep her prices in line with the competition. She was, first and foremost, a business woman.

"So, we're both awake, you've had some coffee and it appears that Fudge is awake, too. Do you want to learn more about your gift?"

I sighed. As a thirty-year-old, single Virgo, I was set in my ways and didn't like change. Discovering I'm a witch is a *big* change, I would say. "I suppose," I answered.

Gregory started. "So, we know you're an Earth-affinity but I don't know what else you know."

"Neither do I."

"Not to worry. Tell me what you see." He held out both hands, palms up.

"Red sparkly balls. Two of them, one in each hand."

"Good. You can see energy flows. That makes things much easier."

"It does?"

"Yes. Some witches can't and it makes it more difficult to train them because they can't see what they're doing. Can you feel them?"

I concentrated on those balls. "They give off something…tingly?"

"More good. Now, I want you to hold out your hands the same as me and think about making a ball of energy, just as I did. If you can see and feel the energy I've shown you, you can also feel it around you. Think of it as something you can mold, perhaps like dough. Pull it into your hands and shape it into a ball."

Fudge came out from Gregory's room, hopped up on the couch and put his paw on my thigh. What was the cat doing in his room and why, all of a sudden, was he being more than just a cat?

Something tapped the back of my head, but when I raised my hand and felt, nothing was there.

"Is there something wrong, Amy?" Gregory asked.

"I just felt a tap on the back of my head. Is this place haunted or something?"

"I've never heard of a haunting here. Focus, please?"

Fudge's paw pressed harder into my thigh. Thankfully, he had his claws sheathed or I'd have had five puncture wounds to deal with. I looked down at him and I could swear he winked at me!

I closed my eyes and imagining the room, tried to find something like Gregory's energy balls in the air. I felt some pressure at the back of my head and then I felt tingly, something like when you're outside and it's misting rain. You don't exactly feel the raindrops but more a caress of moisture on your skin.

I opened my eyes and saw the entire room sparkling, as if everything were dusted with fairy dust. I could see some lines of sparkle coming from various parts of the room and the closer they got to Gregory, the redder they got, until they ended at the deep red balls in his hands.

How do you turn sparkles into dough, much less into a ball?

(Damn, girl. Do I have to do all the work for you? I want to play, not teach.)

I felt that pressure on the back of my head again then it came to me. The sparkles were glitter. All I had to do was make a ball of glitter and the glue holding it together was my will. I envisioned a clump of glitter in my hand in the shape of a ball and as I watched, the sparkles coalesced in my hands. As they did, a ball formed. Much to my surprise, as it formed, the glitter changed from silver-white to forest green.

Gregory smiled. "Definitely Earth-affinity. Look at that gorgeous tree-green. And quick, too."

I looked at the clock on the VCR above the television. It had taken fifteen minutes. "What do you mean, quick?" I asked.

"Most people can only do that with hours of practice. You got it in less than one. However, I think you had help." He looked down at Fudge and smiled. Fudge had a smug look on his face. Well, smugger than normal.

"Oh, damn," I said. "You said I'd be able to feel Fudge when I was doing magic." I looked at Gregory and then down at the cat. "You're the pressure in the back of my head, right?" I swear the cat started preening.

"You're lucky to have a familiar," Gregory told me. "Not everyone gets them but as you've just discovered, they can really help."

"I thought every witch or wizard had a familiar," I said. "Don't you?"

"No. Never have. From what I understand, there aren't as many familiars as there are witches and wizards so they're assigned by the Familiar Council to people who they deem deserving of the honor."

"There's a Familiar Council?"

"There is a ruling council for everything that's not mundane, except ogres. They're not as organized. You have already had dealings with the Vampire Council. At some point, you will have to appear before the Witches' Council, your ruling body, to get registered. Although, perhaps not. You have a familiar and that may automatically have registered you. I believe they talk to each other but I'm not certain. At any rate, you will get a notice of appearance if you have to."

Now in addition to mundane law and the Internal Revenue Service, I had to keep up with magical laws, too? I was getting a headache and said as much.

"Not to worry. As long as you don't kill anyone with your magic, you will be just fine. Using it for murder is about the only prohibition. The registration is more for your magical signature. Everyone's is different, just as everyone's DNA is different. You will learn that. Back to the energy."

Over the next hour, I learned how to not only make balls but pull things toward me and throw a magical punch. The couch pillows got a good workout and I only broke one bottle of Scotch on the bar, which Gregory quickly made disappear by evaporating the liquid and "sweeping" the glass into the trash.

The crash of the bottle woke Tony up and he opened the bedroom door just in time to have a pillow fly into his face. "Nice wakeup call," he growled.

I blushed. "Sorry. I was trying to make it fly around the room and you opening the door changed the flow."

"And in that, there is a lesson," Gregory said. "You need to keep a tighter hold of whatever you're moving so a change in the air current doesn't disrupt the motion. Now that Tony is up, I suggest we suspend lessons. We have a drive to make, I think."

Gregory and I had finished the first pot of coffee, so I made another for us to "start our day" with. Although I'd had almost no sleep, I really didn't feel that bad and it didn't feel like a caffeine buzz. I asked Gregory.

"Whenever you work with energy a lot, you always retain some inside. Under normal circumstances, I would take you outside to ground the excess but since you didn't really sleep, I will let you keep it. It will help you get through the day but it's not a practice you should become accustomed to. You can literally burn yourself out by retaining energy that doesn't really belong in you.

"I've seen it happen," he continued. "It's not a pretty sight. Have you ever seen anyone Tasered? It's rather like that. The body just collapses from complete synaptic overload, except you don't recover from this type of electrical shock."

I'd seen videos of cops being Tasered so they would know what the target was feeling. I didn't want to experience the same thing. "So, you'll teach me to get rid of the excess energy, right?"

"This afternoon, yes, when it will be okay for you to get sleepy. Perhaps on our way back from wherever we're headed. It's easy enough."

We drank coffee, watched the morning news, ate room service breakfast and then took our showers. By nine, Gregory had called for the rental car. As I put my jacket on, Fudge clawed my pants leg. I took that as a sign he needed to go with us, so zipped the jacket part way up to make a cradle for him. Gregory just raised an eyebrow but said nothing. Shortly thereafter, we were in the car with Gregory driving and Tony navigating. Fudge and I stretched out across the back seat, watching the scenery flash by.

Even on a Sunday morning, Atlanta's interstates were busy. Gregory smoothly maneuvered the car through traffic. There was a bit of an awkward moment as we all searched our pockets for fifty cents in change to get us through a toll booth but shortly thereafter, the indications of civilization started to thin. The highway even lost its exits and became a four-lane road with stoplights.

We came upon one intersection with one of the largest outlet malls I've ever seen. Minnesota has a couple but I'd only visited them once each as they're a bit of a drive from The Cities. Although I don't much like to shop, the thought of the bargains awaiting almost had me drooling. Unfortunately, it wasn't yet open. I filed the location in the back of my mind for future reference.

"Go just a bit farther," Tony said. "There's too much interference here but it looks like it'll thin out and I'll be able to get a better sniff."

"Wait," I cried. "There's a Starbucks sign up ahead on the right. I want more coffee."

Gregory sighed, pulled into the shopping center and we all got a caffeine fix: regular coffee for Gregory and Tony; I got my favorite venti latte. Fudge got a small cup of milk. Yes, I know milk is bad for cats, especially male ones, but I like to give him a treat every now and again.

(I *always* deserve treats! I know about the milk. It is taught to us at a very early age. Alcohol is bad for humans, yet they drink it. Everything in moderation.)

"If you're satisfied, may we get back to the matter at hand?" Gregory asked me when we were back in the car.

"Sorry. But you know how addicted I am to this stuff," I pouted. Gregory pulled back out onto the highway.

Five minutes later, Tony told Gregory to pull over. "The traffic is really thin and I think the air should be clear enough for me to get a sense of direction, if they haven't masked it," he said.

Gregory pulled over and killed the engine. Tony got out, shut his door, walked a ways away from the car and, raising his nose to the sky, turned a slow circle. He turned a second time, eventually stopping when he faced the direction we were heading. After one last sniff, he got back into the car.

"They're really not *that* smart," he said after taking a drink of his coffee. "If they were, they would have wiped the bag with disinfectant or something like that after finding the hair. As it is, I get a very faint scent of it, still north of here. According to the signs, there's another town up the road. Let's stop there, too."

Ten minutes later, we pulled off the highway and drove into a quaint little town with the equally quaint name of Dahlonega. Like most small towns, it was centered on a square and looked like a typical tourist trap with shops selling everything from antiques to ice cream. The one detail that *was* different about this town was the "Gold Rush Museum" prominent on the square in the old building that was probably once the courthouse. Naturally, nothing appeared open, yet, it being Sunday morning and all.

Curious, I pulled out my phone and did an Internet search on the town. As I read, something clicked in my mind. "Hey guys," I said. "Did you know there was a gold rush in Georgia before the one in California?"

"Yes," Gregory said, concurrent with Tony's "No, really?"

"According to Wikipedia, it sounds like this gold rush was the reason for the Cherokee removal. White miners trespassed on Cherokee land," I said for Tony's benefit. Then to both, "You know, an abandoned mine fits the picture of the place in my dreams."

Gregory pulled into a parking spot on the square. "Then perhaps we are in the right area. Let's get out and under the pretense of stretching our legs, Tony, take another sniff or two."

As much as I hated it, we cracked the windows and left Fudge in the car. Gregory and I strolled around the square, looking into shop windows. Tony walked on his own and wandered down a side street. I pulled Gregory into the only shop that appeared open: the Dahlonega General Store.

"Oooh, look at all the rocks," I cooed. I was a sucker for pretty stones and one entire wall was devoted to trays of them.

"Hmmm," Gregory mused. "Which ones are you drawn to?"

"They're all so pretty, but nothing's set in jewelry." I pointed to a geode. "Apart from putting it on the coffee table, what would I do with something that large?"

"Consider this a teaching moment," Gregory said quietly. "Quiet your mind and tell me which ones call to you. Ignore the 'pretty' for the moment."

I sighed. I guess I was going to have to get used to this witchcraft crap pervading everything. I closed my eyes and recalling what I'd experienced of energy earlier in the morning, felt around. Metaphysically-speaking, of course. Tingles came from everywhere: weak ones from the staff and customers in the store; stronger, older ones from the building itself; and yet even stronger and older ones from the stones surrounding me, although some of *those* tingles felt a little off.

"Separate the wheat from the chaff," Gregory whispered in my ear. "Identify the stones then find the song."

I opened my eyes and looked at him. "Song?"

He shrugged his shoulders. "That's what I call it. If you have a close affinity to something, it will 'speak' to you in an unusual way. Song is the only way I have to describe it."

"Ooookaaay," I said. "I've got the stones separated from everything else but why does some of the energy feel weird?"

"I can't tell you for certain because Earth isn't my element but my guess is you're feeling the effects of the stones being polished. Go on, now. See if any of them sing to you."

I closed my eyes again. There was a strong, not-off tingle coming from my left. I turned, opened my eyes and looked straight at a container of chunks of not-quite-gold-looking rocks. The sign said, "Pyrite. Fool's Gold." I pointed. "Those feel the, um, cleanest, for lack of a better word."

Gregory laughed. "Appropriate for your particular situation. If I recall correctly, pyrite is good for focus and clarity. A small piece of it in your pocket might help you with all the lessons you will be enduring over the next several years. Pick out one piece that feels right."

I shrugged my shoulders. Whatever. I rummaged around in the bin until I closed my fingers over one piece that virtually hummed when I touched it. "This one," I said as I pulled it out from the depths.

"Good. Go pay the man your dollar plus tax. We should find Tony."

I did as I was told and slipped the rock into my pocket. Somehow, it felt right having that small weight there. We walked out of the store and almost bumped into Tony.

"What, no huge shopping bags?" He smiled at me.

"Not from there. Most of it is touristy stuff. Where did you go?"

"Been walking around the side streets, trying to get a direction. It's kind of difficult with all the odors coming from the buildings but I think they're northeast of here."

"We're in the right area, then. I wonder how we find an abandoned gold mine up in them thar hills?" Gregory mused.

"It's nearly noon. Jarvis should be up. Let me call and see if he's got any ideas," Tony said as he pulled his phone out of his pocket.

Yes, it was almost noon and several hours since I'd had breakfast. I looked around the square with my stomach as Tony talked with Jarvis. Someone related to a café catty-corner from where we were standing was opening its door and putting one of those blackboard signs out on the sidewalk.

I pointed. "I'm hungry and they're open. Can we get something to eat?"

Tony tapped his phone then looked at Gregory. "Jarvis is going to make a couple of calls and get back to me. I suggest we feed the girl and then head back to the city. There's not much we can do until we've got a better idea of location and we need to be back there in the morning to get the money, anyway."

Gregory nodded. "I agree. I could do with a bite to eat but Amy, we should let Fudge out of the car for a bit, first."

Damn, I'd forgotten the cat again. I wasn't used to having him along wherever I went. We went back to the car. After Gregory had unlocked it, I scooped up Fudge and, carrying him over to the wee lawn in front of the museum, put him down. With a glare, he walked over to the shrubs next to the building and I swear let out a sigh as he peed. After scratching in the mulch, he came back to me without a single detour to smell other things. He was continually surprising me.

We put Fudge back in the car with a promise to bring him some food and went to the café I'd seen to eat. The only thing I could find appealing on the menu was a salad – everything else was fried and although I was calmer than I'd been earlier, I didn't think grease would settle well.

After lunch, Gregory pulled me back over to the lawn by the museum. "There is nothing important left to do this afternoon. I want you to release the energy you've picked up today. It's easiest at the beginning if you do it in bare feet but it's a little chilly today for that. So, I want you to feel inside yourself and take hold of the energy that you know isn't yours. When you're ready, crouch down, pretend you're examining the grass and imagine that excess energy flowing out your hands into the ground."

Separating out energy was getting easier. After only a minute or two of comparing the way I felt now to what was normal, I found a knot of "foreign" energy just below my breastbone. I mentally grabbed hold of that knot, unraveled it like a ball of yarn and moved the string up my torso, around to my shoulders, then down my arms, forcing it out of my hands. Once the end of the last string disappeared into the earth, I felt really tired.

"Good girl!" Gregory exclaimed. "You're catching on a lot faster than I would have anticipated. You will probably doze off on the way back to the city but that's to be expected since you really didn't sleep last night."

We piled back into the car and as Gregory followed the side roads to the highway that would take us back to downtown Atlanta, I gave Fudge the pieces of a hamburger that Tony had saved for him. The meat hadn't quite disappeared before I fell asleep.

Chapter 7

I must have been a lot more tired than I thought. The next thing I knew, I woke to strengthening light coming through the window of the hotel bedroom. My stomach was growling, too. Looking at the clock, I saw it was just after six o'clock and since Tony and Fudge were sound asleep on either side of me, I knew it had to be morning. The smell of coffee had me trying to get out of bed without disturbing either of the other occupants. I noticed I was in my nightgown (it had better have been Tony) so pulled on a robe and padded into the living room. Fudge woke and followed.

"Good morning!" Gregory greeted me with a cup of steaming elixir. "I know you want this first, but after that, drink some juice or eat some fruit. You need fuel and fructose is the quickest available form until I can order some breakfast."

He was right. I couldn't even think about any kind of food until I was completely awake, which usually meant copious amounts of coffee.

"How do you feel this morning?" he asked.

I thought about it for a moment. "Apart from being hungry, I've had a good night's sleep. That much is obvious. Nearly seventeen hours, though?"

"You've done things with your energy in the past two days that you've never done before. Except for the sore muscles part, think of it as if you ran a marathon without ever having run one before. You will get used to it in time but ..."

"But what?"

"You need to eat something other than a salad at meals. It's not enough fuel and you will find yourself running on fumes. Yes, you can borrow energy from around you but as I said before, it's not something you can continually do without burnout. Naturally fueling yourself so your personal reserves don't get depleted is the best way to go."

I frowned. "So why didn't you tell me this at lunch yesterday?"

"You're upset at sleeping so long, aren't you? Experience is the best teacher." He grinned. "Don't feel bad. I slept an entire day after my first lesson and was caned for missing my chores."

More background on Gregory. I'd never thought about it but the more I was learning about him, the more I thought I could write him into one of my stories. I probed further. "Caned?"

"Literally. I was raised on a farm by my grandparents and Grandfather had lost part of one leg in the war. If I misbehaved, he would hit my backside with his cane. I got some nasty bruises but I learned to do as I was told rather quickly."

"The war?" I wanted to know how old Gregory really was. Yes, we females want to know everything.

"Amy, I'm not going to tell you my exact age if that's what you're feeling around for. But Grandfather lost his leg in the French and Indian War. He was lucky to have survived."

Gregory was *old* by my reckoning but only looked to be in his forties. I refilled my coffee cup. "So who gave you the magical lessons? It couldn't have been your grandfather if you got caned for missing chores after a lesson like that."

Gregory sighed. "You're not going to let this go, are you?"

"Nope."

"My abilities come from my maternal grandmother and although they skipped my mother, she was aware of what Grandmama could do. When I started manifesting at age ten, it scared the bejasus out of my father, who wanted me out of his house. Mother convinced my grandparents to take me in.

"Remember, that wasn't too long after the Salem scare. Magical people were still secretive and other paranormal-types stayed hidden. My grandfather didn't know a damned thing about Grandmama's abilities, except that she was the healer in the area. No one thought anything about that since herbs and folk medicine were women's work.

"She taught me the basics while we were out of his sight, doing chores like feeding the chickens or working in the kitchen garden. When she'd taken me as far as a witch can, she passed me on to a wizard who owned the neighboring property by getting me a job with him felling timber."

He refilled both our cups and while starting a fresh pot, continued, "So, as you're good with numbers, you can figure out about how old I am and by that, you know I have a *lot* more experience than Cassandra. But there's only so much I can help you with because females, or witches and males, or wizards, go about their magic somewhat differently."

"Why is that?" I asked. "Isn't magic just magic?"

"Yes and no," he answered. "I'm not certain but my guess is it has to do with our hormones. At least in my experience, wizards tend to use the brute force of the energy whereas witches…weave it. There is no difference in outcome but to me, witches' magic seems gentle, even when they're walloping on someone and trust me, I've seen witches fight with magic."

"That doesn't make sense," I said.

"Yes. I don't know any other way to describe it. It's another one of those things you'll have to figure out for yourself."

Tony came out of the bedroom and without a word, poured himself a cup of coffee. "Are you two going to talk about magic the whole time?"

"Sorry," Gregory told him. "But the faster she learns about herself, the easier it will be on all of us – especially you. Never had sex with an out-of-control witch, have you?"

"What?" Tony choked on his coffee.

Gregory grinned. "Remember me saying she had to get control of her emotions? Earthquakes don't only happen when Earth witches are angry and you should see what happens with an out-of-control Air witch."

"Holy shit," I said. "This is *so* not a conversation I want to be having with the two of you right now. Can we change the subject, please?"

Both men chuckled. "I don't know. I'd kind of like to hear about Gregory's wild sexual encounters," Tony teased. But rather than pursue the subject, he sat down and opened his laptop.

My phone rang at a very opportune moment. It wasn't even seven-thirty his time and yet Martin was at his desk. "Write down this name and address," he told me. After I did so and repeated it back, he said, "Be very, very nice when you go to pick up the money. I called in a lot of favors and now I owe one to him, which I don't like. He's expecting you at ten sharp. Oh, and dress like you're going to the office. He doesn't like what he considers low class attire."

After I hung up, I told the guys what Martin had said and added, "I didn't think to bring a suit with me so I hope my slacks and blouse will do."

"They won't," Gregory replied. "I know about him. You thought the people Ev deals with are snobbish? He has them beat hands down. Tony, look up that address, will you? We need to know how long it will take us to get there. Amy, which suit out of your closet do you want?"

Shit. A guy-not-my-boyfriend looking into my closet. At least I had underwear so he didn't have to go magically snooping through my drawers, too! I heaved a sigh and described what I called my "banker's suit" to him: navy blue, severe cut, skirt a little longer than I normally wear them. I usually only wore it when I met with Ev's bankers or attorneys.

Gregory closed his eyes and a few seconds later the suit, still on its hanger, landed on the couch next to me. A small smile crossed his face and then he rose and looked over Tony's shoulder. "It looks like it will take us about twenty minutes. Are you coming with or staying here?"

Tony replied, "Unless you think something will go haywire and you'll need me, I'll stay here. I have emails to answer and I'm still waiting on Jarvis to call back. It'll be easier here if I have to take notes."

"I can't see where anything could go wrong. We're just picking up a satchel as far as I know and unless I miss my guess, we will be in the very best part of town. What do you want for breakfast?"

While I showered, Gregory ordered breakfast. I stepped out of the shower to the yummy smell of bacon and eggs. My stomach growled even louder than it had before and I decided to dry my hair and dress after I'd eaten.

About an hour later Gregory and I were in a limo, being whisked to the home of our loan shark. At least that's the way I thought of him. The guy was getting twenty percent interest when, if there had been time, I could have gotten five percent from the bank.

I'll admit: I was thoroughly impressed when we pulled into the guy's driveway. The home of a business associate, vampire and agent-to-the-stars John Minton, had *nothing* on this. The two-block-long driveway wound its way through what appeared to be an old pine forest peppered with blooming azaleas and dogwoods. At the top of the hill sat a castle. Well, it looked like a castle. The whole thing was granite blocks, from the main house to the large garage — with a granite porte-cochere between.

Gregory told the driver to wait. We walked up the wide flagstone steps to an oversized front door and when Gregory rang the bell, we could hear chimes echoing inside. In just a few moments, a fully-liveried butler opened the door, inquired after our needs, then ushered us through the entryway and into the library but not before I got a good look at a wide reception hall with a double staircase up to the second floor landing.

Trying to kill time, we both looked at the bookshelves lining the walls. No paperbacks for this guy or even everyday hardbound books. Everything in sight was leather-bound with gilt titles on the spines. I heard a throat clear behind me and turned...

To find the ugliest dwarf I'd ever seen dressed in what was obviously a custom-made suit. Admittedly, I'd never seen an *attractive* dwarf but this guy took the cake. Instead of just a gnarled countenance, his was gnarled and horribly scarred, like someone had stuck his head into a vat of boiling oil. The scarring covered not only his face but his whole head so he only had tufts of hair growing here and there. But shrewd, sharp blue eyes peered at us out of the disfigurement.

"Good morning. I presume you are Amy and Gregory?" Ugly asked.

Gregory answered that we were and asked if the man had something for us. "Of course," the dwarf replied. "I assume Martin made the terms of the loan clear?"

I nodded, desperately not wanting to look him directly in the face so soon after I'd eaten, yet I knew I had to. "Yes, he did. The principal will be repaid one week from today together with the agreed-upon interest."

The blue eyes looked at me with curiosity. "Good. Then here is your money. Martin has the information to wire the repayment to my account. I wish you well." He dropped a small leather bag on the floor, abruptly turned and left us alone in the library.

I turned to Gregory. "What…"

He shushed me. "At the hotel and no earlier," he quietly said as the butler arrived to escort us out. We heard, "I bid you good day" as the door silently shut behind us.

Since I couldn't voice the question I was dying to ask, the ride back to the hotel and up to the room was quiet. Once our door closed, I started.

"He's the ugliest being I've ever seen. What in the hell happened to him?"

Gregory grimaced. "I don't know him personally so don't know all the details but the rumor is when he was young, he was working at a fast food restaurant and someone threw a full fryer of hot oil onto him. He received millions in a lawsuit and parlayed that into ownership of a group of fast food franchises that made him even more millions. He's not on Forbes' Top 100 list of millionaires but close to it."

"Did you see that house?" I asked. "And a butler in tails? That's a little over the top, if you ask me."

"Everyone has their foibles. Tony, have you heard from Jarvis?"

Tony nodded. "He called about a half hour ago. One of his guys knows a guy who knows a guy who knows of three abandoned mines within fifteen miles of where we were yesterday and a half dozen more within fifty. It cost me but a couple of Jarvis' lieutenants are checking those places out tonight. I should know something by nine or ten o'clock."

"Ev will reimburse you whatever it cost," I said.

"I know. I'm not worried about that at all," he said, yet he frowned while speaking.

"So what's on your mind? You look upset about something," Gregory commented.

"I'm supposed to be back in LA tomorrow for some meetings. I've spoken with my boss and told him I've got a personal issue to deal with but he's not happy with me."

"So, go," Gregory said. "Introduce me to Jarvis and I can take it from here."

"I can't do that and you *know* I can't," Tony retorted. "It's bad enough that I'm not part of Jarvis' clan but all the help would disappear if I wasn't here to facilitate things."

Gregory sighed. "Oh, I know. I just hoped maybe weres had decided to cease being so insular. You're not going to lose your job, are you?"

"No. Hal will rant and rave for about a week, probably call me all sorts of names but in the end, he'd be hard-pressed to replace me. Besides, I already rescheduled those meetings for Friday, figuring we'd be here at least another day or two. A slight inconvenience that's happened before."

"Whoever these jokers are, they're screwing up a bunch of lives," I fumed. "While I'm glad for your help, I'm sorry this is causing you so much trouble, Tony. Oh, shit. I'd better call Sally and check in. I haven't talked with her since Friday morning. Ev will kill me if the company goes to pot while he's sitting in some dank cave getting beaten up."

I was getting really mad again. I started shaking and all of a sudden, Fudge came running out of the bedroom and literally leapt into my arms, purring as loudly as I'd ever heard him.

"Fudge has the right of it," Gregory said soothingly. "Get hold of your emotions. We don't need another earthquake."

Crap. I couldn't even get good and mad anymore. I took several deep breaths to calm myself. "Thanks," I said as a burrowed my face into Fudge's fur.

"Call Sally. I'm sure everything is fine or she would have called you but it will make you feel better. We don't have anything else to do until the next note shows up. Me? I'm going to change into some more comfortable clothing and go for a walk." Gregory went into his bedroom and closed the door.

"Are you *sure* you can stay?" I asked Tony.

Tony crossed the room, took Fudge from me and after putting him on the floor, took me into his arms. "Yes, Doll. I'm fine. Face time is good but I really can handle most everything by email and telephone. I'm more concerned about you. You're dealing with an awful lot right now, what with finding out you're a witch right in the middle of dealing with your boss being kidnapped."

I sniffled a little. "I've dealt with a lot of stressful things in my life but I must admit this is probably the worst. I have faith in you and Gregory that we'll get Ev back but the money part is worrying me and I definitely have no idea how to handle this witch thing."

He kissed the top of my head. "Trust me, I know how difficult it is to deal with a new self and you don't have quite the change to adjust to that I did. You're lucky that the best person to help you adapt is also your best friend who knows you well. Right now just try to keep a check on your red-haired temper. We'll get Ev back and if I have anything to say about it, we'll get the money back, too."

He hugged me and pushed me toward the bedroom. "Change into something more comfortable than that suit and call Sally. You'll feel better. I have some more emails to send."

Chapter 8

Under Fudge's close supervision, I changed back into jeans and a T-shirt, then sat on the bed and called Sally.

"Hey, how's it going?" she asked after recognizing my voice.

"We're still, um, negotiating with the kidnappers. I'm more concerned with what's happening back there."

"Oh, everything is fine. The weekend reports had nothing unusual in them and I've started processing payroll for you. Omar came in a little while ago to see Ev. When I told him Ev was out of touch, he just shrugged his shoulders and left a message for Ev to call when he got back. Truth be told, I'm a little bored. I'll bet things are a lot more exciting down there. I heard there was a minor earthquake on Saturday."

She had no idea but I wasn't about to relate the past three days on the telephone. "We'll hopefully be back tomorrow or Wednesday. Keep the home fires burning, huh?"

"Will do. Call if there's anything I can do on this end."

I ended the call feeling a little better. I had faith that Sally could handle almost anything but nonetheless, I wasn't accustomed to not having my finger on the pulse of the business. Fudge followed me out into the living room. As I sat on the couch and reached for the television remote, another note landed on the coffee table with a "poof".

We assume you have the additional funds by this time.
Check into the Days Inn in Dahlonega by five. We will let
you know the exchange arrangements this evening.

Shit. Jarvis' boys weren't supposed to check out the possible locations until nightfall. If the kidnappers wanted the exchange to happen before we knew which cave they were using, there was a good possibility we wouldn't be able to rescue Ev *and* keep the money.

"So now what?" I asked Tony.

"First, call Gregory and get him back here. It sounds like they want the exchange to happen tonight, which means we have to either move up our own timetable or change plans. I have to talk to Jarvis."

I called Gregory as instructed and in less than ten minutes he was back in the suite, reading the note.

"They're getting sloppy in their eagerness. This one has a hint of a signature on it," he said with a smile. "One more like this and I will be able to go to the Councils to get a name."

"And that does us good because…?" I said.

"Once I know *who* it is, I will know what their element is and quite possibly how strong they are. That will let me formulate a plan to counteract whatever spells they've managed to bind Ev with."

"Oh." Strangely, I, a writer, was at a loss for words. Once again, I was way out of my element.

"Jarvis says there's nothing they can do until nightfall," Tony said after closing his phone. "Most of the guys have jobs and besides, it's not like we can transform and roam around during daylight without drawing attention."

"I understand. We may have to delay the exchange," Gregory answered. "In the meantime, I suggest we all pack up. Whatever happens from here will take place up in the mountains so we no longer need this hotel as a base." He picked up the phone and made arrangements for us to check out.

Since all I could do was what I was told, I went into the bedroom and packed my bag, then took care of Fudge's things. I felt bad using the wastebasket to put his litter in but there was nothing else to do with it. I consoled myself with the fact that the housekeeping staff had probably seen and smelled worse. At least the bin had a liner that I knotted closed.

Gregory came into the bedroom. "All packed up? Good." With a wave of his hands, Fudge's now-empty litter box, bag of litter, food dish and food container disappeared.

"They're back at your apartment," he said after seeing my inquiring look. "It's much easier than carrying it all with us, don't you think? I will retrieve them once we're settled in the new hotel."

"So if you can just whisk things through the ether, why do I have to empty the litter box? Can't you just make that go somewhere, too?"

"To where?" he replied. "I have to know where I'm taking something from or sending something to. I have no idea where garbage dumps are and even if I did, there's the issue of packaging. I could move the box with the litter in it but then we'd need another box. Or I could move each clump of used litter, each piece of feces and each kernel of unused litter individually. Time- and energy-consuming, to say the least."

Another "Oh" escaped my lips.

"Shall we?" Gregory asked with a sweep of his arm. I put my jacket on and as before, zipped it partway to make a pouch for Fudge who settled himself against my stomach. While not uncomfortable, the added weight made me feel awkward. I had a notion that this might be how a pregnant woman felt. Thankfully, the thought was fleeting. That wasn't something I wanted to dwell on.

We stopped for lunch on the way and pulled into the parking lot of the Dahlonega Days Inn just after three o'clock. Opening the door to our room, I realized that I had been terribly spoiled the last few days.

"Someone must have an interest in this business," Tony grimaced. "I haven't stayed in a place this small in years."

"I have but it wasn't quite this basic," I countered. "At least it's clean."

Fudge jumped out of his jacket-pouch and proceeded to investigate every corner of the room. It didn't take long and when he was done, he trotted over to me with his head held high and tail erect. I gathered him back into my arms as a knock sounded at our door.

Tony admitted Gregory, who had the room next to ours. Gregory closed his eyes, waved his hand and Fudge's accoutrements appeared under the sink next to the bathroom. He looked at me. "Amy, I'm going to do something to you you're not going to like."

My eyes popped. "You're *what?*"

"We need to delay the exchange. Whoever is spearheading this, David most likely, has keyed everything to you. If you're sick, *you* can't make the exchange, which is what I think they want. Hopefully, that will buy us enough time for Jarvis' people to do their scouting."

"How will they know? Apart from hangovers, I don't get sick. And how can you make me sick?" I *so* did not like where this was heading.

"Remember, all the notes have appeared in the room where you happen to be. Therefore, we know their witch or wizard is able to keep tabs on you." Gregory's voice was calm and I could tell he was trying to keep me that way. "It will be nothing serious, I promise. But it's springtime down here. I can pull enough pollen out of the air to give *anyone* an allergic reaction. You'll just have the standard head cold symptoms until late tonight when I banish the pollen from your system."

"But, but," I stuttered.

"That's brilliant!" Tony cried.

"I'm sorry, Amy, but it was the best solution I could think of. We *need* the delay if we're going to have any chance of thwarting the kidnappers' plans."

"But I've never been sick."

"That's due to your witch's immune system. Like other long-lived beings, we seem to be very resistant to bacteria, viruses and the like that generally affect the human population. It's probably one of the reasons that, while human in most other respects, we live much longer lives.

"Notice I said resistant, not impervious. We *can* get sick. It just takes a lot more of whatever - it - is to affect us. I will wager the only time you get a hangover is when you really go overboard on the alcohol, right?"

All this time I believed I didn't get hangovers because I was careful with my drinking. But the more I thought about it, the more I remembered times that I hadn't drunk any water and still hadn't gotten a hangover. He was correct and I admitted as much.

"Alcohol is a poison. Where your human friends may have a whopping hangover after only five or six drinks, it takes a lot more for the poison to overpower your system. Naturally, it all depends on body size, metabolism, et cetera but…"

"I see what you're saying," I cut him off. "But can't you come up with something else? I have friends who get spring or fall allergies and I don't want to be that miserable."

"Sorry," he said with a wry grin. "I honestly did think on it during the whole drive up here but that was my best shot. Unless you have another idea…"

I didn't. "This totally sucks. You're sure it'll be short-term?"

"I promise. You will feel fine before you go to sleep."

"Okay," I sighed. "Then go for it. Let's get it over with."

Gregory opened the door and after peering out at the street, presumably to ensure he wasn't being watched, moved his hands around. It looked like he was pulling water toward himself, sort of like you do when you're splashing yourself in the tub. I felt a breeze stir my hair, even though the trees outside gave no hint of wind. A cloud of dust gathered in front of him. With an exclamation, he turned and pushed the cloud my way.

Fudge sneezed, then so did I. Again. And again. My head felt like one of my stuffed animals - filled with batting. My eyes itched and started watering. I ran over to the tissue box so cleverly built into the sink vanity and used half of it, trying to clear my nose.

"I feel awful," I moaned.

"I'm so sorry," Tony put his arm around me. "I had allergies before I was turned and remember how miserable they were. At least yours will be short-lived."

"Oh, that's a consolation. How do people deal with this year after year?" I sneezed and blew my nose again.

"Put her to bed," Gregory told him. "These types of hotels don't have room service so I'm going to go see where we can get dinner from. Call me when we get a note."

Tony got my nightgown out of my case and helped me into bed. He even brought the box of tissues over to the bedside table after filling the litter box, food and water dishes. He and Fudge arranged themselves to either side of me and we all lay there, watching inane afternoon television.

Without anything to capture my attention and my eyes wanting to close anyways, I fell asleep at some point. The next thing I knew, I was being jostled awake.

"Doll, the next note just popped in," Tony's voice said as I felt a rough tongue licking my nose. That didn't feel so good on a spot sore from using so much cheap tissue earlier. I pushed Fudge aside, sat up and blew my nose yet again.

"Ow. Gregory had better be good at healing, too. My nose feels like I've peeled about five layers of skin off," I whined.

"Only a little longer. I promise. Read the note while I call Gregory."

Miss McCollum,

Tony let Gregory in as I read.

"My eyes are watering so badly I can't see much of the television, let alone drive," I griped. "Your nasty ploy worked, Gregory, but how do we tell them?"

"It will be pizza for dinner," he said as he arranged himself in one of the two chairs at the tiny table. "If everything is working as usual, you should be able to write your reply as you did with the original note and it will return to them."

"Okay. How much longer do I have to be sick?"

"Until we get their answer, I'd think. We need to ensure they know you're really sick. May I see the note, please?"

I handed it to him and after a moment, he said, "Whoever sent this got careful again. No signature this time. Damn." He gave the note back to me saying, "Here's what you write."

I grabbed the pen from the bedside table and took his dictation:

I can't drive anywhere tonight. I have a cold or something and am too sick. Will you accept delivery from Gregory or Tony? Amy

Without meaning to, I sneezed on the paper just as I was signing my name. The paper disappeared with the last stroke of the Y.

"Beautiful touch," Gregory exclaimed.

"I couldn't help myself," I pointed out.

"I know but that parchment is now damp and it will just emphasize the fact that you're sick. I know you want the all-meat special, Tony but Amy, what do you like on your pizza?"

I didn't have much of an appetite and said so. "Once again, I will remind you that you need to eat," Gregory admonished.

"I know what you said. I just feel like shit and want to go back to sleep. I usually get a vegetarian pizza."

"I can eat either so I will order one meat and one vegetarian. Have a snooze while we wait for delivery of both food and the next note. I suspect they're scrambling since we've put a monkey wrench into their timetable."

I settled back down then sat back up. "Make sure there's enough so Fudge gets one slice."

Gregory looked at my cat, who stared back at him. "A cat eats pizza?" He laughed.

"Just the sauce and cheese," I said. "But we've always shared and I'm not going to stop now."

Gregory laughed again and looking at Fudge, said, "Not a problem, my friend. You will get your piece, too."

Fudge meowed in reply and we both snuggled back under the covers while Gregory called the number on the card he found on top of the television. Tony pulled out his phone and dialed. I drifted off to the sound of Gregory placing the order and Tony saying, "Jarvis, the drop point is someplace called R Ranch."

I awoke to a loud banging on the door. Whoever it was either didn't know their own strength or thought the motel rooms were cavernous.

"Damn, man. A simple rap would have been sufficient." Gregory greeted the delivery guy, handed him some money and took possession of a couple of pizza boxes and a bag with soda bottles and something else in it. He placed it all on the table and gently closed the door.

"Teenagers!" Gregory swore. "Insolent."

"Calm yourself, man," Tony chided. "He looked like a linebacker. Probably didn't know he was knocking so hard."

"Oh, I know. It just irritated me," Gregory said as he got plastic cups off the vanity and after pouring a shot from a hip flask that magically appeared in his hand, filled the rest of each cup with tonic from one of the bottles in the bag. He handed a drink to me and Tony and took a swig from his.

"Fudge gets the first slice," I said.

"I figured as much," Tony said as he pulled paper plates and napkins out of the bag. Fudge hopped off the bed and nuzzled Tony's leg as he duly put the first slice on a plate, then set it on the floor over by Fudge's food dish. Fudge trotted behind him and immediately dug in, daintily picking off all the vegetables, being sure to eat every last iota of cheese off each one before setting them aside.

The men watched him with interest while devouring their own dinner. "He's so meticulous about everything," Tony said while Gregory commented, "I've never seen a cat eating pizza!"

Me? I was trying to chew and breathe at the same time. Given that I couldn't breathe through my nose, I was having difficulty. The pizza didn't taste like anything more than cardboard, either. I gave up after one slice and after blowing my nose yet again, curled back under the bed covers.

"How much longer?" I groused.

"Don't know," Gregory said as he cleaned up, putting all the paper into the wastebasket and putting one box with a couple of uneaten slices on what passed for a dresser. "We need to ensure they're positive you're too sick to do anything tonight. Anything good on TV?"

I resolved to sleep until I could be magically cured of this affliction, especially since Tony found a basketball game on one of the few channels the motel got. It figured. I felt like shit and the only thing on television to distract me was my least-favorite sport. Fudge resumed his position next to me and I fell asleep to his quiet purr.

"Hey, Doll, wake up," Tony whispered as he shook my shoulder. "The next note is here."

I groaned, sat up and sneezed. Loudly. Gregory stirred in the chair he'd fallen asleep in. As I blew my nose for the hundredth time in just a few hours, he reached over and grabbed both a piece of parchment and a bottle off the bed next to me.

"Looks like it worked," he chortled, holding the bottle up so I could see the label. "Nyquil" it read. Still laughing, he read the note out loud.

> *We will NOT allow either the wizard or were to interfere any more than they already have. You have 24 hours to feel well enough to drive. Same instructions, tomorrow night.*

"Can I be made well, now?" I asked.

"Give it a few more hours. I saw someone in the trees across the road awhile ago so I think this place is being watched," Gregory was still chuckling. "Once they're certain we're all bedded down for the night, they will probably go away. Just as I pulled the pollen from outside, I need to put it back outside and I don't want anyone seeing that. Let's all pretend like we're going to bed. I will return after midnight and do it then."

Great. I looked at the clock. Still at least another two hours of feeling miserable. "The sooner the better," I said as Gregory left our room for his.

"All for a good cause, Doll," Tony tried to console me. "You bought us the time we need to hopefully find out where Ev is being held."

"Yeah, yeah. I'm a hero. This sucks," I pouted as I slid back down under the covers, pulling the tissue box with me.

"Go to sleep. I'll wake you when Gregory comes back," he answered, tucking me in as if I were a little kid.

***

"It's a good thing you don't get sick. You make a terrible patient," Gregory said to me several hours later as we stepped out of the hotel room onto the walkway.

"What did you expect?" I retorted. "I've never been sick and you inflict that on me?"

"All for a good cause."

"I know. Tony said the same thing. Can we get on with it?"

There was just enough light from the dim lamps along the wall for me to see the glint in Gregory's eyes. He was highly amused – at my expense. I would find a way to pay him back. Wait. No, I wouldn't. This was all to save Ev. I'd get my pound of flesh from *him* once he was back safely.

"You have to help with this one," Gregory told me.

"Huh?"

"All that pollen is now residing in your body, causing the allergic reaction. I need you to envision all of it floating from your nose, sinuses and eyes, through your mucous membranes and blood vessels and gathering together in your throat. When I say 'now', cough hard."

"Are you sure we're not being watched? I'm not real comfortable standing out here in the middle of the night in my pajamas."

"Yes, Tony and I both checked the area a few minutes ago. Do you want to get rid of this or not?"

Did I! I closed my eyes and did as Gregory had instructed, envisioning all those little pollen bastards being rounded up and

73

corralled until I felt a huge lump at the back of my throat. I heard "now" and opening my eyes, coughed as instructed.

When I opened my eyes, I saw Gregory making a pulling motion toward him with both hands and tasted dust as I coughed out not just air, but a cloud. Gregory continued his pulling motion and the cloud followed his hands. With a grunt, he pushed the cloud toward the street. I could see it disperse before it got as far as the streetlights.

"Feel any better?" he asked.

I could breathe again! If I wasn't concerned about making more of a spectacle of myself than I already had by being outside in my night dress, I would have whooped for joy. I took a long breath and let it out.

"My eyes are still a little itchy and I still feel a little congested but I can breathe. Thank you."

"You should be right as rain in a few minutes. It will take a bit for the residual effects to wear off."

We heard Tony's cell phone ring and almost jammed ourselves in the door, both trying to get in to hear at the same time. At this time of night, it could only be one person. Jarvis.

"Yes. Yes. Wonderful. There's a Waffle House down at the corner from our hotel. Meet you there at nine for breakfast? Good. See you then." Tony smiled at us as he closed his phone.

"Telling Jarvis about the R Ranch made things a lot easier. They found the abandoned mine Ev is being held in about six miles away from there. It's currently being guarded by three dwarves and a were no one recognized so he's a rogue.

"As you heard, we're meeting for breakfast at nine. Jarvis and his two lieutenants, who work for him, will take the day off and meet us. That's only seven hours from now so I suggest we get what sleep we can."

"I didn't realize they were going to help with the rescue, too," Gregory said.

"I arranged it with Jarvis the first time I spoke with him. I figured reinforcements might be necessary. And it'll only cost us half the agreed-upon price. Jarvis is looking forward to taking care of the rogue himself. Feeling better, Doll?"

I was feeling better by the minute and said so.

"Let's take Tony's suggestion and get some sleep. I will collect you shortly before nine. I suggest wearing something comfortable enough for hiking. Good night." Gregory closed our door behind him.

"Doll, I need to warn you about something," Tony said as he stripped to his shorts in preparation for bed.

"What's that?" I asked as I crawled back under the covers. Fudge stood expectantly on the floor next to the bed, ready to hop up and make his customary nest out of my hair.

"I'm hoping it won't get nasty but if it does, a were fight isn't pretty and in this case, may be to the death. If the rogue doesn't bow to Jarvis' authority, the lieutenants will kill him. Since I know we can't leave you behind, I thought I should prepare you for something ugly."

"What?" I almost screamed.

"Shh. I know there's no one in the room on the other side of us but you don't need to wake the entire motel."

"What do you mean, to the death?" I said, a little more quietly.

"What were you thinking? We'd march up to the mouth of the mine and they'd sweetly deliver Ev to us without argument? If it had been a normal kidnapping, we'd have already exchanged the money for Ev by now. But it's not normal, is it? You heard Gregory the other day. Whoever it is, whether it's this David person or not, isn't playing by the rules. Adding a rogue were into the mix with the clan leader and his looeys involved just adds fuel to the fire."

"No, I didn't expect them to hand Ev over without argument. I don't know what I thought but bloodshed certainly wasn't in any part of my imagination unless it was just a cut or a scrape from rocks. You're certain about all this?" I shuddered.

"That's why it hurts me that we can't leave you here while we go get Ev. I've been in a scrap or two and I'm certain Gregory has but you haven't. There's going to be a fight, Doll. I don't know how bad of one but you need to prepare yourself for the worst."

"You couldn't wait until morning to tell me, could you?" I shivered. Tony pulled me into his arms.

"We won't have much time in the morning and I wanted you to have some time to steel yourself."

"Great. Nice dreams you're giving me, dog. Turn the television back on. I'm not sure I'm going to sleep much."

Tony reached over me for the remote and turned the television to cartoons. I laid my head on his shoulder while Fudge arranged my hair to his liking and after a couple of turns, flopped down against my back. Within minutes, both my guys were snoring softly.

I kept company with Tom and Jerry until sometime later, my eyes finally closed.

Chapter 9

The following morning saw us sitting at the Waffle House, across the table from three rugged-looking men. The clan leader, Jarvis, could have been Tony's brother: a little over six feet tall, built like a wide receiver with dark hair and eyes. They even looked a little alike, except Jarvis had some gray in his hair where Tony did not. What really separated the two was Jarvis' thick southern accent. I found it difficult to understand him at times. The other two men's speech was no different.

Jarvis eyed me up and down. "You're awfully small. Are you sure you want to go with us?"

After Tony's warning of violence the night before, I wasn't certain I wanted any part of it. However, Ev was my boss/friend/family and I felt a certain obligation to do so. I didn't trust my voice so simply nodded.

"In that case, here's how I think we should handle it." Jarvis proceeded to describe the layout of the land, and explain that we were going to climb up the back of the hill and approach the mine from upslope which, today, would also be upwind.

"Gregory, I'd like you to bind any magical types we may find. We'll identify them for you by smell. Sam and I will deal with any weres. Tony, while we're dealing with the outside guards, you and Jimmy go into the mine and take care of anybody there. You, little lady, stay upslope until one of us tells you it's safe to come down. Is everyone clear?"

We all nodded and rose as one. Gregory paid the bill at the cash register then we all trooped out to one of the largest pickup trucks I'd ever seen. It was big enough that all six of us could sit in the cab, although it was a little cramped because Gregory and I were the two smallest people and he was no shrimp. Two large leather satchels sat at our feet.

Twenty minutes later, we were in a parking lot with signage indicating a state park. "Ready for a hike?" Jarvis asked as we piled out. "It'll take us about a half hour to get where we need to be. There are water bottles in the cooler in the back. Everyone take at least one."

Jimmy led the way. If I hadn't been busy watching where my feet went, I'd have marveled at the scenery. Although it was not truly an old-growth forest, my guess was most of the trees were about fifty years old. The deciduous trees were starting to leaf out and the white dogwood flowers against the dark green of the pines made it look like a green bouquet with baby's breath. It was almost as pretty as some areas of the Boundary Waters I'd been to.

Up we climbed. I was grateful for all the bike riding I did around the lakes in Minneapolis. Otherwise, my legs would probably have collapsed about half-way to our destination. I'd almost finished my bottle of water and was starting to get a little winded when Jimmy held up his hand, indicating we were supposed to stop.

He turned back to us and quietly said, "The mine is just over then down this ridge about fifty feet. Stay here. I'll go look then come back and report." He kicked off his shoes and right before my eyes, he shimmered and in his place stood a wolf. Jimmy was a blond man and the wolf had beautiful gold and white fur, sort of like a wolfy golden retriever. I gulped. If I hadn't known he was friendly, I would have hightailed it. The wolf gave what was probably a (very toothy) grin in my direction, his tongue lolling and tail wagging just like that golden retriever.

"I wish I could do it that effortlessly," Tony whispered. "I still rip my clothes."

"You'll get there, youngster," Jarvis whispered back as Jimmy silently bounded up the ridge and out of sight.

I'd just finished taking the last swig of my water and was wondering what was taking so long when Jimmy came striding down the hill in human form. He crouched down, and drawing a diagram in the dirt with a stick, said quietly,

"From the top of the ridge looking down, the entrance is here, about fifty feet away. There's one were to either side of the opening and although I can't see them, I can smell a wizard and another male were somewhere. I'm guessing they're just inside. I couldn't smell any dwarves but if they're around, they must be farther into the mine. Neither of the weres I could see is ours and neither looks very alert. They're just squatting, smoking cigarettes and talking."

Jarvis nodded. "Gregory, you go with Tony and Jimmy into the mine. Otherwise the plan stays the same. Little lady, you stay here until someone comes to get you." I grimaced. Oh, not at the admonishment to stay behind. I knew I wouldn't be any help in the fight that was sure to come. But that "Little Lady" epithet was starting to get to me.

Tony gave me a peck on the cheek, took his shoes off and hung his jacket on a nearby tree limb. "See you in a bit, Doll," he said as he shimmered right along with the other three, except instead of his clothes transforming with him, his shirt and pants ripped as his body reformed itself. Once in wolf form, he kicked the pieces of cloth away from him. The wolf looked at me and I think he shrugged his shoulders.

"Do please stay here, Amy," Gregory said. "We will come get you when it's safe. In the meantime, try not to get angry about anything. That's a mine underneath us and it probably has loose rocks." He gave me a quick hug then with a nod at the wolves, followed them up the ridge.

Shortly, I heard shouts, then growling and snarls. *Lots* of growling and snarls. *Loud* growling and snarls. It seemed to go on forever. Finally, curiosity got the better of me. I crawled up the hill as quietly as I could and looked over the ridge to see what was happening.

I'd never before seen a dog fight. I think I had now. Three wolves were circling two, every now and again lunging forward with a snap of jaws. As I watched the curious fight, two wolves tumbled into view, legs and paws locked in a vicious embrace and each trying to bite the other's neck. Finally, one of the wolves got a good bite in and with a quick jerk of his head, snapped the neck of the other, who went limp. The victorious wolf disentangled himself, stood next to his victim and howled.

That was enough to distract the two encircled wolves and the other three also went in for the kill. I felt bile rise in my throat as I watched them efficiently dispatch their quarry. The other three also let out a howl. As I surveyed the carnage, I realized that the first to die had the same markings as the wolf who had, just a few brief minutes before, kicked off pieces of torn clothing in front of me.

At that point, I saw nothing but red. I'm sure I screamed but the next thing I knew, I was racing down the slope, hurling balls of green energy at the wolf who had killed my lover. The first knocked him to the ground, a couple went wide of their mark and went into the trees and a couple may even have hit a good guy. I didn't care.

As I slid down the scree I felt a rumbling below my feet. I paid no attention to anything except the pain in my heart and the fervent desire to kill the gray wolf. I threw energy balls until I had nothing left with which to make them. I skittered with the uneven footing, fell on my ass and proceeded to burst into tears. I tried throwing another ball but only a wee bit of light flickered in my palm. The next thing I knew, a dark brown ball of fur barreled into my chest and knocked me on my back.

Amidst the tears and heaving sobs, I felt calming energy wash over me and the vibration of a purr on my chest. My blurry vision told me that Fudge was the barreling ball of fur. A pair of feet came into view, then knees, then a kindly face that looked so much like an older version of Tony. I heard Fudge hiss then resume his purring.

"I'm so sorry, little lady," Jarvis' voice said. "You weren't meant to see the fight, just in case something like this happened."

"He said he knew how to handle himself," I sobbed. "How could he lose?"

"It happens. We're all good at fights because that's how we play. The other guy was just better this time. I hate to ask it of you but could you calm down? We need your help. And cat? I'm not going to harm her."

I sat up, cradling Fudge in my arms and nuzzled his fur. He never stopped purring. "I want to go home," I bawled. "I want to go to sleep and wake up to find this has just been a nightmare. I want…"

Jarvis interrupted my plaint. "Little lady, we still need to get your boss and Gregory out of the mine. There's been an earthquake and the entrance is blocked. By the way, no one told us you were a witch. It's a good thing you don't know how to throw killing energy."

That made me sit up straight. Oh, shit. I'd gotten mad when I wasn't supposed to and now Ev *and* Gregory were in trouble because of me. That also sort of explained Fudge's presence, although how he got to me was a mystery. I buried my face in Fudge's fur, trying to get myself under control – I *had* to so I could help my friends. Jarvis waited patiently.

My sobs finally subsided to sniffles. "What can I do? I'm not strong enough to move boulders."

Jarvis smiled. "None of us are. But I can talk to Gregory through the rocks and he tells me you should be able to sense which ones are okay to move without bringing anything more down. He'll do the heavy lifting."

Jarvis helped me stand and as I cradled Fudge, I looked around me. Tony's body, still in wolf form, lay a few feet in front of me. I walked over, squatted down and ran my hands along coarse fur and strong shoulders. I felt myself start to get angry again and Fudge batted my face with his paw. My reminder to keep my emotions under control. Jarvis cleared his throat.

"We'll take care of him, I promise. The one who killed him is also dead. I made certain of that. I know you're grieving but…"

I looked at Jarvis and then past him to Sam and Jimmy. They all had scratches here and there but those were healing even as I watched. I got myself together as best I could and looked back at Jarvis. "What do I need to do?"

He motioned me over to what had been the entrance to the mine that was now blocked with boulders, smaller rocks and dirt. "There's a small opening, here. You can talk to Gregory through it."

I walked over to the mess and did indeed see a small space between a couple of boulders. After another sniffle escaped, I took a deep breath to center myself then shouted, "Gregory, are you okay?"

"You do not need to shout," came the reply. "I'm only about six feet away from you. The better question is, are *you* alright and is Fudge with you?"

"No to the first, yes to the second. How did Fudge get here and what do I need to do? How's Ev?"

"I sent for Fudge as soon as I felt the ground shift. I'm sorry about Tony but that's why we wanted you to stay behind. Ev needs medical attention so we have to clear the opening to get him out. This is what I want you to do, with Fudge's help."

He told me to use my senses to probe the pile of rocks to see how they were fitted together. It was sort of like playing Jenga. We had to figure out which rocks to move without making any more come down. "Fudge can help you see the structure of the pile, understand where the stress points are and which ones I can safely move. If I can clear a three or four foot hole, I can levitate Ev out of here."

"Okay. Give me a minute or two to figure it out. How do I let you know which rocks?"

"Wrap a tendril of energy around the good ones. I will see it."

"I don't know if I have anything left. The last ball I tried to throw just fizzled in my hand."

"Well, that's a good thing. Jarvis said you gave him a good-sized bruise with one. Do the same thing we practiced in the hotel. Find it around you and use that."

I closed my eyes and extended my senses to the jumble of rocks in front of me. I could feel the pressure of Fudge in the back of my brain, guiding me until I could see the pile as a completed jigsaw puzzle that had to be carefully taken apart. I sure caused a mess. But the more I – we – looked, the more I could see which ones could be moved without causing the top of the mine entrance to fully collapse.

I changed my focus to the area around me, to find some energy to borrow. I didn't have to look far. The trees, the ground…everything radiated energy. I thought back to what Gregory had taught me and pulled the glitter not into a ball but into a string that I wrapped around the first rock to be moved.

"Stand at an angle from the entrance," I heard. "I have to push them out as there's no room in here."

Jarvis, who had been standing next to me the entire time, pulled me by my free arm (Fudge still sat in the other with his front paws on my shoulder) and we moved to our left. I heard a grunt, then the rock I'd marked fell out of its spot and rolled downhill, smashing into a tree at the edge of the clearing.

"Good start, Amy," Gregory called. "Next?"

I marked the next and that one rolled out and down, smashing into the first. And so it went. Slowly. Thirty minutes later, I thought I was going to drop from exhaustion when Gregory climbed out of the hole we'd made. He came over to me and gave me a hug.

"We did it!" He let go. "Jarvis, we need to make a litter. I don't think Ev can walk far and especially not back down to the truck. I have prisoners I will need to pay attention to so I can't levitate him that far."

Jarvis snapped his fingers. Sam and Jimmy disappeared up over the crest of the ridge. "We have a tarp in the truck. That and a couple of small trees for poles ought to do it."

When Jarvis' men had left, Gregory put his arm around me once again. "I know this is a difficult time. Can you hold it together a little longer?"

I felt the tears I'd been holding back threaten to spill out again. I sniffled a couple of times, willed myself to be strong and nodded. "Yes, I'll be okay."

"Good girl." Gregory nodded, climbed back into the hole and very shortly, Ev's body came floating through, just like you see in the movies. He was lying on his back, surrounded by a blanket of red energy. Once Ev cleared the hole, Gregory's upper body appeared. Gregory's hands were in front of him, obviously guiding the ogre. As his hands lowered, so did Ev until he was laying on the ground at my feet. The red blanket disappeared. Ev looked up at me through swollen green and yellow eyes.

"Gregory tells me I have you to thank for finding me. How did you know?" he croaked.

Jarvis squatted down, pulled a water bottle out of his back pocket and gave Ev a sip. Ev eyed him as best he could. "A werewolf, too? I have a feeling I'm not going to like the whole story."

"Lie still," I admonished him. "We'll tell you the whole story but you've got some healing to do first."

Ev coughed and Jarvis gave him another sip of water. Sam and Jimmy reappeared with a tarp, some rope and a couple of saplings they'd obviously ripped from the ground on their way back. After stripping the branches off, they constructed a very serviceable litter. While they'd been working, Gregory, a dwarf and another man had crawled through the hole. Both the dwarf and man looked somewhat worse for wear with cuts and two black eyes each. Gregory had left their legs free so they could walk but otherwise, they were wrapped in red energy like a mummy.

The dwarf was the fired guard, David. I walked over and punched him in the face as hard as I could. "You bastard," I yelled. "I could kill you for what you've done."

Gregory pulled me away. "He will be taken care of by the Dwarf Council, Amy, as this wizard will answer to the Wizards' Council. Let justice run its course." I stuck my now-bruised fist in my mouth and tearfully nodded. When he saw that I'd calmed a bit, he let go of me and turned to Jarvis.

"Jarvis, I need your claws. I'm going to have to loosen these two for a second to get Ev onto the litter."

Jarvis grinned. "Happy to help." He walked over to the two, held out his hands in front of them and we all watched his fingers grow into some nasty-looking claws. He then walked behind the prisoners and placed one hand on each neck. "Twitch and I'll sink these into your jugulars."

The red wrappings faded but didn't quite disappear completely as Gregory reformed the red blanket and gently moved Ev over to the litter. Once Ev was settled, he turned his attention back to the prisoners and the red energy glowed brightly once again. Jarvis took his hands away from the necks and his fingers returned to normal.

"Amy, it will take all four of us on the litter. I'm fairly certain I can hold my concentration but I want you to watch these two and if you see the energy fade, alert me. Ev, I'm sorry but you will be jostled a bit. It's not a smooth path. But you will see a healer soon."

Ev groaned and nodded. Fudge hopped out of my arms and started up the hill. We all followed … David and the wizard in front, the three weres and Gregory carrying Ev, then me. I paused and looked back at Tony's body lying in the clearing. Jarvis saw me.

"I promise, we'll come back shortly to take care of him. He'll be cremated tonight. I'll call his clan leader who will call his parents and employer." I swallowed hard and nodding, said a silent goodbye as I turned to follow everyone up the hill.

Chapter 10

The walk back to the truck took longer than the walk up the ridge. The guys were being very careful, trying not to jostle Ev any more than they had to. I kept my eye on the prisoners but the color of Gregory's bindings never faded. Without much to do, my mind went back to the events of the previous hours and I felt myself starting to both cry and get angry at the same time. I knew now that I had to keep a lid on my emotions and choked them down. I damned near fell flat on my face when Fudge twined himself around my legs, seeking attention. I reached down, picked him up and immediately calmed as I felt his purring.

While Fudge kept me from causing another earthquake, his presence didn't stop me from reliving the events of the last few hours over and over. By the time we reached the parking lot, all I could do was drop Fudge, run behind a tree and empty my stomach. As I crouched, shaking and feeling like shit, Gregory came over and put his arm around me.

"Now that I have a signal on my mobile, a helicopter will be here shortly to transport you to the airport. Ev wants to be treated back home so I've arranged for a medical plane. I have to stay for a few hours to wait for the dwarf and magical authorities to come get our prisoners so you will have to accompany Ev home. Are you up for it?"

I didn't have much of a choice, did I? I swallowed and nodded.

"Good. We have other things to talk about but they will wait until Ev's in the hospital. An ambulance will meet you at Flying Cloud. Once you've checked Ev in and seen him settled in his room, I suggest you go home. Sally can handle everything for one more day and I will meet you in the office tomorrow morning."

I nodded again. It was good that Gregory could take charge because I certainly couldn't do anything at that point but follow instructions. At the moment, my only thought was I wanted to brush my teeth.

"I don't have a toothbrush or toothpaste, but swish this around your mouth. It will make you feel better." Gregory handed me a travel-size bottle of mouthwash. I duly swished and spit. It did make me feel better.

A minute later, the purse I'd left in Jarvis' truck appeared at my feet. Gregory smiled. "I assumed you'd need it. As soon as I get rid of the prisoners, I will check us out of the hotel and transport everything to your apartment."

The sound of a helicopter broke through my grief fog and I felt the gale of its blades blow my hair and push me onto my butt. The wind subsided as the pilot turned the machine off. Two medical types jumped out with boxes in their hands and headed over to where Ev lay on the ground. As I watched, Gregory joined them and apparently gave them some instructions. Once Ev was strapped on their gurney and transferred to the helicopter, he motioned me over.

"These people are mundanes and won't accept a cat on board. Neither will the medical plane. So I'm going to send Fudge home. You need to get on board now. I will see you in the morning."

Gregory kissed the top of my head and with his hand on my back, guided me to the helicopter. While the medic strapped me into my seat, the motor roared and the rotor blades started turning. Gregory held Fudge in his arms, shielding him against the wind and waved to me.

The flight home was uneventful. The medics in the helicopter had given Ev something to knock him out so the transfer to the private ambulance plane, the flight to Minneapolis and the transfer to the hospital went smoothly. That gave me about four hours to wallow in my grief but not as much as I would have liked – I remembered that I had to keep a tight lid on my emotions. Who knew what I might do to a flying conveyance? It's probably a good thing I wasn't on a conventional plane with a fully-stocked bar.

I got Ev settled in his overly-large bed in a private room at St. Aloysius' Hospital – the only one in the Cities that treated non-humans. He was still knocked out via some powerful drugs and had what seemed like twenty IVs going at once. The wizard doctor told me that Ev had a broken jaw, a broken nose, two cracked ribs and more bruises than he could count. In addition, he was severely dehydrated and slightly starved.

"He's an ogre so I can't use magic to make him well. He should be ready to go home in three or four days but it's going to be a couple of weeks before he's fully healed. I'll keep you apprised."

I could only nod, ensure the desk had my cell number and head home. I was about to crawl into a taxi when a car screeched to a stop behind it. Cassandra jumped out of the passenger side and enveloped me in a big hug.

"Honey, we just heard from Gregory. Are you okay?"

"No." I started sobbing into her shoulder. I felt another arm around both of us and knew it was Tommy from the ever-present scent of coffee, bread and herbs.

"Come on. Let's get you home," Tommy said as he waved the taxi off. I let them tuck me into the back of the car, Cassandra crawling in beside me and rewrapping me in her long arms.

"I won't ask you to tell me what happened right now. I got the gist of it from Gregory. But you know I'm – we're here for you." Her voice soothed me and I sobbed myself to sleep on her shoulder, only to be woken again shortly thereafter as we stopped in front of my apartment building.

Cassandra saw me to the door and opened it with her key. "I hope you don't mind but I called Elinda and Marge. I suck at sleep spells and you need some dreamless sleep right now. They're waiting for you inside." She hugged me and pushed me through the door – right into Marge's ample bosom.

Marge and Elinda were like my grandmothers – always ready to lend an ear or to help where they could – and that included bringing me homemade cakes and cookies on a regular basis. I saw Elinda in my kitchen, doing something at the stove. Marge kept her arm around me as she guided me to the bedroom.

"I'm so, so sorry, honey. Cassandra told me a little of what's happened to you in the last few days. She's right – you need dreamless sleep and I'm going to make sure you get it. Climb into your jammies and crawl into bed. I'll be right back."

Fudge was already curled up on one of the pillows and he meowed softly as I did as I was told plus one other thing: I brushed my teeth. I'd just pulled the covers up to my chin when she reappeared with a mug in her hand.

"Drink this. It'll nourish you so you don't have to try to choke down food. It's not hot so you can down it."

I sat up and mechanically drank the liquid, grateful that, although slightly woodsy-tasting, it wasn't too bad.

Marge took the mug from my hand and smiled at me. "Lie back down and get comfortable. Fudge, you know what to do."

Fudge, without his usual kneading in my hair, curled up right next to me and I felt the now-familiar pressure at the back of my head. Marge closed her eyes, extended her hands and I could see and feel gentle tendrils of energy wrapping themselves around me, forcing the tense muscles to relax. My eyes closed and the last thing I remember is hearing *"Sleep well, my human. I will keep watch"* in my head.

When I opened my eyes, it was to a view of chocolate brown fur. Fudge had draped himself over my head again. This time, however, he moved before I had a chance to sneeze into his stomach, which would have necessitated another thorough grooming. The smell of coffee accompanied Cassandra's voice saying, "Mornin'. How ya feelin'?"

The events of the prior day slammed back into me and I pulled the covers all the way over my head. "Like shit," I mumbled. "What are you doing here?"

"You didn't think we'd leave you alone to wallow, did you? Marge, Elinda and I are taking turns until we're sure you've got a good handle on everything. Here, drink this. It's some of Gregory's Italian stuff I found in your suitcase which, by the way, is still in the middle of your living room." She handed me one of the two steaming mugs she was carrying then sat on my cedar chest.

After taking a sip from her mug and moaning a little with pleasure, she continued, "You've been through some awful crap in the last few days, not the least of which is your powers not just blossoming but rocketing off. Couple that with the horrible emotions you must be feeling and we think you need supervising. No arguing, either, because it's already been decided."

I glared at her. "What? I'm a little kid who can't tuck myself in at night? I don't need anyone hovering. You know I like my privacy."

"Amy, this is different. According to Gregory, you can cause earthquakes if you lose control. That's dangerous. A mundane who's been through what you have can lose it on a moment's notice. *You* can't afford to lose it. Ever."

I sighed and drank some more coffee. "All this before even one full cup of coffee. I know Marge and Elinda are retired but don't you have a deli to run? And I have to go into the office to take care of stuff that's slid while I was gone."

She grinned. "Yes, I do have a deli to run. And for the first time in our lives, we're both going to bring our cats to work. Familiars can talk to each other, you know, and Fudge can tell Merlin if anything is happening that means I need to run upstairs."

Someone had been doing some blabbing and his initials were Gregory Tremayne. I looked at the clock.

"Holy shit. It's already nine. Who's in the deli? I gotta get to the office."

"Calm down. Tommy opened the store for me this morning and Charlie's coming in early. Sally is already at her desk and Gregory won't be there until about noon. We have plenty of time. I need a refill and I know you do, too. We need to talk and the couch is a lot more comfortable than this chest. Come into the living room."

I duly padded after her and after refilling both our mugs, she curled up on one end of the sofa while I tucked my feet underneath myself in the recliner. Fudge hopped onto the chair arm and leaned against me.

"So, talk," she said. "Tell me in your own words what happened. Don't leave out anything, including how you felt while wielding energy. Filter out the rage if you can. I need to know how you process things."

For the next hour, I related everything I could remember. Strangely, I felt no rage or deep sorrow when I told her of Tony's death. I felt detached, somehow. I said as much.

Cassandra nodded at my cat. "That's Fudge at work. He's dampening your emotional centers. There are times we have work to do when strong emotions would screw up the spell. Familiars can block the stronger emotions so they don't come through in our magic. Once he releases his block, you'll feel them again. It kinda sucks in a way but on the other hand, it's helpful at times."

I looked at my cat and then at her. "This is weird," I said.

"You've got a lot of stuff to get used to. Fudge's abilities are just one of the weird things that are going to become normal. Familiars are much smarter than pets. Of course, they have to be. Fudge has been living with you for what? Five years, now? He knows you better than you know yourself. He knows when to help and when to stay out of things, including your head. I grew up with Merlin so I'm used to it. You'll get used to it in time, too."

My jaw dropped. "Wait. You *grew up* with Merlin? He's over thirty? Twenty years old is ancient for a cat." I looked at Fudge. "How long do you guys live, anyways?"

Fudge preened a little as Cassandra answered me. "They live as long as we do in this body. This body will die when you do and the spirit will reincarnate in another body when and where it's needed. Fudge and Merlin are probably a thousand years old."

More weird crap to process. My cat is a feline Yoda. Joy. But as long as we were on the subject of familiars…

"Does Merlin talk to you in your head? Gregory said they don't but I distinctly hear someone talking to me in English at times and I know it's not coming from my ears, if you get my drift."

Her eyes widened. "That's really rare. I know what Merlin's thinking but it's more of a feeling. He obviously understands what I'm saying but we don't converse, for lack of a better word. My great-aunt could hear her bulldog, Spike, speak, though. You're one of the lucky ones. You can have an actual conversation with him!"

"I am older than that moving picture character. He was only nine hundred as you humans count years. There are many of us who have lived long enough to develop telepathy with humans. If the youngster, Merlin as she calls him, behaves, perhaps I will teach him to have mind speech with his human."

My eyes widened as I looked down at my cat. He just looked back at me with a totally expressionless face.

"You have a lot of learning to do in a fairly short period of time," Cassandra continued. "Fudge can help with some things, like controlling your emotions and being something of a memory bank, but there are laws and methodology and stuff like that I'll need to teach you. From now until I deem otherwise, Sundays will be devoted to magical work."

I glared at her again. "I have things to do, you know. Like a job, my writing – oh hell, I'm even later than I was past a deadline. My editor is going to kill me." I looked at the clock again. It was ten-thirty. "I gotta get moving. I promise I'll be at your house at noon on Sunday, okay?"

"Make it eleven and you're eating both lunch and supper with us. Bring a notebook or your laptop. Whatever you're most comfortable taking notes on. Mom has given me permission to make a copy of my workbook for you so you'll have immediate reference material. But arrange your schedule so you have time during the week for studying. Like I said, you've got a lot of catching up to do.

I'm headed to the deli. I'll be bringing your lunch up so I'll see you in a bit."

She gave me a hug and headed out the door without another word. Fudge got off the arm of the chair and all of a sudden, I felt a wave of both sorrow and anger wash over me. I slumped back into the chair, not wanting to move.

"*I let go of the block,*" I heard. "*You must learn to deal with this as any human must.*"

He was right. I pushed myself out of the chair and headed for the shower.

After I dressed, it dawned on me that I was supposed to take Fudge to work with me. I didn't have a carrier for him, and I certainly didn't want cat hair all over my suit before I even set foot in the office.

"*Unlike dogs, I do not need a leash. I will walk beside you,*" he said. Having someone else in my head was going to take some getting used to.

"Why am I now just hearing you?" I asked him – out loud.

"*I have always been here. But your magical abilities had to completely manifest before your conscious mind would acknowledge me. Now, so other humans do not think you are completely crazy, I suggest you learn to think to me rather than speak aloud.*"

I know we got some funny looks. A human walking on the sidewalk with a cat trotting alongside. Daintily, I might add. It was still early spring in the frozen north and I'm sure the concrete was a little cold on the paws. "Do I need to get you booties or something to keep your paws warm?" I asked, er, thought.

"***Please*** *do not insult my dignity in that way. I have walked farther on much colder surfaces. I will be fine. Watch where you are walking instead of looking at me. You are going to trip on that tree root.*"

I looked up too late. I stubbed my toe on said tree root and damned near fell flat on my face. Thankfully, I didn't and there wasn't anyone looking to see my face flush deep red with embarrassment – and a wee bit of anger that my shoe was scuffed. I hated polishing my shoes – it was so messy. I heard a small chuckle in my head and walked with an eye on my path the rest of the way to the office.

Sally came around her desk and gave me a big hug before I could even get my coat off. Then, looking down at me she said, "Are you okay? I can keep things going just fine if you want to take a few days off."

"I wish people would quit asking me that," I replied. "No, I'm not okay but I will be. Work is the best medicine."

"All right but if you need to get out of here, you just get up and leave. No one will blame you. Why is there a cat with you? Did he follow you here?"

"Well, yes, in a way he did follow me. This is my familiar, Fudge. Fudge, this is Sally. Apparently I have some magical issues to work through and he's here to help. At least that's what he and Cassandra say."

"Wow. A familiar, huh? Jack is going to be jealous. No one in his family ever got assigned one. What issues?"

I sighed. Here we go again. "That earthquake you read about in Atlanta? The one that broke some dishes? That, apparently, was me. When I get highly pissed, which I was at that moment, I can cause them. So, Fudge is here to help me keep a lid on my emotions. Cassandra's familiar is down in the deli with her so I have a bunch of babysitters. If you don't mind, I'd really rather not rehash everything for the second time today. I promise I'll tell you everything but not right now. What's been happening while I was gone?"

She smiled in understanding. "Don't worry about it. Pour yourself a cup of coffee and go sit down. My notes are on your desk. There were only a few things I didn't feel comfortable handling so it shouldn't take too long to get back up to speed. I'll be here if you need me."

I sat down to ten pages of meticulous notes, detailing not only calls and emails but *exactly* what time the message came in, what time she answered, how she dealt with whatever it was and anything I had to do was highlighted. She was even more anal about things than I! Thankfully, the highlights were few and far between. Ev couldn't have chosen a better time of the year to get kidnapped.

"Martin's on the phone," Sally's voice said over the intercom. "He says it's important."

"It is," I sighed back while picking up the receiver.

"Good morning," I said.

"Mornin' Amy," his gruff voice was cheery. "I wanted to ask you which account you want to take the loan interest out of since all the principal has been repaid. I know it's not due until Monday but we may as well take care of it now and reduce the total amount of interest a bit."

Repaid? They got all the money back? To be honest, the money end of things never crossed my mind with everything else that had happened. I took a quick peek at the computer and told Martin which account to use. As I hung up, I saw Gregory leaning against the door jamb with a smile on his face.

"You have Jarvis to thank for that," he said. "He and his group tracked down everyone involved…all ten of them. Five were rogue weres and because he puts a bounty on those, he decided against getting paid for their services. Hello, Fudge."

I blew out a puff of air in relief. Now that I was in work mode, I realized that having to rearrange portfolios to accommodate such a loss would have been a major pain. I was indeed grateful to Jarvis for not demanding payment, although it would have been his right to do so.

"I presume you've already been to see Ev this morning. How is he?" I asked.

"Grumpy, which is a good sign. They took out most of his IVs this morning. I left when the nurse told him he'd have to be on a soft diet until his jaw healed. I know ogres heal almost as quickly as weres but it's still going to be a week or so before he will be able to really chew anything. I didn't want to stick around to hear the argument."

I grinned. Better someone else than me nursing him. Given that Ev flew off the handle at the slightest provocation, I could imagine the argument that ensued.

"Speaking of nurses, has anyone called Marianna?" I asked.

"I called her when I landed in Minneapolis last night. She ran right over to the hospital and I don't think she's left yet. She was sleeping in the chair when I arrived there this morning. She's how they snatched Ev, you know."

I raised my eyebrows. "Huh? How?"

"I got Ev to tell me this morning when Marianna went to get some breakfast. Someone called him with her mobile, apparently able to effectively imitate her, said she was in hospital in Atlanta after a car accident and could he come be with her? That was the call he got at Cassandra and Tommy's reception. Loverboy had me drop him at Flying Cloud without telling me where he was going or why.

"He felt a little sheepish saying anything to me. Apparently, he's really smitten with her. They snatched him at his hotel down there. *I* learned that one of the wizards had obtained an ancient spell specifically designed to bring down an ogre which, by the way, I now know and have made the council aware of."

Gregory moved from the doorway to one of the chairs in my office. Setting his coffee cup on my desk, he continued.

"All the bumps and bruises are from David and his cronies taking out David's anger on Ev when he was tied up. I hope they have a boxing gym or the equivalent in prison. They're not going to be seeing the outside for quite some time and this time it's dwarf, not human prison. Even for the wizards. It's not going to be a fun time."

Gregory coughed. "Marianna is feeling a bit sheepish as well. Someone stole her mobile out of her bag at one of the parties they attended a fortnight ago and because she was staying home where she has a land line, she didn't bother calling her provider until Wednesday.

"If Ev had bothered to *think*, he would have remembered she said she was staying in. If he'd told me what was happening, I could have confirmed her location before he went haring off. But neither thing happened so here we are with a banged up, angry but thankfully not dead ogre on our hands."

"This is all so surreal to me. You say it happens often?" I asked.

"Oh, all the time. You noticed Martin didn't even bat an eyelash. It's just the brutality that was unusual. But now that Ev knows what to expect, I suspect he will be a little more cautious in the future. He's young, you know, and this was a painful learning experience. He's going to be upset about the interest on the loan, too."

"How long can we keep him out of the office? The longer I can postpone his ranting around here, the better."

Gregory grinned. "Marianna's going to try to keep him out of your hair for another week. That should give you enough time to figure out how to tell him you're a witch."

I grimaced. "You keep coming back to that subject. What's he got against witches?"

"I will let you find that one out for yourself. Just let me know when you're going to tell him. I want to see this one. I saw Merlin downstairs and Fudge's presence up here tells me that Cassandra has already been at work on you. Pay attention to her, Amy. Your power is serious business.

"I have to go ready the house for Ev. He doesn't want to sleep upstairs until he's fully healed so I have some rearranging to do. If you need me, you know how to get hold of me."

Gregory turned and, saying something quietly to Sally, held the door open for Cassandra on his way out. Cassandra dropped a plate of something on Sally's desk then brought my lunch in to me. She put a plate of cat food on the floor next to where Fudge had curled up.

"I talked with Gregory before he came up here. Sounds like everything came out fairly well in the end but I don't want to be here when Ev finally comes back to work. He's grumpy enough on a normal basis. We're busy. Gotta run. See you later."

I munched on my sandwich while going back through Sally's notes. At least once a month, guards had to be rearranged to accommodate personalities and requests. This job fell to me in Ev's absence. After perusing personnel files, I figured out who needed to be with whom and where, and made the appropriate phone calls. Thankfully, I'd been with Ev long enough that I was taken at my word and no one felt a need to consult with him. I didn't want to have to lie to explain why *he* wasn't making the changes.

Chapter 11

When we (Fudge and I) got home from work later that afternoon, Elinda was waiting for us. I swore I was going to change the locks and not give out any keys.

"Hi, Darlin'," she greeted me. "I hope you don't mind but I let myself in." Well, duh. Otherwise, how would she be greeting me at the door? I had a feeling I wasn't going to get my nap.

"Did you have a good day? Here, I made some cookies for you to snack on." She took my coat from me while guiding me to the kitchen where there was a plate of still-warm chocolate-chocolate chip cookies, complete with a glass of milk. Elinda was indeed a grandmother. Fudge eyed the glass of milk and with a sigh, took a drink from his water bowl.

"I take it your day went well," she continued.

I finally had a chance to get a word in edgewise. "I'm fine. Nothing set me off at the office and I have things to do here, nothing of which is going to get me angry. Fudge is here to keep an eye on me. Thanks for the snack but you can go back upstairs."

"Sorry, darlin', but no. Consider me your psychotherapist. You need to work through your feelings about what happened and the earlier we do that, the better off you're going to be in the long run. Mundane people who have experienced extreme emotional trauma can re-experience the event and lose their cool on a moment's notice. All they do is get angry and/or cry. You can do a lot more damage.

"So, we're going to talk about it and Fudge is going to be here to help. The cookies were on purpose. They're fuel for what you're about to do." The expression on her face brooked no argument.

A snarky response came out of my mouth. "If it's fuel, shouldn't the snack have been something healthier then, like a peanut butter sandwich?"

She smiled. "Chocolate is good for the soul. Trust me. Finish your milk then sit."

My well-meaning aunt had tried to get me to go to therapy after my folks were killed in a car crash and I wouldn't have anything to do with it. I hated talking about my feelings with anyone else. I'd rather just work through them myself. Although I considered Elinda part of my family, I still didn't want to "talk about it". But I could tell she wasn't going to let it go. I sat in the recliner as instructed, Fudge crawling into my lap.

"Tell me what happened," she started.

"I went through all this with Cassandra this morning," I protested.

"I have some skills Cassandra doesn't have," she answered. "Talk."

So, yet again, I related the past several days' events. I will admit it got easier with every retelling. She would stop me and ask questions at certain points, making me analyze why I felt what I did. Periodically, she'd feed me another cookie or two. They tasted good but also seemed to give me the energy to continue talking in a way I wasn't accustomed to.

Three hours later, Marge walked in with a huge tray holding four plates – three human-sized and one obviously meant for Fudge. It was dinner time. "How's it going?" she asked.

"She's making excellent progress. Better than I expected, actually," Elinda replied.

We ate the most excellent pot roast and while Marge piled the plates back on the tray to take them back upstairs, Elinda continued her interrogation.

"Let's examine how you're currently feeling about Tony's death."

I thought about it. Strangely, although I was still upset, there wasn't the horrible ache in my heart that I'd felt the previous day. When I told her this, she smiled.

"This is the point we all wanted you to get to and you've gotten there much more quickly than anyone I know who's lost someone close to them. You don't lose your control when thinking about a traumatic event."

I looked down at Fudge who had been taking his after-dinner bath in my lap. *"What? I was not doing anything,"* he said in between licks of fur.

I switched my view to Elinda. "What, exactly, has been happening here the last couple of hours?"

She smiled once again. "I really was a psychiatrist in my working life. I have a gift for drawing out and then smoothing over emotions. The cookies are spelled to help with that."

"But I didn't see any energy waves coming off you." I was confused.

"Unless you're a *very* gifted Air witch, this type of energy usually isn't visible. It's too delicate. I rarely have to use it but both Gregory and Cassandra told me you're stronger than a lot of witches. Since your affinity is with Earth, I figured it would be best to get this all over quickly so you didn't bring our home down around our ears. Your boss pisses you off too often."

Well, she *was* right about Ev irritating me. I just didn't think I'd ever gotten *that* mad at him. However, I did feel very calm, except for the fact that there were all these people talking about me behind my back. I said as much.

"We all care so much for you, darlin', that we don't want anything to happen to you." Her voice soothed me even more. "But there's more to it. Witches and wizards are bound by law to protect the environment and the greater community. As you've discovered, your gifts can be destructive. It's our duty to do what we can to prevent that destruction. So yes, we've talked about you but it was for not only your good but the greater good as well."

"Humph. Okay. My turn," I said. "How did you know Fudge was a familiar? Cassandra tells me you had to know in order to send him to me in Atlanta."

She grinned. "That gift I have? It extends to the energy animals give off. I knew Fudge was a familiar from the day he ran through your window screen. Although he was just a kitten at the time, he felt old."

"So why haven't you said anything all these years?"

"Because it wasn't my place to do so. Had your gift not manifested, Fudge would have allowed his body to age naturally and moved on to another body for another witch. The fact that he is a familiar wouldn't have mattered. But that's all a moot point, now. You are and he is."

She stretched. "My work is done and I'm beat. You won't need any of us to stay with you and I'll call Cassandra to tell her she needn't come over in the morning. Fudge can handle anything you dream about. I'm for bed."

Fudge hopped off my lap and twined his way between Elinda's legs, nearly tripping her as she made her way to the door. "I know," she laughed and gave him a scratch between the ears.

I must have had a quizzical look on my face. "He was giving off energy that said he was thankful I'd done what I did. I made his job a lot easier."

So she couldn't actually hear him. For some reason, that pleased me. I wanted to keep my talking cat all to myself. I hugged her at the door and although it was early, felt like I could sleep for days. I, too, headed toward bed.

The next morning *finally* saw me back to my normal routine: up with the sun, checking email and social networking while inhaling my half-pot of coffee. I grimaced at the emails. My editor had sent several about missing my deadline, the last being a shout I heard by virtue of "WHERE THE HELL ARE YOU?" in all caps. I fired off a reply, explaining that a business emergency had come up but everything was okay, now, and I'd be getting everything I owed to her within a couple of days.

Work was normal, too. Well, as normal as it could be, given the nature of the business, its employees and clientele. I only had one complaint to deal with: a dwarf guard had gotten drunk at a party and passed out in his charge's lap in the limo. This was the first infraction from the guard so I made the calls, soothed the client's ruffled feathers, shouted at the guard (making his hangover worse, I'm sure) and made notes in the files for future reference.

The only thing not-normal was Fudge insisting that as long as he was going to work with me, he needed his things. I refused to haul everything back and forth and ended up calling Sally before she left the house and asking her to stop on her way to buy a litter box, litter, dishes and a small bag of his favorite dry food. She laughed and agreed to do so, ending her call with, "Spoiled, aren't we?"

Gregory called with an update on Ev's condition. He was being discharged from the hospital and was meekly going along with Marianna's suggestion that he avoid the stress of work for a few more days. Gregory had hidden Ev's cell phone so he wouldn't be trying to conduct business behind Marianna's back, giving me even more respite.

That night, Fudge and I shared a microwavable shrimp dinner while I did a final read-through on the manuscript I owed my editor. It would take another night to get it to the point I was comfortable sending it off but *normalcy*. I could get into it.

Normalcy was blown all to hell on Sunday. At eleven on the dot that morning, I let myself into Cassandra's house, notebook and Fudge in tow.

"Hiya," she greeted me with a fresh cup of coffee. "Ready to get down to work?" Fudge wandered over and touched noses with Merlin.

I hadn't even managed to get my coat off. No polite chit-chat, just, "Ready to get down to work". I had a feeling I wasn't going to like this visit very much.

"This is for you." She dropped two three-inch black ring-binders on the coffee table with a thunk. "They are your study and reference material. Thankfully, we're both Earth witches so there's nothing to adapt to another affinity. These are copies of my books."

Lovely. I had another book to write, editing looming on the horizon and Cassandra was talking about school.

"I can't tell you how much I *don't* want to be a witch," I groaned. "I like my life just the way it is."

"You've said that before but you don't have any choice. Magic isn't a faucet you can turn on and off. So, whether you use it or not, you have to learn to live with it.

"First, even though you live in a building with wards and all, these books can't be out in the open for prying eyes to see. I'd suggest you keep them on the shelf in your closet. Or in a cupboard. Anyways, hidden from view but somewhere you can easily get to them.

"Second, you need to read the first one cover-to-cover and commit it to memory in a short period of time. It's the law book – both those that have been laid down by the Council and those that just *are* ... sort of like the laws of physics you studied in school. I want you to start now. I'll be in the workroom so just ask your questions as you come to them – I'll be able to hear you."

She left me to myself in the living room. Merlin followed her, Fudge curled up next to me on the couch.

"I know you are not interested in magic but at least read this first book," he said. *"These are things you **need** to know."* Then, it was apparently bath time.

So, I picked up the first book. It looked like nothing more than a binder she'd bought at an office supply store but when I opened the cover, I felt a tingle in my fingers. "What's the tingle?" I hollered.

"It binds the book to you and your magic. Mundanes will see nothing but a printed manuscript of one of your books. Witches and wizards will be able to read the standard stuff like the laws but nothing you personally write in it. Other magical-types will know it's magic but will see nothing but blank paper. The second book will feel the same the first time you open it," came the reply.

I just had to ask. "So if mundanes see one of my manuscripts, what do they see in yours?"

"Each book is spelled to match the owner. Mine is supposedly a cookbook. I think Mom's is the same. I just figured you weren't much of a recipe collector so I connected it to your writing. Start reading."

I opened the book. Rather than the expected white paper and computerized printing, the paper looked like parchment and the writing was all calligraphic. I closed the binder and looked at it on edge. It looked like computer paper. When I re-opened the book, it was all parchment and calligraphy again. Cool!

I started reading. It may have been pretty but it was *boring*. The first two pages were a list of the members of the Witches' Council and where they were located. As I watched, one of the member's locations blurred and changed from "Davenport, Iowa, United States" to "Moline, Illinois, United States". Not surprisingly, Cassandra's mother was on page two.

The next page was a list of the Midwest United States contacts for the other councils. I only knew one name: the local representative for the Vampire Council. We'd unfortunately met over that brouhaha with the lovesick vampire the prior fall.

The next nine pages were specific instructions on how to contact a Council member, which member you should contact when, why you would want to do so, penalties for frivolous contact or failure to report something…*rules*.

Page thirteen had one sentence on it, "Thou shalt not use thy gifts to kill."

Page fourteen was yet another single sentence, "Thou shalt protect the Earth, thy Mother".

Page fifteen, too: "Thou shalt cultivate the gift thou hast been Blessed with".

Page sixteen was headed "Earth" and a diagram that looked like DaVinci's "Vitruvian Man" but instead of being surrounded by a square and circle, it was superimposed on a drawing of the Earth and had all sorts of lines from the body to the earth.

The next countless number of pages went on to explain how someone who had an affinity for Earth could affect their surroundings, the potential for good and the potential for bad. The first bad thing mentioned was earthquakes. Oops.

The second big concern was causing a volcano to erupt. Everything had examples and apparently, the famous eruption of Mt. Vesuvius was caused by a pissed off witch. An "oops" of epic proportions. Since she died during the eruption and subsequent burying in ash of Herculaneum, they couldn't kill her for it but death *was* one of the penalties for not keeping your temper under control.

All penalties were imposed by the Witches' Council but it only required a simple majority of the thirteen to punish by death. Not even a super-majority like ten or something. I looked up to see Cassandra sitting in the chair opposite, watching me.

"So how come no one's yelled at me?" I asked.

"Because of a few things." The corners of her mouth quirked up in a half smile. "First, your gift manifested so powerfully and so quickly that no one had a chance to do anything about it. Second, you only caused minor damage.

"Third and most important, both Mom and Fudge interceded for you. The Elders were all for at least slapping your hand but Mom convinced them that you were surrounded by people who could train you quickly and Fudge promised to keep a lid on your temper if you couldn't immediately do it on your own."

I looked down at my cat who stopped preening long enough to say, *"Because of my age, I have some sway with the Councils. They know I will keep my promises. I did not want you discouraged before you had even begun."*

I looked back at Cassandra. "So you're saying I *have* to do all the mumbo-jumbo you and Tommy do in your workroom? Where am I supposed to put all that crap in my apartment?"

She laughed. "Absolutely not. I like to cook, whether it's food or a spell. So does Tommy. You don't *have* to use your gift for anything. You *do* have to be aware of it and *how* to use it, if it becomes necessary that you do so. That said, I'll bet you find something you like to do and when that happens, you'll make room for it, whether it's in your apartment or in your schedule.

"It's lunch time. Let's take a break and eat. You need to finish reading that first book but do it at home. We'll do practical stuff after lunch."

Lunch wasn't anything really good like she cooked up in the deli – just grilled cheese sandwiches. Because she usually whipped up something I wouldn't normally cook at home – and I was a master at grilled cheese – I teased her about it.

"Hey, it takes a lot of work to teach you, y'know. I decided to be lazy with the food end of things today. Besides, this requires minimal cleanup." Another bite, then, "I have a question."

"What? You're the teacher and you're asking *me* a question?"

"Hush. How do you get ideas for your books and then transform them to stories?"

"Um. I never really thought about it. I just write. Why? And I thought I was supposed to be working on mumbo-jumbo today."

She wrinkled her nose. "I don't really have a lesson plan. Because I grew up with it, there's no formal schooling that I'm aware of. I'm trying to figure out the best way to teach *you*. So, think about it and give me an answer. I think it'll be a clue as to what the next step is and how I get it through your thick skull."

I thought. "Well, you know most of the characters are based on someone I know or someone I've met." I hadn't yet told her that she and Tommy were the basis for the protagonists in the book I'd just submitted. Their pre-nuptial arguments were too precious to pass up. "I take those people, put them in a situation I dream up and then as they deal with their problems, the book sort of writes itself. I write an outline but nine times of ten, the characters themselves change the story and its outcome, blowing the outline all to hell. I don't know how else to explain it. How does that relate to witchcraft?"

"Like your writing, it's hard to explain. So much of what we do is based on intuition – just knowing what's needed in a certain situation. It's that 'gut feeling' people talk about all the time. You write using your gut feeling of what needs to happen when. I think I'm going to work on plants next."

After lunch, she took me into her greenhouse, both cats following. "I understand Gregory did a lot of energy work with you and what you did at the fight kinda shows that he did. So, I'm not going to focus on that with you right now. The greenhouse is a good place to get you used to plant energy. Let's start with one of the friendliest I know, peppermint. Focus on the plant and tell me what feelings you get or what your gut tells you."

I tried not to feel silly when I stared at the plant. But all of a sudden, I got the same feeling like you do when you open the refrigerator door on a hot day – a wash of cool air.

"It's in the second book but I'll tell you that means in healing it'll bring down fevers. For spellwork, I use it if a situation needs "cooling off". Naturally, it has other uses but generally speaking, the first impression you get is the one where it'll work best for you."

"What do you mean by that?" I asked.

"For the most part, every plant has more than one medicinal or magical property. The overlap is mind-boggling. So if you need something for a specific situation and you don't have it, there's almost always a substitute. Because *your* energy goes into anything you do, the better your connection with the plant, the easier the work, whether you're drinking tea for an illness or casting a spell for something."

I shrugged my shoulders. I didn't get sick so I had no idea about illness – unless you counted the occasional hangover. Ibuprofen and gallons of water healed me there.

Over the next couple of hours, she introduced me to about half the plants she had, some in flats ready to go into the ground when it got warm enough, some that were permanent residents in the greenhouse.

Peppermint wasn't the only one I got something off of. Basil gave me an image of Martin – it must be good for money; off sage I got a hot, desert-dry wind – drying; mugwort made me giddy but I felt a cocoon surround me – you can get high off it but it's good for protection; and so on. I wrote all my impressions in my notebook which, according to Cassandra, I'd be transferring to the second binder.

Then there were the plants where no matter how hard I focused, I got nothing. Feverfew? Lavender? One of her ferns? Zip. "Don't worry about it," she said. "Some are easier than others, and some you'll never form a true connection with. Just make notes of what I tell you in case you need them for something." I furiously scribbled.

All of a sudden, I heard Cassandra yell, "Hey!" I looked up from my writing to see her shooing both cats away from a plant in a deep pot. I could see the soil was disturbed and both of them had sheepish looks on their faces.

"You know better," she chided Merlin. "*I'm sorry, I could not help myself,*" I heard from Fudge.

She sighed. "I should have known better. They were after the valerian root."

"Valerian? Is that a form of catnip?" I asked, pen poised to write down her answer.

"No. Believe it or not, some cats don't like catnip. However, some react to valerian or chamomile in the same way. I knew about Merlin's affinity for valerian and it appears Fudge has the same love for the herb. Here. Smell this." She held out a large amber jar with the lid off.

I took a whiff and almost choked. "Eeew. That smells like freshly-worn gym shoes."

She laughed as she screwed the lid back on. "I know, right? But cats seem to like it. I'll give you a little in a muslin bag for Fudge to play with once in a while."

I recorded her comments about valerian being good for sleep in my notebook while she smoothed the dirt back over the roots in the pot, apologizing to the plant all the while. (Tea? No thank you. It probably tastes just as bad as it smells. Capsules, if you please.) After that, I yawned and rubbed my temples.

"Enough for one day?" she asked.

"I think so. My head is about to burst with all this…and I'm wondering just when I'm ever going to need all of it."

"Knowledge is power," Fudge said. *"You do not know what will happen in the future when some of this may be needed. A future, I might add, that is going to be much longer than you had originally anticipated. Things change in a long lifetime, believe me."*

"I know it's a lot to absorb in a short period of time but you never know when it might come in handy," Cassandra admonished me. "Do you still want to stay for supper? You're welcome, you know. Tommy should be home in a few and I need to get things started."

As much as I loved their cooking, I thought I needed to go home and relax, so I said no to the invitation.

"In that case, take your books with you. You need to finish reading the first one before next Sunday. There *will* be a quiz!"

This bites. I was back in school and just like when I was a kid, it was obligatory. It would have been one thing if I'd found something I truly was interested in and had voluntarily sought education on the subject. This business about learning to be a witch wasn't a subject I would have chosen but there were too many people around me insisting I learn that I wouldn't be able to duck it or play hooky. Not to mention that fancy-lettered "Thou shalt cultivate the gift thou hast been Blessed with" sounded awfully ominous. I had a feeling I wasn't going to get much recreational reading done.

I trudged home in the darkening afternoon, tucking my chin into my coat and still feeling a bit guilty about Fudge's bare paws on the cold sidewalk. A bite in the air told me we were going to be getting a late spring snow. I hated when it did that. You get all used to warming temperatures, fewer layers of clothes and spring flowers then bam! Mother Nature makes everything all cold and white again. The farmers must have been heaving a lot of sighs.

When I got home, I dropped the binders on my coffee table then decided there was still time for a nap before choosing what to eat for dinner. I automatically checked my phone for a message from Tony. A flood of tears accompanied the realization that there wouldn't be any more long phone calls, short text messages or flowers delivered to my desk every Monday morning. I plopped onto the couch, sobbing.

Fudge hopped on my lap. *"It is going to be okay. The hole will heal and there will be scar tissue."*

I hiccupped. "You're going to let me cry?"

*"Of course. Tears are a necessary part of healing. You **are** human, you know, and humans cry when they are sad. As long as you do not start throwing off disruptive energy, I will not stand in the way of your healing."*

I curled up on the couch and allowed the tears to flow freely. Fudge nestled next to me, purring loudly. At some point, I cried myself to sleep…

And woke up with Fudge batting my nose – at least he was using soft paws. *"I am hungry and you have not refilled my dish today."*

"I was *sleeping* and you woke me up to feed you? Selfish, much?" I grumbled as I felt around for the switch on the lamp. I had no idea how long I'd been out but the sun was completely down and it was pitch dark in my apartment.

"Well, you need to eat something, too."

My stomach chose that moment to growl. *"See?"* I looked through sticky eyes at the clock. It was after ten. My stomach may have been hungry but the rest of me wasn't. All I wanted to do was go back to that dark, dreamless sleep. But I knew Fudge was right. I couldn't go more than twelve hours without food or I'd get light-headed and nauseated. I uncurled myself, padded into the kitchen and put a scoop of food in Fudge's dish, mentally reviewing the contents of the refrigerator to see if I had anything that didn't require a lot of chewing and choking down. Turns out dinner wasn't

in the refrigerator. I heated a bowl of soup in the microwave,
downed it then headed for bed.

Chapter 12

They should outlaw Mondays. They suck.

Oh, the first few hours of this particular Monday were as good as any Monday is ever going to be. But the shit hit the fan when a strong odor let me know that the opening of the front door wasn't a visitor but Ev coming back to work.

I got up from my desk to go greet him. I gave him the once-over, seeing no indication of trauma except for the bulge in his jaw where the swelling hadn't quite subsided and a few fading bruises. "Welcome back! How are you feeling?"

"Like shit. I still can't chew real food and it hurts to breathe. The doctor bills are going to be astronomical. How much interest did we have to pay to that shark in Atlanta?"

Wow. I guess I got the answer to my question. Grumpy *and* thinking about money, which he didn't usually do. He scowled when I told him to the penny how much the interest was. "I suppose it's not deductible, is it?"

I shook my head. "You know better. We've talked a lot over the years about what's business and what's personal. This falls under the personal category."

Ev turned his head when a sneeze came from behind me, then peered in my office door. "What's your cat doing here?"

"We have a lot of things to talk about," I answered, mentally fortifying myself for the conversation to come. "I just made a fresh pot of coffee. Let me refill my cup and get my notes. I'll meet you in your office."

While I was talking, the door opened and Gregory walked in with a couple of Cassandra's bear claws on a plate balanced on top of a cup I knew contained coffee. He grinned. "Good. I arrived just in time for the show. Ev, these are soft. Want one?"

Ev growled, snatched one of the sweets and stalked off to his office with Gregory right behind him. I grabbed my notes and coffee cup from my desk, detoured into the kitchen for more caffeine and followed, seating myself where I usually did for our morning catch-ups. Gregory leaned against the wall, sipping his coffee.

I opened my mouth to start filling him in on what had happened in his absence but he held up a hand, forestalling me. "What's Fudge doing here? Your cat has never come to the office with you before."

I fidgeted in my chair. "Well, some things *have* happened since you've been gone. One of them means that Fudge has to accompany me wherever I go for a while."

He raised an eyebrow. "And?"

I looked at Gregory, who shrugged his shoulders. No support from that direction. "Um. Turns out I'm a witch and Fudge is my familiar. Bad things can happen if I lose my temper. He's here to help me keep control of my emotions until I can do it on my own."

Ev shot to his feet which, apparently, wasn't a good thing to do. He put his hand to his side, right where the broken ribs were. "What? What do you mean you're a witch? We've been together for ages and you're just now telling me? Don't you think maybe that's something you should have mentioned when I interviewed you?"

"Ev," I said, trying to make my voice calm. "I didn't know back then. I found out less than two weeks ago."

He came around from behind his desk and loomed over me. "What do you mean you just found out? Witches are born that way. You should have said something. I can't work with a witch."

"Whoa," Gregory interjected. "Calm down, man. You're still healing, remember? And you work with wizards all the time."

"Wizards are guys. They're not devious like witches."

I was taken aback. I stood and, craning my neck, looked him as close as to the eye as I could get. "You mean to tell me this changes everything that's happened over the last eight years? Devious? You call busting my ass to get and keep *your* business running smoothly devious? You call flying all the way down to Atlanta, traipsing in the woods and watching my boyfriend be killed to save *your* ass devious?"

"Amy," Gregory cautioned.

Fudge came running into the office and with one smooth motion, sprang into my arms. He sneezed again then I heard "*Calm yourself*". Another sneeze followed.

I took a big gulp of air and, unclenching my fists, twined my fingers in Fudge's fur. Fudge sneezed again, turned his head and nuzzled into my armpit. *"Your deodorant smells much better than the ogre."*

"I can't work with a witch, I just can't," Ev said. "I'm sorry Amy, but our relationship has to end. Please clean out your office."

My jaw dropped. "What? You're firing me? One little quirk in my DNA comes to light – something I can't do a damned thing about and you're firing me? You malodorous bastard. Fine. I'm outta here." I turned on my heel, walked from his office to mine, grabbed my purse and coat and left with Fudge still in my arms. Barely noticing that the monitor on Sally's desk made a zapping sound as I passed, I made certain to slam the door on my way out, stomped all the way down the stairs and slammed the outer door, just for good measure.

I'd gotten just a couple of steps down the sidewalk when Fudge said, *"If you do not calm yourself, I will have to do it for you. You are giving off more than sparks."* I stopped dead in my tracks. I couldn't even be furious anymore. Earthquakes were not good anytime and unheard of in Minnesota. *"Untrue. You can be furious. Just cold rage instead of boiling mad."*

I closed my eyes, took several deep breaths and waited for my racing heart to slow. *"Better."* Fudge jumped out of my arms and started walking toward home. *"Coming?"* I brought my focus back to my surroundings, put my coat on, slung my purse over my shoulder and followed.

Remembering "cold rage" instead of "boiling mad", I stomped into my apartment, slammed that door, flung my coat and purse on the sofa and began to pace. "That bastard," I muttered to myself. "After all I've done for him, he fires me over something I can't control."

I continued my march around and around the living room, Fudge matching me step for step. Oh, it wasn't the paycheck. I didn't need that – I made enough money off my writing to support myself. It was the *principle* of the thing. I'd known about my witchiness for less than two weeks, really hadn't a clue what to do about or with it and thanks to Ev, my life gets turned upside-down yet again. The match-making demon who made my life hell was his fault. Come to think of it, so was the lovesick vampire. Maybe I *was* better off not working for him anymore.

Then I sagged onto the chair and started crying. I *liked* my job. Keeping his business in order was an outlet for the anal-retentive part of me. I also couldn't deny that I got the majority of the characters in my books from the people I'd met working for Ev.

I had no idea how long I cried but after some time, there was a knock on the door. "Go away," I cried.

Gregory's voice came through the steel. "Open up, Amy. We need to talk."

I didn't want to talk to anyone; I just wanted to wallow in my sorrow. "I don't want to. Go away."

I heard some murmuring then footsteps back up the stairs. Good. I was alone with my thoughts and my cat.

A couple of minutes later, the back door opened and Gregory slipped past Marge, who had the key to my apartment in her hand. "It's for your own good," she said before closing the door and leaving us alone. Gregory walked over, opened the front door and admitted both Sally and Cassandra. I glared at them all.

"You should know I just quit," Gregory said.

"Me, too," Sally added.

"Ev's off his rocker," Cassandra piped in.

I stared. "What? Why?"

They all started talking at once and I couldn't make heads or tails of what *anyone* was saying. "Shit. One at a time, guys. Gregory, you first."

Gregory' usually smiling visage was serious. "I knew Ev didn't like witches…at all. I am honestly surprised he's had as much to do with Cassandra as he has. He had a bad experience with one about forty years ago. His love life, naturally. But I never dreamed he'd fire you over being one. I assumed he'd just throw one of his tantrums then calm down and realize you weren't like that *one* woman.

"If he cannot work with a witch, especially one who has done him nothing but good over the years, I can't see why he would want to work with any magical people at all and told him as much. As I'm a magical person working even more closely with him than you, I said I couldn't fathom him wanting me around and tendered my resignation."

Sally picked up where Gregory left off. "I came in early today because I was bored and caught the tail end of Gregory's lecture. Ev offered me your job. I told him I didn't need to work and the only reason I did was because it was part-time and I enjoyed working with you. Because I'm married to a wizard, I could probably get Jack to cook up something *devious* so Ev was better off without me around and I quit then and there."

I looked at Cassandra. "And you're here because …?"

She grinned. "Gregory grabbed me on the way out – right in the middle of catering prep, I might add – thinking maybe I could provide some moral support. I can. I hold the lease to Ev's office and although he may not remember, I'm sure *you* know it's up for renewal in two months. He probably doesn't want to lease space from a devious witch, right?"

"Why are you doing all this?" I sniffled.

"Oh, hell, Amy. First, we're your friends." Cassandra reached over to my desk and handed me a tissue from the box I kept there. (I *did* cry when I wrote mushy scenes.)

"More important, Ev needs to learn a lesson," Gregory added. "He's perfectly within his rights to avoid witches in his personal life but given the nature of his business, he can't *not* deal with witches."

"And he also needs to learn that just because you're now a witch, that's not going to change who you are and what you do for him," Sally chimed in.

I sniffled a little more. Cassandra handed me another tissue. "So now what?" I asked.

Gregory chuckled. "I give him less than a week before he comes crawling. You have spoiled him, you know. I'm not sure he knows his bank balances, much less how to do payroll."

For the first time in a couple of hours I smiled. "Ev has access to my computer and Ed can figure out my systems. However, once Ed tells him how much it's going to cost for a CPA to do just that part of my job, Ev is going to throw a *good* tantrum. So, you think he'll ask me back. Should I go?"

Gregory's smile widened. "Not at first. Remind him that he thinks witches are devious and you wouldn't want any suspicion to fall on you for anything."

"Oooh. We witches *can* be devious," Cassandra's eyes twinkled. "You already have a new job working for me. Witches have to stick together, you know!"

"What? You need help?" I'm sure my eyes were big as saucers.

"I'm kidding," she said. "I'm fine. But Ev doesn't have to know that. Make him beg you to come back. I'm hoping he'll even feel compelled to talk to me about it. He'll get an earful if he does."

Everyone knew Ev was an abject failure at the business end of business. That's why he'd hired me in the first place. It was just a question of how long he'd hold off calling me and how much of a mess I'd have to clean up when I finally agreed to go back.

"Hey, what if he decides to hire someone new?" I asked.

"He won't," Gregory answered. "Apart from his love life, he hates change and it appears even the love life is settling down. We just have to hang on until his ego decides to take the blow. Will you be okay waiting this out?"

I nodded. "I have plenty of things to keep me busy and enough money to live on. I'll be fine. I know Sally doesn't need to work but what about you?"

"I don't need to work, either. I'm old enough to have amassed a fair amount of savings and Martin has done an excellent job with my portfolio even in this horrible economy. As we discussed in Atlanta, I do it because of the challenges it presents. You can't tell me working for Ev isn't a challenge!"

Cassandra clapped her hands in glee. "You have *daytime* as well as *nighttime*, now. I won't hear any excuse for not studying!" Fudge butted his head against my leg in agreement.

I sighed. "Yes, I know. It really was on this week's agenda."

They rose as one. "Well, we will let you get to it, then," Gregory said as they headed toward the door.

"You have my number. I'm back when you are," Sally told me.

Maybe a short vacation was a good thing. I could do the studying for Cassandra *and* start the next book without the interruption of a nine-to-five job.

My stomach rumbled. It was noonish and for the first time in months, I had to make lunch during the week. Quickly changing from my suit to sweats, I put a peanut butter sandwich together and sat down with a novel. Work – whether it be studying or writing – could wait one more day. Fudge turned his nose up at my sandwich and, curling up next to me in the chair, started in on his hourly bath.

Chapter 13

Although technically unemployed, I woke with the sun, my normal routine so ingrained that I couldn't go back to sleep. It felt strange to have a leisurely weekend morning on a Tuesday.

Once I was ready for work (that thought elicited an internal snort), I flipped a coin to decide whether I'd write or study on this first day of my "vacation". I sighed. Studying won.

"Read completely through the first book," Fudge advised. *"This is what you **need** to know to survive in this world."*

I looked down at my cat. I swear, put a pair of glasses on him and he'd have the same expression as my economics professor in college.

"I am not joking, my human. Knowing these laws will keep your head on your shoulders – literally."

"Why do you always refer to me as 'my human'? I have a name, you know. And yes, Cassandra explained all that to me on Sunday."

*"Sorry, Amy. Habit. Witches and familiars were not that **familiar** with each other. For hundreds of years, I was accustomed to being addressed as 'familiar' and nothing more. It has only been in the last few centuries that I have been viewed as something akin to a pet and been given a name. It probably started when familiars had to be seen as pets for the witch to live.*

"I am aware that the other human – Cassandra – said you needed to know the laws. I really wanted to stress that. The laws the Council have laid down are one thing but how your magic works is the most important part. You really can kill yourself without outside help and I would not like for that to happen."

Studying. Ugh. I hadn't done that since college – a lifetime ago. I sighed, refilled my coffee cup and, grabbing the binder that now said "Book One" on the cover, sat down to read.

I skimmed through the first part that I'd already read and committed the essential parts to memory. Well, except for the

Council list. I knew if I had contact with them, it'd be them calling me.

Flipping through to the section that started with "Earth", I took a hard look at the witch's version of The Vitruvian Man then started reading in earnest:

"Earth practitioners, of all the elements, have the greatest connection to the Mother. Air is thin in a cave deep underground. Water is scant in the desert. Fire can draw but faint energy from the Sun's reflected light of the Moon. But just as the Mother combines every element to make and sustain life, only Earth can draw strong energy *wherever* you may be. For even if you are soaring above the clouds or floating upon the ocean, Earth is always beneath you."

That made sense. I flipped the page.

Oh. My. God. The beginning of a section about geology. My eyes started glazing immediately. Science was *never* an interest of mine. I only took high school biology because I needed a year of science to get into the college I'd never finished. Descriptions of various types of rock and earth swam before my eyes.

"***Pay attention****! You would not move five pounds of sand the same way you would a five-pound piece of granite, would you? You need to know the difference. Your magic works differently depending on what type of Earth is beneath you.*"

"Do I not have any privacy in my own mind anymore?"

"*Not when you are doing anything magically-related. As in studying. I try to stay out the rest of the time. Human thoughts are **too** strange most of the time.*"

I snorted. "I suppose I'd be just *thrilled* with yours if I could read them, huh?"

"*Well, of course. I have had well over a thousand of your years of experience in many areas. We could have marvelous philosophical discussions but your human mind would not begin to comprehend the subject matter. Back to studying.*"

So, familiars, even in (especially in?) cat form thought they were superior to humans. I snickered and thought of the joke about cats, opposable thumbs and can openers. A metaphoric slap upside my head had me laughing even more as I turned my attention back to the text.

Well, shit. I really was back in school. I grabbed a pencil and started making notes in the margins.

Three hours later, my brain was about as full of sedimentary, metamorphic and igneous rocks and all their stony permutations as it could be. I saw the next section was headed "Ley Lines", whatever those were. It was definitely time for a break. Since I was going to have to feed myself lunch for an unknown number of days and didn't want to go anywhere near the deli and its upstairs neighbor, I made a grocery list.

I had just finished putting the groceries away when there was a knock at the door. The peephole told me it was Gregory, so I let him in with, "What are you doing here?"

"I thought I'd bring you this." He handed me a small piece of flexible rubber. Just what every girl needs. I raised an eyebrow in inquiry.

"It's to protect your mobile. I am surprised you haven't blown it up already."

"Huh?"

"Your energy spikes can burn up the circuits in some of today's technology. Your temper tantrum yesterday blew out Sally's computer monitor. As you usually keep your mobile on you, I'm surprised it's still working."

I grabbed my phone out of my purse and looked at it. It still had the same lock screen and signal strength but I noticed the battery was showing low even though I'd put it on the charger when I got home the day before and had only taken it off when I left for the grocery store two hours earlier. I showed it to Gregory.

"Ah, yes. It's going haywire but not as bad as some. Apparently, you drain batteries. How is your watch?"

Although I wore one, it was because I felt strange without it, not because I looked at it all the time. There were clocks on *everything* so the watch was more decoration than anything else. I had put it on that morning out of habit but didn't remember when I'd last consulted it for the time. When I looked down, the second hand wasn't moving. The battery was dead. I took it off and tossed it on my desk.

"You may as well forget about wearing it unless you want to replace the battery every hour or so. Those don't hold as much juice as other things." He fitted the piece of rubber over my cell phone. "This should protect your phone and its battery so you can use it. You will have to charge it more often but it should be good otherwise."

"What about my computer?" My life was on that thing and if I couldn't use a computer, I was thoroughly screwed.

"It's an expensive one, isn't it?" He asked. "One you can drop and it will still function? One you can spill coffee on and it will work?"

I nodded. I'm a klutz at the best of times. After the third spilled cup of coffee had shorted out a keyboard, I'd splurged on an industrial-strength laptop. (Industrial-strength does not equal pissed-off-vampire-proof. Trust me on this one.)

"Then you should be okay. Those are well-shielded. I would just ensure it's turned off when you're doing energy work of any kind."

"Well, thanks for the present, but what are you *really* doing here?" I asked him.

Gregory gave a little smile – the one that said he had something up his sleeve. "We're going to be neighbors for a bit so I thought I'd do the neighborly thing and come introduce myself."

I think my jaw hit the floor and went straight through it to bedrock. "What? Why? Where?"

"As I no longer work for Ev, I felt it only right to move out of the cottage. I called James and he had an open apartment in the building next to this one. No garden but I know it's only short term. If everything goes according to plan, I should be back at the cottage and garden within a couple of weeks so I won't miss spring planting.

"Being next door and unoccupied with other things means I can help you with your studying, if you like. Although we're different elements, I've been around long enough to know the basics of all four."

I was dumbfounded. He didn't say as much but I knew I had just acquired yet *another* babysitter. All I could spit out was, "Why is everyone so bloody concerned about me?"

"Amy, although they're not unheard of, late bloomers are rare. Powers generally *start* to manifest at puberty and there is usually a magical relative around to help guide the new witch or wizard. You don't have that relative. Plus, your powers just blew up instead of easing their way in, rather like a dam that just burst instead of starting to leak. So, we're all concerned for both you and your environment."

I screwed up my face at him. "Did you plan all this? Did Mr. Owens kick someone out so you could move in?"

He laughed. "Absolutely not. Like I said, I didn't expect Ev to fire you. James really did have an empty apartment that he was *just* about to advertise. It suited both our purposes that I take it for a few weeks. If he finds a suitable tenant before Ev gets his act together, I will just move somewhere else. In the meantime, Cassandra has a deli to run but I'm nearby and at loose ends."

I mused out loud. "If everyone's that concerned, why aren't Elinda and Marge down here badgering me, too?"

"For one thing, they're both Air, like I am. For another, neither is as old as I am, nor have they traveled much, so they don't have the body of knowledge I've amassed. Lastly, and I'm speculating here, I think they'd rather be the grandmothers who soothe hurt feelings than the teachers who must sometimes be harsh."

I knew I had to accept my quirky DNA and at least learn enough to not cause a building to collapse when I got mad. Whether I would do anything with it beyond that, I wasn't sure. I had come to trust Gregory over the years – who wouldn't after seeing him pull Ev out of some tricky situations? I also knew that Cassandra hadn't planned on taking time to teach me and was squeezing me in. She had the deli and her new husband to pay attention to. Plus, it felt too weird to have my best friend as a teacher.

"Okay. You can teach. But on *my* schedule. If I'm not going to the office, I don't want to study every single minute. I want to have a fair amount of time to write. Deal?"

He nodded. "Deal. It looks like you just went shopping. Do you have enough for lunch for two? I'm hungry."

Over grilled cheese sandwiches (I *did* mention I'm the grilled cheese queen, didn't I?) we set up a schedule. He got three hours in the morning for teaching plus one weekend day. The rest of the time was mine. I finally got around to asking about Ev.

"Haven't seen him since we argued while I was packing," Gregory said around a mouthful of Cheddar and Pepper Jack – my favorite combination. "He hasn't called, either, which suggests his ego is still getting in the way. He probably either called Marianna or took a taxi to work since he doesn't drive."

That was fast. "Although you think Ev will come to his senses soon, you knew you'd move?"

"Of course," a slight chuckle escaped. "You have to remember that Ev is still very much a child in some respects. Standard ogre temper tantrums aside, he needs to learn that not everything goes according to *his* plan in this world. He's a likeable person and has played on that but it's nothing compared to how the magical community sticks together. Leaving the cottage is just another way of telling him I'm on your side, not his.

"I believe Cassandra delivered the non-renewal of the lease this morning. At least she said she was going to. He should be in a right tizzy about now. His ego won't let him remember how difficult it was to get decent, inexpensive office space in the first place or what a mess things were before you showed up. I suspect there will be a couple of fist-sized holes in the wall that will have to be repaired before Cassandra will give him back the security deposit."

I knew Ev would have a lot of difficulty managing things in my absence. Hell, the last time I took a few days off mid-week, he was beside himself when I returned. But I also knew his ego. We'd had more than one *discussion* about how to do things. Rather than get into a shouting match and unforgivably bruise his ego by reminding him what a mess he'd made of the paperwork in the beginning, I'd acquiesced to his methods – on the surface. I kept doing things the most logical way, just rearranged the reports he got so he *thought* he'd won the argument.

Then I got to thinking about moving the office. He had a cushy deal with Cassandra. The rent was probably thirty percent below market and the office was conveniently located. Then there were the benefits of Cassandra's wards and food almost immediately at hand. He was going to have to shell out a good deal more money to replicate what he now had anywhere else. Plus, organizing the entire office for a move? I wondered if Marianna would help.

Moving. Packing. "Hey, I didn't hear any big trucks outside. Did you just magic all your stuff?"

Gregory grinned. "Of course. I keep crates in the garage for the small things and as I've moved quite a bit in my life, packing is almost as easy as breathing. It only took me a little over three hours to pack everything. Between me and James, it took about an hour to do the actual moving. That's one of the reasons I was hungry."

"So, you're friends with Mr. Owens?" Curiosity was always my weak point.

"*I'm* how Ev got you this apartment. James and I have been crossing paths for the better part of a century. I ran into him at a grocery store of all places right after Ev and I moved here. I wouldn't say we're bosom buddies but acquaintances who do each other favors, yes.

"Ev told me he had hired you but that you were an out-of-towner. I knew James owned several apartment buildings and called him to see if he had anything available. It was just luck that he had a building with a vacancy in the same neighborhood as the office. I told Ev and the rest you know."

Even though I'd seen hints of it before, I was beginning to realize just how tightly-knit the magical community was. Everyone seemed to know everyone else. I had to remind myself that I was now a part of it. The thought didn't thrill me too much. I liked my privacy.

I made a face. "So Mr. Owens now knows about me? How far has the word spread that Amy can do magic?"

"No, he doesn't know about you," Gregory soothed. "I just told him Ev and I had a spat and I thought it best to get out of the way for a bit. *That* he understood, as would most who know or know of Ev. I won't say anything to anyone unless I feel it's in *your* best interest that they know. I need to go unpack but may we talk about your studies for a moment before I do?"

After I'd told him about my Sunday session with Cassandra and what I'd read that morning, he made a face.

"I don't want to belittle Cassandra but she took the easiest route for her. Plants are her love and you will have to learn about them, too. But you obviously need to work on the rocks part of it first. Study books are magically-geared toward teaching what isn't immediately available in living, breathing form. That's why the geology came up first in yours. I would wager it's the same in her book as her mother is a big plant person, too."

I asked a question I was dying to know the answer to. "Do wizards have books, too?"

"Now they do, yes," he replied. "When I came into my power, very few people knew how to read or write. Everything was passed down by word of mouth and committed to memory. I still prefer that method but I recognize that not everyone learns that way. So, we will combine reading with practical exercises. I will speak with Cassandra about taking over for her. You need to progress the way your book is written."

"She'll probably be relieved," I told him. "I know teaching me wasn't exactly on her agenda but her folks are too far away."

Gregory headed toward the door. "I will see you tomorrow morning at nine. Re-read the chapter you read this morning before I get here."

"Wait," I called after him. "It took me three hours to get through it this morning. I have to start studying at six?"

All he did was grin as he shut the door behind him. I grumbled then realized it was only one o'clock. There was plenty of time to write…a book about an older, single wizard taking up with a young, fledgling witch.

Chapter 14

And so it went for the rest of the week. I was up with the dawn each morning, taking only a half hour for social networking before reading that same damned chapter over and over. Gregory was promptly at my door at nine. At least he brought a pound of his special coffee so there was something really tasty to sip on as he drilled me about the different kinds of rock and soil. How I *hated* science!

I thought Saturday morning was going to be more of the same but when he knocked on my door at nine, he had car keys in his hand. "Come. Practical lesson time." He turned and walked back up the stairs to the sidewalk.

I ran to the kitchen, grabbed a travel mug and filled it to the top. I gathered my coat, cell phone and purse and was just about to close the door behind me when Fudge darted past me and up the stairs. I finished closing and locking the door and followed, to see Gregory open the passenger door of that Hummer and allow Fudge to hop in the front seat.

"The Hummer's yours?" I asked.

"Yes. I wanted an off-road vehicle for myself. Ev thought being able to get around even in the worst snow was a good idea so he purchased it but it's in my name. If things don't work out the way I think they will, I will definitely be downgrading to something smaller."

I clambered in. With a vehicle that large, Fudge had plenty of room to sprawl between us on the seat – right in front of the heater. He looked smug.

"Where are we going?"

"Somewhere you can work on your lessons without drawing attention. Drink your coffee. It will take us a couple of hours."

He turned the radio on and we rode in companionable silence, listening to the strains of classical music, punctuated by Fudge's little feline snores. I watched the scenery of farmland and stands of trees along Interstate 35. The same route I'd taken to spend a romantic weekend with Tony just a few months prior. The one that had started out romantic and ended with us having to call the posse in Minneapolis to bail us out of a magical jam. I realized that except for that one moment of weakness a week earlier when I knew I'd never hear from him again, I hadn't thought of him. Not really in love with him? Too many other things occupying my mind? But the hole that was there was at least scabbed over, if not healed. I didn't even have to choke back a tear. I felt a little guilty.

"Do not feel guilty," Fudge sleepily said into my mind. *"I do not believe you were truly attached to him. He was convenient. But he was a dog. It was never going to be a permanent arrangement."*

"I thought you stayed out of my mind unless something magical was going on."

"I do. Your thoughts were strong enough to wake me and I felt it necessary to answer."

I harrumphed at him. He just started snoring again.

My curiosity was piqued when we got off at the exit that would take us to Mille Lacs Lake.

"A lake? There are several in Minneapolis. And I'm supposedly Earth, not Water."

"Remember your teaching. There is Earth wherever you are. There is a park on the edge of the lake that will be virtually deserted this time of year. I know it well and there are nice, secluded spots where we won't be observed, even by wanderers."

He parked in the back corner of a lot that held only two other cars – one of them was a Park Ranger's vehicle. "It's only a five-minute walk," he said as he refilled our travel mugs from a thermos. "I suggest you take advantage of the facilities here. You don't look like much of a rustic camper."

He was right. I wasn't and after nearly two hours, I needed to get rid of some coffee. I availed myself of the port-a-potty and followed him onto and then off of a ready-made hiking trail, heading deeper into woods that would be lush in a few months. At this time of year, it was mostly bare-branched hardwoods dotted with a pine here and there. The deeper we got, the less sun peeked through and we could still see piles of snow snuggled at the base of some trees. The air was crisp and cleaner-smelling than that of the city but even so, I pulled the collar of my coat closer.

Fudge seemed to be enjoying himself. He explored to both sides of us, sniffing this and that, following a scent then abandoning it only to pick up on another. Gregory damned near stepped on him as he came to a halt in a clearing and said, "Here is where we will work". Fudge immediately stopped his sniffing around and, scuffing a hole in the leaves, rested his butt on the soil, looking attentive.

I put my mug down on a rock level enough to hold it, stuck my already-gloved hands in my coat pockets and tried to pull my coat closer to me. It was chilly. Through the trees, I'd noticed that ice still crusted the lake, although it was more black than white and slush was visible on the surface. Ice-out was coming; the fishermen and boaters would be happy. "What am I supposed to do?" I asked.

"First, identify the type of Earth you're on. Then, break it down for me. How much is hard – or rocks and how much is soft – soil or sand."

Logic told me I was standing on sedimentary rock. After all, the entire area had been under a glacier a couple of times – or so I'd been told. But I knew that wasn't what Gregory was asking. So, I closed my eyes and felt around with what, after my experience at the abandoned mine, I had started calling my "witchy senses", Fudge's pressure in my head helping me out.

"Sedimentary above metamorphic. Most of the metamorphic is too deep for me to do anything with…I can barely feel it. But there are big chunks of granite both above ground and not too far buried in the soil. Probably eighty percent of what surrounds me is kinda loose soil with the other twenty being either that granite or rock-hard clay." I opened one eye to peer at him. "Right?"

"I have no idea. You're the Earth element here," he grinned as he took a swig of coffee.

I opened the other eye. "Huh? You don't know if I'm right?"

"No. My knowledge of rocks extends to those in a jewelry setting."

"Then how did you know about all this when you were drilling me this week?"

"Mostly, I just read up on the subject that first night after I unpacked. The Internet is a wonderful resource in some regards. I've also picked up a little over the years from hanging around with old wizards who enjoy debating archaeological finds.

"But this isn't a science class. It's all about knowing what surrounds you and what you can do with it. For example, the air here is lighter than it is just a hundred yards away over the lake.

Slightly less moisture. Therefore, it requires a different way of working with it than if I were sitting in a boat on the water. You need to be able to tell the difference with *your* element."

"Remember what I said about the difference between moving sand and granite." Fudge just had to add his two cents' in.

I glared at him and turned back to Gregory. "I don't get why I need to know about moving dirt or rocks. I'm a city girl and I don't do gardening."

"I understand that you don't really want to use your gift, Amy," he sighed. "But just for example: we live in Tornado Alley. What if your brick apartment building took a direct hit from one? Knowing you can, would you use magic to carefully move the debris away from you or would you use your hands to try to dig yourself out from under a ton of unstable rubble? How about if you were out of the building and came home to find your neighbors and Fudge trapped? That scenario isn't much different from what you did for Ev and me."

My heart jumped at that thought. A twister had taken out a good portion of an area just a few blocks away only two years prior. Several homes were just *gone* and more were grotesque versions of their former selves. People were still rebuilding. The thought of losing my home and all my things in the blink of an eye, regardless of insurance, was frightening.

"More importantly," he continued, "you can draw strength from Earth. The harder the earth, the more energy encapsulated in it. Therefore, rock has more encased energy than loamy garden soil, which has more than sand. Now, instead of simply identifying the kind of earth, feel for the energy."

I blew out a breath. I could see his point but, geez. School. For a subject I didn't want to learn. I did as I was told, this time with my eyes open.

"Look for clumps of that substance you call glitter," I heard.

"I know. Shut up," I murmured back.

Although I wouldn't admit it, that analogy helped. The piece of granite my mug was sitting on was chock-full of glitter while the rest of the ground was sparkly but not mirror-shiny. The sparkle thinned as my eye looked closer to the lake, which had a somewhat sandy shoreline.

"See it?" Gregory asked.

"Yes."

"Good. Now you have to look for something else. Any time you're dealing with earth, there are going to be plant roots. You don't want to starve the plants so you have to be careful how much energy you pull from where. Yes, it replenishes but if you take enough, it will be a long time coming back. Look again. The tree roots should be very visible to you."

Crap. I was already known as a plant-killer. A friend had given me a houseplant "guaranteed to grow for even the blackest thumb" when I was in college. Is there a color darker than black? I killed it. I didn't even trust myself with one of those "air plants" you see in stores.

I felt around again with those witchy senses. The deeper underground I went, the more different the tingles became. I could tell the difference between the small pieces of granite (or whatever it was – hard rock) and the looser soil that compacted farther down but there was a third kind of tingle. It felt…alive. I know that's not a good explanation because energy is energy but that's what my brain came up with.

That "alive" tingle was tangled all over the place, like a snake's nest. Although I was standing in a clearing probably fifty feet across, those snakes, big and small, were all entwined under my feet, covering the open space. Logical brain translated that to tree roots.

"Open your eyes," Gregory commanded. "You need to be able to use that sense while the others are still working."

I hadn't even realized I'd closed my eyes and said as much. "That's the reason for practical exercises," he said. While looking directly at me, he held out his hand. In a split-second, I saw a small, sparkly-red tornado whirling above his palm which dissipated a second later.

"Sit and take a break," he told me. "I know this is a lot to cram into a short period of time. You must be feeling overwhelmed."

I sat on the rock next to my mug and gratefully took a swig of the still-warm elixir. "Not overwhelmed, per se. More pissed. Not pissed. Discombobulated. My life has been turned *really* upside down. I like routine. I had a comfortable one. Not anymore."

"Ah, but life is to be *explored*, Amy. Routine is boring. You get in a rut and you become a boring person."

I raised an eyebrow. He coughed. "Well, you were rather boring. When I saw you, all you talked about was work. Even when you were dating someone, you talked about work."

"If you'll recall, that's pretty much all we had in common until this upheaval. I don't talk about my private life with co-workers."

"You did with Sally," he countered.

"She's a girl. It's different. And I didn't tell her all that much, anyways. I don't even tell Cassandra everything."

It was his turn to raise an eyebrow. "I thought best friends shared *everything.*"

"Not this one. Cassandra knows more than anyone else but deepest, darkest secrets are still very deep and very dark."

He hummed a little tune to himself as I drained my coffee. Then he looked sternly down at me and said, "Some secrets are worth keeping, even to yourself. But stretching your horizons a bit is no bad thing. You were uncomfortable the first few times you went to a party with Ev, weren't you? Yet you figured out how to deal with it and in the meantime, if I recall our conversation correctly, were able to parlay the people you met at those parties into a nice side job. So, you're just stretching your horizons again. This time in a different direction."

My butt was getting cold. I stood. "At least I won't have to ask Cassandra how a witch would respond in a certain situation anymore, that much is true."

Gregory grinned. "See? Advantages. One more exercise then we will head back to the city. I will even treat you to lunch on the way home."

The last was the most tiring. Isn't it always? He had me draw energy from the soil, not the nice piece of granite I'd sat on and the couple more like it in the clearing. I had to avoid the tree roots, form it into a ball in my hand then allow it to dissipate back to where I'd originally got it from. Avoiding tree roots was almost impossible, given where I was standing. I had to find those little pieces of hard rock scattered around to get enough to form a decent energy ball. I had to repeat the exercise countless times until it only took me a second or two to form a ball the size of an orange.

"That's enough for today. It will come even faster with practice," Gregory told me as he picked up his coffee mug and prepared to leave the peaceful clearing.

"I thought I had to learn how to move stuff?" I was tired but still wanted to get *all* my lessons out of the way. I had a book to work on.

"I'd be willing to wager you can do it now," he countered. "Okay, one last thing before we go. That piece of granite your mug is sitting on? Move it to your right just a little, then back to its original spot. It's no different than what you did with the couch pillow at the hotel."

I eyed the …boulder. It wasn't huge but nine cubic feet of granite weighed a *lot*, I was certain.

"Contain the energy you see with your will, then move your container where you want it to go. The energy weighs nothing. It is easy."

"For you to say," I thought back. Once again, I felt the pressure of Fudge in the back of my head. I saw the rock's energy sparkles, imagined a Tupperware container holding those sparkles, then "saw" the container move over a foot and settle back down to the ground. Then I "moved" the container back. Fudge was right. It was no more difficult than moving my leftover spaghetti from one spot on the kitchen counter to another.

"Oh, well done, Amy!" Gregory clapped his hands. "Now that you know you can move a small boulder, you should be able to move anything else. Out of curiosity, how did you do it?"

He laughed when I told him about the Tupperware. "I know a young Air witch who envisions a blow-dryer to move things with air. Whatever works. Ready to go?"

I was. "How did you find this place?" I asked, trudging behind him while Fudge explored off the trail again.

"State and national parks are wonderful places for city folks to go, even the magical ones. I've been to nearly all of the ones within a hundred miles or so of home in the time I've been here. Late fall and early spring are fantastic times to be alone in the woods…it's not warm enough for campers, too wet for hikers, and no snow for skiers. This particular park seems to be nearly deserted in the off-season so I come here often. In the summer I usually avoid the lakes in the cities, as well as the larger lakes, like this one, because there are too many people. There are plenty of places to go for solitude without driving all the way up to the Boundary Waters. You just have to search them out."

Gregory was just a fount of information. Although a friend owned a cabin up north and I borrowed it on occasion, it wasn't always available. Something closer to get out of the noise in the city would be nice.

I hauled my little self up into the monstrosity that was the Hummer and asked if he would share his list of places to go. He nodded as Fudge curled up on the seat, looking expectantly at the heating vent. I had to admit, he had a good idea. I was chilled but not to the point of uncontrollable shivering. Fudge at least had a fur coat.

*"That does not mean I do not feel the cold. As a matter of fact, I feel it more than you do. I have a higher natural body temperature. The only reason neither of us is shivering is because **I** can take it. You were warming yourself a bit with the energy."*

"Oh shut up," I said. Apparently, out loud.

Gregory gave me a gimlet eye.

"I wasn't talking to you," I retorted.

Gregory choked. "Fudge *talks* to you? How old is he?"

"No idea. He claims over a thousand years. Will you turn the heater on?"

Gregory started the car and turned the heater on full blast. "You are *so* lucky, Amy. I've only known a few witches and wizards who got a very old familiar. They know so much. Treasure him."

Fudge preened. I thumped him on his head but he continued looking smug. A minute or two later, warm air was coming out of the vents. Fudge and I leaned into it.

Chapter 15

All that fresh air and exercise must have done me some good. I didn't wake when the sun hit my window Sunday morning. Some time after the sunlight had moved across my bedroom floor I woke in a panic, thinking Gregory would be knocking on my door for lessons in just a second or two, only to remember that he'd given me Sunday off with the admonishment that I should at least read the next chapter in my workbook. Wasn't going to happen. I was accustomed to writing at least one full day every weekend and I wasn't about to break up my routine completely. Not to mention that all the time I'd been spending with him recently meant I had more information with which to flesh out my new wizard character – I wanted to get it all down.

So, I wrote all day Sunday. Monday was back to my new routine: up with the dawn, check social networking, read a chapter in my magic book, lecture by Gregory, write in the afternoon and evening.

Tuesday was the same except I was beginning to worry about my job. It had been over a week and no one had heard from Ev. Not even Cassandra. She said he'd stormed out after she delivered the non-renewal notice and she hadn't heard a sound from upstairs since then. I mentioned it to Gregory who simply shrugged his shoulders and said, "He's probably off pouting. He does that fairly well. I'm not going to worry until it's been two weeks. Then I will start looking for him."

Since the next chapter in my workbook was on ley lines (*really* concentrated Earth energy that runs in lines all over the world), I had to venture outside in the cool spring weather once again on Saturday. (I'm a warm-weather person. Anything below 50°F is cold. Don't ask me what I'm doing in Minnesota. I should be in the Caribbean.) We didn't have to go far, though. A park on the north shore of Medicine Lake was only thirty minutes away.

It was a nice day and a Saturday so people were out enjoying the weather. Parents supervised their children on the playground, joggers bounced along and power walkers strutted their stuff while dodging those ambulating at a more leisurely pace along the walking trails. Others sat on the beach, staring longingly at the still-frigid water.

Because of the public nature of the park, Fudge had grudgingly agreed to wear a leash that Gregory had thoughtfully brought with him. "*I look ridiculous. It is too tight. It itches.*" When I told him it was either that or stay in the vehicle because of leash laws, he acquiesced but the grumbling continued.

"No overt displays, Amy," Gregory cautioned as we walked along the path. Hopefully, we just looked like a couple out for a Saturday stroll with their pet cat. (A cat walking docilely on a leash caused more than one jogger and walker to miss their stride.)

"Well, duh. All these people around. What am I supposed to do?" The entire area was a river of energy glitter, except for the path we were walking on. Whoever built it knew about shielding or something. I wanted to crawl under the timber walkway to find out what they'd used. But I didn't. I can behave like a normal person on occasion.

He gestured. "We're going to sit on that bench over there and enjoy people watching. While *I* people watch, I want *you* to experience the ley line. We will be sitting almost right in the middle of it."

My feet began tingling almost as soon as we left the path. That was weird because I'd been told the synthetic soles of my tennis shoes would shield me. By the time we got to the bench, I was shaking. I wasn't sure I could sit without vibrating apart. I managed to find the bench and park myself on it but I couldn't help but feel like I was going explode into a messy mass of tissue and blood at any moment.

"*Use your personal shield energy to push* **out** *until you are more comfortable. Then let some seep in. Draw strength from it but do not allow it to overwhelm you.*"

Fudge hopped into my lap and I felt his comforting presence at the back of my head. With his guidance, I did as instructed. Pushing out with my personal shield stopped the shaking almost immediately. Then I opened a small hole and allowed some of the energy to trickle through. Wow. You've heard the term "energy rush"? This was the epitome of that. More than what I'd experienced in Atlanta, I felt not just awake but ready to take on the world.

"*Enough. Do not overload.*" I reluctantly closed the hole I'd made. I turned to Gregory.

"Dizzying, isn't it?" he asked with a grin.

"You can feel it, too?"

"Ley lines are so powerful that anyone can draw from them. Even Ev would feel an energy surge off one when other energies just bounce off him. However, high power equals danger. They are the magical equivalents of electrical high tension wires. You don't want the full power of that wire going directly into your computer. Nor do you want to completely open yourself to a ley line. You would fry yourself in the wink of an eye.

"That said, they're handy for workings that require a *lot* of energy, or for replenishing yours in a hurry. Just don't overload. If you feel a need to come here, I suggest you always bring Fudge because he can stop you if you can't stop yourself."

"I already got that. Can we go? I'm getting jittery again. It's uncomfortable."

He took a long look at me then down at Fudge. "She needs to strengthen her normal shield. Can you work with her on that?" My cat *nodded*. Just like a human. "Good. We can go."

I heaved a sigh of relief and unceremoniously dumping Fudge out of my lap, skittered back to the trail and its shielding. Gregory picked up the end of Fudge's leash and strolled back. As we ambled along, still trying to look like a normal couple (with a cat on a leash), I asked how he knew just where to go and how he managed to feel so calm around that much energy.

"You saw the maps of ley lines in your book. We all have a copy of them. It was just a matter of overlaying the one of North America onto a modern road map. In addition, there's the name of this lake, *Medicine* Lake. I know the official story behind what the Native Americans called it but I think it's hogwash. They know about ley lines just as much as we do.

"My shields are much stronger than yours so the extra energy doesn't affect me unless I want it to. Yours are still at human strength and Fudge can help you with that."

We arrived at the monster car. As soon as I'd shut my door, I heard "*Get this cord off me*". Laughing, I complied with Fudge's demand.

When we arrived back home, Gregory stopped me getting out of the car with a hand on my arm. "No lessons with me next week. I have a few personal things to attend to. Then, if I haven't heard from Ev, I'm going to find out what's going on. If you need me, you have my mobile number. In the meantime, work with Fudge on your shielding and read your book."

"Yes, Master," I grinned as Fudge and I crawled down our side of the car while Gregory simply stepped out of his. "If you hear anything about Ev, let me know?"

"Of course." We both went to our respective buildings. It occurred to me as I walked down to my door that I didn't know *which* apartment Gregory lived in. I'd have to find that out. You never know when I might have to knock on his door.

I was on my third cup of coffee Monday morning, contemplating the next chapter in my workbook (healing with gemstones) when there was a loud pounding on my front door. I'd only opened it a crack when Cassandra pushed her way in.

"Mom just called," she said as I closed the door and turned to her. "They've arrested Gregory in connection with Ev's disappearance."

As my mouth hung open, she walked into the kitchen and poured herself a cup of coffee. I yelled, "What?" at her back.

"According to Mom, Marianna filed a complaint with the Witches' Council last night. She claims Ev hasn't been home in a week, that Gregory was the last to see him and also that Gregory had it in for Ev."

I was flabbergasted. "That is the most ridiculous thing I've ever heard. Why would Gregory do *anything* to Ev? He's got a nice job, a free place to live and from what I've heard and seen, he rather likes Ev."

"You and I both know that but apparently Marianna walked in on an argument while Gregory was packing to move. She claims Gregory said Ev would regret his decision to fire you. Then she said that you and Gregory were an item so naturally, he'd want retribution for your lack of a job."

I spewed my last swig of coffee. "Gregory and me? An item? What *ever* gave her that idea? She knew about my relationship with Tony."

"I have no fucking idea what's going on, but we need to get to the bottom of it. Get dressed. I want you to go into the office to see if there's anything that would give a clue to what happened, where Ev may have gone, all that."

I ducked through the shower, threw some clothes on, poured what coffee was left in the pot into my travel mug and followed her out the door. Fudge, once again, slipped through as I was closing it. *"I have a better nose than you. I might smell something."*

Cassandra continued ranting during the walk to the office. "I wonder what she hates about Gregory? I wonder where Ev went? He doesn't normally disappear for more than a day or two at a time."

"Hang on there," I tried to put some calm into my voice. "We don't know anything at this point. Can you get details of what the Witches' Council is *actually* charging him with and *exactly* what Marianna said?"

"There should be a parchment on either my desk or yours when we get back. Although Mom doesn't know either one well, she smells something fishy, too. Unfortunately, Marianna's family is close to one of the officers, so it'll have to go through the entire process."

I still had my key to the office so as Cassandra went back into the deli, I headed up the stairs. It felt strange to be making that climb after two weeks. When I opened the door, it looked like no one had been there in that time…except for the fist-sized holes in the walls of Ev's office. A light layer of dust covered everything. A smell of burnt coffee filled the air. I went into the kitchen and looked at the pot I'd started that fateful morning. Thank goodness for the auto-off on today's coffeemakers. Otherwise there probably would have been pieces of shattered glass all over.

"Where to start looking…and for what?" I mused out loud. "He gets kidnapped, gets healed and vanishes for another two weeks?"

"Your boss is unpredictable," Fudge reminded me.

"Well, yeah, but he doesn't just leave business unattended for that long," I answered. "Even when I've taken a day or two off, he's always come into the office."

I checked voice mail. According to the phone company's computer, the box was full with one hundred twenty-two messages. I know, I technically didn't work there anymore. But I couldn't believe Ev hadn't checked voice mail. I grabbed a pen and paper and started listening to them all.

Most were just guards leaving their daily check-in. There were two from Ed, the accountant, reminding me about tax stuff; some from client agents asking questions; one from Martin asking about moving money. Nothing out of the ordinary.

I fired up my computer and pulled in all my email messages…just to clean off the server. Scanning them, nothing there looked out of the ordinary, either. But *nothing* had been done since I'd left. I called Sally.

"Hey, how's unemployment?" she asked.

"Normally, I'd say just fine but not today." I filled her in on what was happening. "I don't like the looks of things. Can you come in and help get this place running again? I'd hate for the business to go down the drain, regardless of what Ev might be up to. Dress casual. It's only the two of us and we need to do some dusting."

"Oh, happy days. I've been bored out of my mind. I'll throw something on and be there in about a half hour. What are you going to do?"

I really didn't know and said as much. "Wait for me to get there," she said. "We'll sort stuff out and decide who needs to do what. See ya in a few." She hung up.

While I'd been doing my thing, Fudge had been sniffing virtually every nook and cranny of the office, sneezing every now and again. *"Everything smells two weeks old. Especially that coffee. There are no magical signatures here except you, Gregory and Cassandra. Whatever happened, did not happen here."*

Based on my amateur observation, I agreed with him. "I'm going down to get more coffee and see if Cassandra's got that parchment. Want anything?"

"Not from her but some fresh water in my dish would be appreciated."

So, before I went downstairs, I emptied his dish, rinsed it out and refilled it. *Then* I trooped down the stairs to see what Cassandra had. Thankfully, it was Monday and the deli was closed. Otherwise, she'd have been busier than a bee with no time to chat. I opened the side door that was spelled to only open for those welcome on closed days.

Pausing to fill my cup from the pot on the counter, I walked back through the kitchen to her office. She raised her head from reading something when I cleared my throat.

"I'm going to have to call Mom to get a translation. It's in Latin. I wish those people would get with the twenty-first century, already!"

"Isn't there a translation spell or something?" I figured magic could solve almost anything.

"Only if you want to call Elinda or Marge. It's an Air spell and I'm terrible with Air."

I didn't and knew I wouldn't be any help, either, so I took a seat and a swig as she dialed her mother in Arizona. I cringed when she yelled into the phone, "It's the twenty-first century! They need to do these things in English!"

She made a face, grunted some noncommittal words, apologized for yelling, grunted some more, then hung up. It sounded just like the conversation I would have had with my mother if she were still alive. They understand their kids, even if no one else does.

"An English translation is in the works. For some reason, Gregory's attorney requested it. We need to call him if we don't want to slog through this thing with a Latin dictionary to try to get all the archaic legalese right."

"Who's his attorney?"

"Some guy named Mortimer Blatherton. An English barrister living in Los Angeles. Heard of him?"

I hadn't. "Where's Gregory being held? Can we go visit him?"

"At Council headquarters downtown and no. Only his attorney at this point."

I grimaced. "There's *nothing* upstairs, except piles of work and a burnt pot of coffee. I've called Sally. Regardless of what's happened to Ev, we can't let the company go to the dogs. After we get things sorted up there, I want to have a look around Ev's house. Do you know anyone who can pick locks?"

She made a face then laughed. "Yuck. He didn't turn your pot off, huh? And yes, I think I know someone but we have a problem."

"What's that?"

"It's a Council crime scene. No one but the investigators is supposed to go in. I assume Gregory's attorney will be able to if he wants but he's on a plane right now."

"So I'm the attorney's eyes and ears. Who knows Ev better than me?"

Her phone chimed with a text message. She held up her hand for me to quit talking, typed some stuff on her phone and almost immediately, I got the same chime. I checked my message to see a phone number with a Los Angeles area code.

"It's the attorney's phone number. I assumed you'd want it."

Did I. I was about to dial it when Sally strolled into Cassandra's office.

"It's a good thing you've got a pot going down here. We need a new carafe. Hi."

I gave her the once-over. "*That's* casual?" She always looked stunning but a silk pantsuit seemed overkill for the two of us in a dusty office.

She shrugged. "I don't like denims. The seams chafe. This is what I wear. Are you ready to dig in?"

Cassandra laughed. "You'd never make it in the deli, Sally. Even with an apron I get at least one stain a day. I have things to do, too. Let's all get our work done, Amy call that lawyer, and we'll meet at Cork's at five for drinks and a planning session. Deal?"

I couldn't help but agree. Gregory had been under arrest for less than a day. I didn't see what I could do but try to put the company to rights as much as I could and wait for the attorney to tell me something. Sally and I left Cassandra to her work and went to ours.

Chapter 16

I heaved a sigh when Sally and I walked back into the office. It was déjà vu. The two-foot-tall stack of mail in the corner of the hall coupled with the dust and piles of paper looked just as it had the day of my interview eight years before.

"Open and sort the mail. I'll sling a dust rag," I said. I hated the thought of that pantsuit getting grimy. She nodded and sat down to work. I grabbed the dusting supplies out from under the kitchen sink and, starting with her desk, furiously hit at least the high spots in her office and mine. I ignored Ev's office. Even if he'd been there, he wouldn't notice.

Once I had the surfaces clean enough to put an elbow on, I grabbed the papers off Ev's desk, merged them with the ones on mine and also sorted. I prioritized the emails in my inbox and printed out the most urgent stuff. Between the two of us, the "gotta do *right now*" stack was a little over two inches thick. I sorted that down into two and handed one to her.

"Pay bills. I'll start returning the most urgent phone calls. If anyone calls for Ev, he's unavailable but you don't know where he is."

"I got that much. But first, I have a problem."

I raised an eyebrow.

"My monitor isn't working. I kind of need to see what I'm doing."

"It is your fault. Remember leaving here angry? There was a puff of smoke coming from that direction as we walked by and the wizard said you had fried it."

Crap. "It's my fault. I didn't have control of my emotions when I left. Take the one off Ev's desk for now. I'll have to buy you another one." I made a note on my long list of things to do.

While Sally was swapping monitors, I grabbed the Accounts Payable file and a stack of checks from the locked drawer in my desk

138

and walked them out to her. I was so glad she was up to speed on all the accounting stuff, although she only had access to the accounts payable module.

Once I was certain she had everything she needed, I started making phone calls. The first was to Mr. Blatherton.

"Yes, Miss McCollum. I know who you are. I just landed and am on my way to see Mr. Tremayne now. I will call you again after I have had an opportunity to speak with him. What number shall I use?" His voice was nasal, obviously British and rather aloof-sounding. I gave him my cell number, hung up and dialed another.

Two hours passed in a heartbeat. I got the estimated tax deposit amounts from Ed, conferred with Martin about moving some money from one type of investment to another, declined numerous party invitations on Ev's behalf, said 'I'm sorry, we're full' to requests from managers and agents for our services (Ev would kill me), told a couple of job applicants to email their resumes, and apologizing all over the place, basically covered for Ev's absence.

I was just about to start in on the next pile of paper ("gotta do *today*") when Cassandra came in, balancing three plates on one arm.

"I figured you two would forget to eat so I brought up lunch. Plus, I want to know how things are going up here." She pushed paper away from the edge, put the plates on Sally's desk and pulled up two chairs, indicating I was supposed to eat out there.

I carefully picked off some bits of bacon from my BLT and gave them to Fudge, who had trotted out of his nest in my office and stood expectantly at my feet. Then between bites, I said, "I called the attorney. He said he'd call back after he talked with Gregory. Two hours. Nothing. Loads of crap to catch up on. Thankful for Sally."

Sally smiled. "It's really not all that bad. With two of us, it shouldn't take too long to get back to normal. You just forget you don't have to do it all yourself."

I shrugged. "Yes, you're a huge help but there are some things you can't do. A *lot* of things you can't do. But I *am* grateful you're here. It would take a week, otherwise."

"It's no surprise the attorney hasn't called back," Cassandra interjected, bringing us back to the main subject. "I'm sure there are all sorts of formalities to go through. I'd guess you'll hear from him later this afternoon."

I wasn't the only one who ate fast. We all inhaled our food. Cassandra picked up the plates and heading for the door, said over her shoulder, "Five o'clock at Cork's".

Sally and I went back to our respective piles of paper.

By three-thirty, I was exhausted. Making nice to people over the phone and via email while telling them exactly nothing they needed to know was wearing. Oh, there were a few decisions I could make but most I preferred to leave to Ev. I'd hear less griping afterward.

Sally handed me a stack of checks to sign. "I'll get these in the mail and then I'm going home. I have an appointment in the morning but I should be here around noon. Okay?"

I scribbled my name in the appropriate spot so many times my hand almost went into full rigor mortis. I nodded at her comment, wordlessly handed the stack back to her and started the process of readying my desk for the next day. My cell phone rang.

"Miss McCollum?" the nasally voice on the other end inquired. When I answered in the affirmative, he continued, "Mr. Tremayne is being held on suspicion of murder. The charges were filed by Mr. Angelich's girlfriend, one Marianna Johannsen. However, as there is no body, the case has gone to investigative stage."

I cut him off. "How's Gregory?"

"Although understandably upset, he is quite comfortable. Magical Council prisons are not like human prisons. He has a suite and his needs are met. He did, however, express concern as to your well-being. How shall I answer?"

I thought for a moment. This guy didn't need to know about my personal problems. "Give him this message: Fudge hasn't had a thing to do. He'll understand. Now, if there's no body, why isn't Gregory being released on bail or some equivalent? What can I do to help clear him? The charges are so bogus I can't begin to tell you…"

He cleared his throat. It didn't help clear his sinuses. "The magical community doesn't operate like that, Miss McCollum. Mr. Tremayne will remain confined until the case comes to a close. Obviously, we need to find Mr. Angelich alive and well for Mr. Tremayne to be cleared and released.

"Although the Council's investigative team is, naturally, working on the case, Mr. Tremayne thought you might be helpful in that regard. I'd like to meet you in the morning for an interview. Where would be convenient?"

I gave him the address of the office. We agreed he'd be there at nine sharp. After I hung up, I looked around. Although I'd gotten the dust off the surfaces, the place still looked dingy. I had a little time before meeting Cassandra, so got out the vacuum and finished tidying up. Ev was too cheap to hire a weekly cleaning service so I was used to filling in between their once a month visits.

Sally had lit some of the stash of scented candles we usually burned to disguise Ev's odor and they had taken care of the incinerated coffee aroma. I tossed the carafe in the trash, reminding myself that I still had to go to the store after meeting Cassandra. We needed a new carafe, Sally needed a new monitor and as I discovered when cleaning, the bathroom was out of toilet tissue. Maybe I could cajole Cassandra into driving me to the local Wal-Mart rather than take a taxi. It wasn't *that* far and it would be one-stop shopping.

"I do not wish to go where you are going. Please take me home, first." I nearly jumped out of my skin. I'd totally forgotten Fudge was at the office. Being an experienced Air witch would have come in handy. I looked at the dead watch I'd put on out of habit then looked at the clock on the wall. I could see I would have just enough time to take him home and change into something a little less dusty before walking back to the pub.

"So, I presume you heard from Mr. Blatherton. What did he say?" Cassandra asked as Cork set a glass of Merlot and one of Chardonnay in front of us.

"Blatherton? Who needs a barrister?" Cork growled. We were both used to the part-giant's deep, gravelly voice and didn't think anything of it but the fact that he knew the attorney's name startled both of us.

Cassandra came out of her shock first. "You know him?"

"Crossed paths with the stiff neck a time or two over the pond. Heard he moved over here a few years ago. What are you two involved in that requires the services of a barrister?"

We looked at each other. Cassandra tilted her head toward me.

I answered very quietly, "Ev's disappeared and Gregory is being charged with murder. Blatherton is his attorney – barrister."

Cork's growl deepened. "What a load of bullcrap. I don't know either *that* well but they've been in here more than a time or two. Tremayne would no more kill Angelich than he would his own mother."

I nodded my agreement. "I know that and you know that but the authorities don't. Cassandra and I are trying to figure out what happened and how to find Ev."

"Has anyone traced his cell phone? It's usually glued to him," Cassandra mused.

"I don't know. I do know he's not answering it. I tried and it just went to voice mail. I'm meeting with Blatherton in the morning. I'll know more then. Speaking of tomorrow, can you give me a ride to Wal-Mart? I have to replace the carafe and a couple of other things before then."

After going back and forth for an hour, neither of us could think of anything to do, barring breaking into Ev's house to see if there was anything of interest. *That* would not sit well with the authorities (magical or mundane) so we decided to wait until after I'd had my meeting with the "stiff neck" to make any further plans.

Cassandra did indeed give me a lift to Wal-Mart. She snickered when I picked up a computer monitor that was bigger than Sally's original yet half the price. "I'll bet that's your fault."

"How'd you know?"

"According to Gregory, you were steaming when you left the office that day. The energy a witch gives off when seriously pissed would easily fry anything electronic within a few feet. I'm surprised it was just the monitor and not the entire system."

"Yeah, well. Ev's still paying for it. He was the one that pissed me off to that point," I said as I absent-mindedly pulled the company credit card out of my wallet to pay for my purchases. Then I did a double-take, realizing which card I'd grabbed. Ev really hadn't paid attention to *anything*. It was still good.

I ranted on the drive back to the office. "Devious, huh? I could have cleaned his bank accounts out and gone on a shopping spree with the company's card and *didn't*. What an airhead! He should have cancelled my card and taken my name off the bank's signatory list immediately. He should feel lucky I'm *really* trustworthy, not devious."

Cassandra laughed. "I don't know what that witch did to him but I'd be willing to bet it was a hex and of his own making. Whatever has happened to him, he'll see the light once he comes back to find his company still in business. I'd still like to know what's going on. You don't suppose someone kidnapped him again, do you?"

I sighed. "Again? I'm sure he's made plenty of enemies over the years but did anyone get a ransom note?"

"Yeah, that's the thing, isn't it? If he'd been kidnapped again, *someone* would have gotten a note and they'd probably have contacted you about the money. Everyone knows you run the business for him."

We pulled up in her driveway and she helped me haul my purchases upstairs. I just plunked the packages on the floor inside the office door. I'd have time in the morning to put it all away before Mr. Blatherton arrived.

"G'night," Cassandra waved as she walked up her stairs. "Call me anytime if you hear anything. Otherwise, I'll see you for your normal latte in the morning."

I walked home in the twilight, lost in thought. I didn't think Ev was dead and couldn't see where Marianna thought Gregory had anything to do with his disappearance. Yes, Ev wasn't answering his cell but...I really didn't know what to think of the whole situation.

I continued musing as I made a cup of (decaffeinated) coffee and fired up my own laptop. I knew the job would be different when I took it but a kidnapping and now disappearance of my boss was *really* unusual. Boss? I guessed I still had a job. Or not? I mentally slapped myself and hired myself back – at least temporarily. Sally, too. Until my signatory powers were revoked, I could pay us.

I put the issue of Ev into a corner of my mind and turned my hat around from being an administrative assistant to a romance writer.

"*You should be studying.*"

I grunted at Fudge and opened the word processing document that was the next novel. "My name is Scarlett and I'll study tomorrow." I felt a query in my mind. Apparently, Fudge hadn't read *Gone with the Wind*. "I parodied a famous quote. Never mind. I'll read the next chapter in the morning." Fudge sighed, took up his usual spot next to the keyboard and curled up for a snooze.

Chapter 17

For the first time in a couple of weeks, I dressed in full office mode the next morning, grimacing as I did so. I'd gotten used to sweats, no makeup and hair in a ponytail. But there was this meeting with the lawyer and I felt a need to look *very* professional.

I'd just finished plugging in Sally's new monitor and ensuring it displayed properly when the door opened. (A couple of minutes earlier would have seen me crawling around under her desk in a skirt. Timing is everything.) A thin, sallow man wearing breeches and a tailcoat entered, raised one eyebrow and, in a thin voice said, "Miss McCollum, I presume?"

I couldn't help but stare. What century did this guy think it was? He even had his dishwater-blond hair pulled back into a ponytail with a ribbon. Imagining him in a robe with one of those white wigs was easy. I wondered how many people had told him Halloween was in October, not April.

I cleared my throat, answered that I was, offered him coffee or water and indicated that we should sit in the reception area. Declining a beverage, he sat on the edge of one of the ogre-sized chairs and, opening a notebook (at least this was modern and not a roll of vellum), proceeded to interrogate me.

After thirty minutes of answering questions about what I knew of Ev and Gregory's relationship, Ev's kidnapping and rescue and Gregory's actions during the entire time, I turned the tables on him. "Has anyone used GPS to find his cell phone? Doesn't one of the magical councils have trackers to find Ev with a taglock? What are Marianna's reasons to suspect Gregory?"

Mr. Blatherton inhaled deeply into his bony, hooked nose, fixed his dour expression on me and stated, "The investigation is proceeding apace. However, I am not at liberty to discuss that with you. Mr. Tremayne thought you may have some insight into Mr.

Angelich's disappearance and possibly Miss Johannsen's reasons for accusing him. I am here only because of that. So, shall we continue?"

Another thirty minutes of questions yielded exactly nothing. "I have no idea," was my reply to most of his questions. I really didn't. Sure, Gregory and Ev argued on a regular basis but Ev's a temperamental ogre, for crying out loud. I wasn't at Ev's side twenty-four-seven so had no clue as to why Marianna might want to set Gregory up to take the fall for Ev's disappearance. But she's an ogre, too, and probably throws tantrums just as often as Ev. The whole situation just made my skin crawl.

He rose, obviously disappointed that I couldn't help. I rose with him but wasn't going to let him get away without one final, "There must be *something* I can do to help find Ev and clear Gregory".

He shook his head and with an "I'll be in touch", left. I stared at the closed door for a moment, waiting until I was certain he was gone then headed downstairs.

"Call your Mom. There must be something we can do," I told Cassandra as I barged in the deli's door.

She and the four customers sitting at tables stared at me. Oops. I probably should have been a little more observant before opening my mouth. "My office," she admonished me.

I sheepishly followed her back crossing paths with Charlie, who was taking a bowl of potato salad out to the front cooler. He nodded at me, said "Mornin'" and continued on his way.

"Sorry. Just got done with an hour of questioning from that weirdo lawyer. It was frustrating," I apologized as I sat down in the extra chair.

She sat at the chair behind her desk. "I talked with Mom last night. She – and we – can't get involved in the investigation. She needs to stay impartial and we don't have any standing. All she said was for you to keep the business going as best you could and for all of us to keep a good thought for Ev and Gregory. It's exactly like a mundane missing-person case. All the people who care can only sit and wait for the authorities to do their thing. The only difference is that our investigators have more resources at their disposal than the mundane police."

"The whole thing sets my teeth on edge," I told her. "I can't figure out the rhyme or reason behind any of it. Ev has disappeared before but only for a couple of days. It's been two weeks. And Marianna accusing Gregory has me totally befuddled."

"I know," she tried to soothe me. "Changing the subject, why did you call Mr. Blatherton a weirdo?"

I described him to her. She grinned. "Wow. Straight out of the eighteenth century, huh? That sort of makes sense in a way, though. He *will* have that robe and wig on if it goes to Tribunal, which is a Council trial. They're still really old-fashioned in that regard. If he's that old, he's probably comfortable projecting that image.

"Don't want to cut you off but as always, we both have work to do. I'll let you know if I hear anything from Mom and you call me if you hear anything from anyone."

She stood. It was a dismissal. I knew she was right but…my shoulders sagged as I headed back upstairs and the pile of work still waiting for me.

"*I need fresh water,*" greeted me when I walked in the door. I groaned. I'd forgotten to add Fudge to my morning office routine. I duly refilled his dish and my coffee cup, and sat down to work.

Sally arrived shortly after noon and wordlessly started in on her allocation of catch-up work. The phone rang frequently and I heard her saying the same thing I had in the morning. "I'm sorry, Mr. Angelich isn't available. May I take a message?" and "I'm sorry, he hasn't checked in today" more than once. The calls she forwarded to me nearly always ended with one of the same statements.

About two, the door opened and a strong odor wafted all the way into my office. I was about to jump for joy, thinking Ev was back when a female voice said, "I'm here to take over in Ev's place."

Rather than being elated, I stalked out into the reception area. "Good afternoon, Marianna," I said in my most polite voice. "How may I help you?"

She turned toward me. "As much as I'm devastated at Ev's murder, I thought the best thing I could do to honor his memory was to keep Angelich Security running. Therefore, I'd like his list of calls, please."

I'm sure my eyes had narrowed to slits. I do know I was more than a little hot under the collar. "Excuse me? First, Ev's body hasn't been found so we don't know about any murder. Second, even if we knew for certain he was dead, his will hasn't been read so we don't know what his wishes were concerning the business. Third and most importantly, you know nothing about how this company is run."

She smiled. "Oh, but I *do* know about the company. Ev has confided many secrets to me in our time together."

I smiled back. Through gritted teeth. "I don't mean to be rude, Marianna, but until I see something legal giving you control of the company, *I* will continue on as if he will walk in that door any minute. That doesn't include giving you access to company information. You're welcome to hang out here but you won't be working."

"Oh, but I will, darling," she smiled again. "I have a paper here, signed by Ev, giving me control of the company." She reached into her purse and pulled out one of those legal documents that's backed by a blue piece of paper and stapled at the top. She handed it to me with a flourish.

I scanned the two pages, and on the bottom of the last was a signature I knew well – Ev's. It was dated during the time Ev had been home recuperating from his kidnapping injuries.

I tossed it back to her. "Marianna, I don't know a lot about magical laws but I know something about mundane laws and those *do* apply in this situation. Ev's signature isn't witnessed or notarized. Nor has this been filed in a court. It doesn't have the court's stamp on it. Therefore, it is not a valid legal document and I don't have to do a damned thing about it. May I suggest you go home and wait for the Council to make a determination?"

She stood with her arms crossed and stared at me.

"Human. Amy. Control your emotions." Fudge had a good point. I could feel my anger rising to the point that I wanted to hit something. However, I thought in this instance a show of anger might not be such a bad thing. I glared at her and, feeling for the wood in the door, pulled it open with a yank of energy. I forgot about the latch, though, and the door frame splintered where it pulled the strike plate off.

"Hey, not bad," Sally quipped. Her eyes twinkled at me as she rose to her six-foot-plus height, putting her at eye level with Marianna, whom she fixed with a stern eye.

"Lady, I only know you've slept with Ev." Sally said. "Nothing else. Sex doesn't give anyone standing anywhere but the bedroom. Therefore, I'd say you have no standing in this office. The door's open. I'd hurry out if I were you because Amy *can* hit your ass with the door as it closes."

Marianna eyed the two of us and with a harrumph, turned to leave. "This is my company now. I *will* be back. Trust me. And like Ev, I won't have a witch working for me." She sauntered out.

I grinned at Sally and with a push of energy, slammed the door. We heard an "oof" on the other side. Apparently, I *could* time it right. The door bounced back open without its latch.

Sally smiled at me. "I'll call Johnny to get that fixed. Now, what are we going to do about her?"

"I have no bloody idea. I'm not up on wards yet, but I'd be willing to bet there isn't one that'll keep her out since ogres are immune to most magic. However, I *am* going to call the lawyer to let him know what just happened. I think this has some bearing on Gregory's case, don't you?"

"Yeah, but why would she want this company in the first place? I'll admit I don't know about the finances but seems to me it's not worth that much effort."

I shrugged my shoulders. "Who knows? She's obviously off her rocker if she thinks she can just waltz in and take over. Do me a favor? Go tell Cassandra what just happened and ask her to tell her mother."

"Her mother's on the Council?"

"Yep. And although she's supposed to stay impartial and has told Cassandra we need to stay out of it, I think this is important."

As Sally picked up her phone to call the maintenance man, I walked back into my office and grabbed my cell.

"You did well. You controlled your emotions and channeled your energy effectively. Next time remember that the door latch is made of metals, which are part of Earth. You can unlatch the door, first."

"Always the critic. I haven't work with metals, yet, if you recall," I teased as I found Mr. Blatherton in my contacts and hit "call".

Fifteen minutes later, Mr. Blatherton told me that the events of the last half hour were *very* interesting. "Did you keep the document?" he asked.

"No. I threw it back at her. It has no legal standing in the mundane world."

"A shame, really," he sighed. "It could easily be tested for forgery. However, it does provide me with an excuse to further investigate Miss Johannsen. I'll be in touch."

No goodbye. Just dead air in my ear. I tried to go back to work but instead of reading reports, I mused on Marianna's attempted takeover. For some reason, she wanted Ev's company. Like Sally, I couldn't understand why. As far as I knew, she didn't know a damned thing about personal security and honestly, the business wasn't *that* lucrative. The whole thing was weird.

Sally poked her head in my office, "Johnny's on his way. Cassandra said she'd call her mom and to tell you nice work on the door."

I grinned. "First time I've ever done anything like that. It felt good, though." We both turned back to work.

Within a half hour, I heard hammering. Then Johnny poked his head in my door. "Temporary plates will hold the door closed until I get a new piece of trim for the frame. I'll finish fixing it tomorrow. Tell Ev to be a little gentler the next time, will you?"

I nodded and smiled. It wasn't the first time a door had been broken, just the first that it was *my* fault. I didn't see any harm in letting Johnny think everything was status quo. I glanced at the clock in the corner of my computer screen, realized it was time to quit and head home for my standard nap. Surveying my desk, I could see that only another hour or so and I'd be completely caught up. Having Sally was really a boon and I told her so on my way out the door.

"As you told me during my interview, working here is never dull. See you tomorrow afternoon," she said to my back.

Fudge padded alongside me on the walk home. "*I know you are supposed to be studying stones but perhaps a little experimentation with metals would not be such a bad thing. Your door at home is metal, as is its lock.*"

I looked down at him. "You want me to learn to be a burglar?"

He shook his head. I was still a little weirded out by the fact that my cat not only understood my thoughts but English to boot. "*You are not a thief. However, I heard your ideas about breaking into that ogre's home. If you feel a strong need to do so, it is possible to open doors without tools. I can guide you.*"

My cat was a lock-picker, too? I stared at him…and tripped over that same damned tree root. Once again, I caught myself before I fell flat on my face. That didn't prevent a flush from creeping up my neck, though. I pulled my scarf a little closer.

"*You must become accustomed to mind-speech, otherwise you will harm yourself at some point. I do not require eye contact as it seems humans do when conversing. To somewhat satisfy your curiosity, I can tell you I have served many humans in my lifetime. Not all were what you would call savory characters.*"

That I could buy. I'd been told that there were good and bad witches and wizards just like there were good and bad mundane people. I had no intention of becoming a burglar but the thought of sneaking into Ev's house to see what, if anything, might be there was still in the forefront of my mind. But first, nap!

That evening, I abandoned the chapter on quartz crystals in my book as well as my writing, and took direction from Fudge on how to open a door via magical means. If you think it's a snap, I dare you to try it yourself.

We started with one of my necklaces. Fourteen carat gold isn't pure gold. It's usually a mixture of gold, silver and copper. I followed Fudge's instructions and ended up with a broken clasp.

"It is a little delicate. Perhaps you will have better luck with the door lock, which is much stronger."

I had to look it up on the Internet: the lock on my door is part steel – an alloy, zinc, and brass – another alloy. Different metals have different densities and you have to discern the densest one, grab hold of that, move it and "encourage" the other components of the alloy to go along. Too much pressure applied to the softest metal – the copper in brass, for instance – and you'd break something, rendering the lock impassable.

It didn't help that Fudge's experience was limited to cast-zinc locks and latches, probably explaining in part my failure with the necklace. He'd never worked with alloys, even brass. After two hours, I was sweating and Fudge was panting. We'd managed to move the tumblers properly to unlock the door but hadn't yet gotten around to moving the latch itself. The miracle was that we didn't break my lock in the process. I'd have been very embarrassed to call Mr. Owens with that explanation!

I would never make a good thief. I proposed we nix the idea of me breaking into Ev's house. Two hours with the door not actually yet open was just too long.

"But you must admit, you just learned a little about metals. File it away for future reference. You never know when you might need the knowledge."

He was right but I was exhausted. I put the coffee together for the morning and fell into bed. Fudge beat me to the bedroom and I dropped off to his soft snores.

Chapter 18

Wednesday was a normal day. I managed to completely catch up on the backlog of work and with a sigh, started making the decisions I'd been putting off for Ev: who to place with whom for temporary situations, contract renewals, performance reviews, and the like. If – when – he came back, he'd undoubtedly yell at me for some of them but they could no longer wait.

Thursday started out normally, too: first-thing latte with Cassandra, bugging her for news of the Council's investigation. "No news," she said for the second day in a row. I heaved a sigh and headed upstairs, determined to ensure the company was up to snuff when Ev returned. Yes, I knew I'd been fired but for some reason, I felt compelled to help out where I could. Maybe it was that "family" feeling I'd gotten when rescuing him from the kidnappers.

I was reviewing an employee file to determine whether or not he should get a raise when the outer door flew open, immediately followed by eau de sewer. Marianna appeared in my office doorway, flanked by two human-looking males.

"You may leave. Now. I am in charge of this company and I don't need your assistance," she glared at me.

I closed the file I was working on, slid it into my desk drawer and stood, attempting to appear calm and collected when all I wanted to do was flatten her. "As I told you on Tuesday, the paper you showed me gives you no legal standing. Until I see a fully-executed document or Ev tells me different, I will *not* turn over the company to you. Now, you can leave quietly on your own or I'll call the mundane authorities and have you – and your friends – arrested for trespassing."

"I assumed you'd take the same stance," she sneered. "Jonathan, do your thing."

One of the men made a whirling motion with his hands. I saw dishwater-gray sparkles coalesce into a ball and then he pushed that energy with his hands. "*Amy, watch out,*" was the last thing I heard before the world went dark.

I woke up with a splitting headache. There was no light shining through my eyelids so I chanced opening my eyes. I was lying on what felt like a camping cot, staring at nothing. Wherever I was, it was pitch black. I gingerly sat up, which made my head throb even worse. "Anyone there?" I called.

"*I am here,*" I heard Fudge groan as well.

"Where's here?"

"*I believe I am somewhere near your feet. There is absolutely no light so even I cannot see anything.*"

"My head hurts like hell and you don't sound much better. What happened?"

"*We were hit with a sleeping spell. You first then before I could act, he got me. Whoever that wizard is, he is strong but untrained. Rather than gauge our shields and adjust his spell, he just essentially used a freight train rather than an automobile to power past them. Hence, the headaches. They should go away shortly.*"

"Any idea where we are?"

"*The floor beneath me is packed dirt and I smell nothing but earth. I smell air coming from somewhere but as I said, there is no light for even my eyes to pick up. There is also the smell of your ogre somewhere close, probably within twenty or thirty feet. He does not smell right, though.*"

My ogre. "You mean Ev? And what do you mean he doesn't smell right?"

"*Yes, Ev as you call him. He smells sick.*"

I continued to sit on the edge of the cot, holding my head in my hands, waiting for the jackhammer to cease its pounding. I tried to consider my situation but the pain in my head prevented rational thought. Slowly, the machine quit tormenting me and I slid down to sit on the floor, feeling around myself. Just at the edge of my reach, I came into contact with fur. Leaning over a little farther, I picked up the furball that was Fudge and put him in my lap. I felt a little better immediately.

Fudge didn't move much, which indicated he still wasn't feeling all that great. I tried to gently massage his head and neck but he batted my hands away. "Without being able to see, do you have any suggestions for what we should do?"

"*Give me a few minutes. It hurts to think.*"

"Cats get headaches, huh? You learn something new every day."

"We do not, as a rule, get headaches. Our physiology does not work that way. But yes, a magical whammy will give me a headache. Now hush. I am trying to get rid of it so I can concentrate."

Without being able to see a damned thing, all I could do was sit there and stroke Fudge's back. At least it kept me calm. I wasn't afraid of the dark but even in a fully-darkened bedroom, I could see *something*, even if it was just a dresser-sized blob. Not knowing where I was or how I'd gotten there or how I'd get out was more than a little frightening.

Fudge finally began to purr. I took that as a sign that he was feeling better. "So?"

"I am filthy and would like to bathe. Unfortunately it will have to wait. We need to find out where we are but you stumbling around in the dark will not do a bit of good. It is usually an Air spell, but can you tether a string of energy to me? My nose is better and I can go sniffing around but I have no idea how large the cavern is and do not want to take hours getting back to you."

I closed my eyes (although I couldn't actually see anything, it helped with concentration) and tried to remember my lessons with Gregory and what I'd seen him do. It seemed to me that rather than just a lump of energy, I needed one wound like a ball of yarn, like I'd done at the mine. I concentrated and although I couldn't see the sparkles, I felt the tingle in my palm. Taking one end of my "yarn", I "glued" it to the nape of Fudge's neck.

"That will do nicely. Be sure not to lose the link to me."

"Why can't I see sparkles?"

"Light refraction off the energy is what makes it sparkle to your eyes. There is no light here to reflect."

"Will you keep talking, please?" Other than Fudge's voice in my head, it was almost like being in a sensory-deprivation tank. Oh yes, I could feel and smell the damp earth surrounding me but with no audio or visual, I felt very alone.

His warmth left my lap and I focused on maintaining the yarn end glued to him, while allowing the ball in my hand to slowly unravel. Thankfully, unlike real yarn, mine was infinite in length. I just kept replenishing it with energy from the earth and rocks above and beneath me.

Fudge kept up a running commentary. *"It is about thirty of your paces between the walls in front of and behind you. If you think of front as north, the ogre is half that distance to the northwest. He is asleep but does not dream so the sleep is unnatural. The west wall is five paces farther than his bed and it smells as if he has been using a corner as a litter box. The east wall is only ten paces from where you sit.*

"The walls are rough-hewn and I have located at least one pillar made of the same material as your city sidewalks. The cavern feels man-made. The only wood I smell is above and to your right. There are no tree roots. Air is coming in somewhere near the concentrated wood smell. It still smells like city, not forest but I do not detect heavy car exhaust as when walking to your office."

I was becoming chilled sitting on the damp ground so moved back up to the cot. It definitely was a camping cot: just a simple wooden frame and canvas "bed". They hadn't even bothered with a blanket and it was only April.

I felt Fudge hop on my lap and released not only my link to him but the energy I was holding in my palm.

"Good girl. You are learning your magic quickly." He yawned. *"The wood smell is high above and I did not find anything that would allow us to reach it. I suggest we nap until something happens."*

With a few half-hearted licks to his fur, he curled up for a snooze. Not having any better ideas, I laid down, dislodging him and pulling him against my stomach for warmth. I let my thoughts swirl.

Why was Marianna so interested in Ev's company? It wasn't much in the grand scheme of things – what the pundits would call a "mom-and-pop" business. And if she wanted him out of the way, why not just kill him? Disposing of a body, even one his size, wasn't all that difficult if you thought about it. There were plenty of woods in Minnesota where a body wouldn't be found for weeks, if at all (wild animals have to eat, too, you know). You wouldn't even have to dig a hole to bury it.

I must have drifted off because the next thing I knew, I heard a deep groan and it wasn't from me or Fudge. The cat immediately sat up. *"Tether me again but this time, follow. I will take you to the ogre."*

I did as instructed, this time adding a little tension to the energy leash so I could feel which way Fudge walked. He stopped and I walked right into something, falling over it. The smell told me I was lying on top of Ev. Eeew. Gross.

I scrambled back to my feet just as I heard a grunt and "What?" coming from Ev.

"Um. Ev? You there?" I said quietly.

Another groan. "Who's there?" Ev's speech was slow and thick, as if he were drunk. I'd *never* seen Ev drunk so I assumed he'd been drugged.

"It's me, Amy."

"Amy? What are you doing here? Where are we?" he slurred.

"One of Marianna's minions zapped me and Fudge with a sleeping spell. The next thing I knew I was here. How are you feeling?"

"Like shit. Fuzzy. Nauseated but…hungry. How long have I been here?"

I shrugged my shoulders. Then it dawned on me he couldn't see gestures. "I'm not sure how long I've been here but you'd been missing two weeks the last I knew. Magic bounces off ogres. How'd they get you?"

"I have no idea. One minute I was having a nice dinner with Marianna, the next thing I knew I woke up here. It's all been a blur. Wait. You said one of Marianna's minions. What's she got to do with all this?"

While I filled Ev in on what was happening in the outside world, he groaned and I assumed the popping I heard was his joints as he stretched. I was close enough to feel him rise off his cot but not close enough to grab him before he walked smack into a wall.

"That bitch. I'm going to kill her when I get out of here. How did she get my signature? Ow. I hate not being able to see. Where the hell are we?" he yelled, his voice magnified by our confines.

"Keep your voice down. It echoes in here and hurts my ears. Fudge says we're in some sort of a manmade cavern, probably on the outskirts of the city. Based on his description, I'd say there's a hole somewhere above us with a wooden cover. But there isn't even enough light for him to see."

"You're a witch, aren't you? Can't you just conjure us out of here? Or at least a light?"

"So now my magical abilities are okay?" The sarcasm in my voice had to be evident, even to him.

I heard him heave a sigh. "Where the hell are you? I know you're near where I was lying and I'd like to sit down again soon. My stomach doesn't like standing up."

I felt Fudge leave my side. *"Tell him to get down on his knees and put his hand on my back. He can crawl and I will lead him to you. It is only five paces or so."*

I relayed Fudge's instructions and shortly heard the "swoosh" of Ev's knees on the ground. Then came the sound of wood creaking as Ev sat back down. I continued to stand. It was as close to an unwashed ogre as I wanted to get and the ground was just too damned cold to sit on.

"To answer your question, I told you two weeks ago I'd just found out about being a witch. I'm really new to all of this and haven't the slightest idea what to do. I'm assuming Gregory would know, or even Cassandra or Tommy but I *don't have a fucking clue* about most of it. *New to the magic stuff,* got me?"

"I've never heard of a witch not born to and growing up with magic. Why you? Why now?"

"How the hell should I know? Both Gregory and Cassandra tell me it's rare but not unheard of for powers to manifest late. Cassandra said something about stress. Working for you is definitely stressful. So it's probably your fault.

"As we seem to have time, why don't you tell me why Marianna wants your company so bad and why you fired me?"

"Can't you at least magic up a light? It's dark in here."

I sent a mental query toward Fudge. *"Light requires a manifestation of Fire. You have **never** worked with Fire and it can be dangerous, especially in an enclosure. One misstep and you will incinerate all three of us. This is why I did not suggest it in the first place."*

"I wouldn't suggest me conjuring a light unless you like to be crispy," I told Ev. "I'd have no idea how to control the fire needed."

"Okay, okay, fine. We'll sit here in the dark. It's all fuzzy but if I recall, at some point, someone's going to give us some food. I hope it's soon. I'm hungry."

A hungry Ev was a grumpy (grump*ier*) Ev. I had to take his mind off food. "So, back to Marianna and the reason I was fired?"

"That bitch," he said again. "She's been asking me questions about the company for weeks. The last night we were together, she was commenting about the parties and clubs I took her to. I don't know, maybe she thinks the company is glamorous or something. Anyways, she was glowing about it all and the fact that I had the time and money to go partying a few times a week. I just thought she was interested in *me* when all along, she's wanted to get her fingers into my business. Fucking gold digger."

I could tell he was fuming. I would be, too. I was, actually. Not only was it the principle of the thing, she'd kidnapped *me*. But there was an ace up my/our sleeve. "She can act the executive all she wants but she has no access to the money. Martin won't let her. She'll be hard pressed to pay bills or payroll unless she's got a lot of her own."

"I know that and you know that but if she fucks up my business, there will be hell to pay. It took me years to build it and she can tear it all down with a few misplaced words. But you're right, she doesn't have access to the money and I don't think she has enough of her own. Small consolation."

"We'll get out of here at some point," I tried to soothe him. "The authorities have been looking for you and I assume they'll start looking for me. Sally would have noticed that I didn't leave a note and I always do if I'm going to be out when she comes in."

"What do you mean Sally would miss you? I fired you and she quit!"

"I rehired myself when they arrested Gregory and you turned out to be definitely missing. I brought Sally back, too, because the piles of work were too high for me to deal with alone."

He sighed. "That's another thing I'm going to get out of her hide. She framed Gregory because he's the one person who can find me wherever I am. I don't know how but he can. I made the mistake of commenting on it one night when she didn't like the fact that he was always nearby. I told her it wouldn't matter how close he was."

"Big mouth. About my job," I prompted.

"I'm sorry, Amy. I had a run-in with a witch about forty years ago that…didn't sit well."

"I know spells just bounce off you so what did she do? Hex your shorts so you had a permanent snuggie? Short-sheet your bed? Oooh. I'll be she hexed your bed so you couldn't have sex in it. Come on. Tell me."

"I…"

His explanation was interrupted by the sound of wood scraping. We both rose at the sound and a little bit of light leaked in when the cover was removed. I made my way over to the spot and looked up. A hand held a lantern, allowing me to get a glimpse of my jail. Then the light moved and Marianna's face came into view.

"Good evening, darling. And witch. It's dinner time." Her voice drifted down. "I do hope you enjoy roast beef and vegetables. I can't say I went to the effort of cooking it myself but it should be tasty nonetheless. I know the restaurant's chef personally."

"What do you think you're doing, Marianna?" Ev roared. "Let us out of here now!"

"Now, now, darling. Once it's an accepted the fact that I run your company, you can come out and play my husband. Since I have the paperwork turning it over to me, people will eventually come around. But that will take awhile. So, enjoy your vacation. I know how much you like vacations."

Ev roared again. I covered my ears. Fudge yowled. "I never signed any such paper. You won't get away with it. Everyone knows it's my company."

She snickered. "Yes, darling. But you're not around to run it and I have that paper. So, everyone will eventually accept me."

A tray on a rope was lowered down to us. On it were two plates of food and a couple of jugs of what appeared to be water. One plate was much larger than the other, the smaller obviously meant for me. I didn't see anything for Fudge.

"Hey," I yelled up. "My cat's down here, too. Doesn't he get to eat?"

Her sneering voice returned, "Who gives a damn about a cat, especially a witch's familiar? You can share your food with him if he's that important. Take the food off the tray and eat. I'm not going to leave it there all night. I have a party to go to as the new head of Angelich Security and don't want to be late for my debut."

While she was talking, I was trying to gauge the distance between the floor and the hole. Fudge had his neck craned, as well. It was probably twenty feet, which was too high for even Ev to jump. By what little light filtered in, I could see the hole was about three feet from the nearest wall. It gave me some things to think about. I grabbed the plates while Ev took the jugs of water.

We quickly ate the food, me sharing what I had with Fudge, who ate sparingly. "*I can go longer without food than you. However, I do need water and cannot drink out of the container. Please finish eating so you can use the plate as a dish.*"

After I'd gulped down over half of one jug, I trickled the rest onto the plate. Fudge lapped it up almost as quickly as the droplets hit.

"I need to go, whether you're finished eating or not. Put your plates back on the tray."

"Hey, what about a light? It's pitch black down here," I called up as I duly put everything back on the tray. "A blanket or two wouldn't go amiss, either. It's chilly."

"If you behave, I'll bring what you ask in the morning. In the meantime, enjoy your evening." She pulled the tray back up and we were plunged into darkness again as the cover slid over the hole. I heard something that sounded like a padlock snick closed.

I yawned. All of a sudden, I was *very* sleepy. From the little light I'd had, I knew my cot was about ten steps away and I gingerly stepped in that direction. *"One step to your right,"* another sleepy voice said. I bumped into the cot, fell onto it and blacked out.

Chapter 19

I woke with sleep-encrusted eyes, a cotton mouth and a swimming head. It felt just like one of my rare hangovers but I'd had no alcohol in a couple of days, by my reckoning. Then it came to me: the bitch had drugged me! While I lay there feeling awful, I noticed Fudge's body against my side. That made me panic. He'd eaten the same food and drunk the same water. Cats' metabolisms were completely different from humans' and vets were careful when they administered drugs of any kind. Was he okay?

I started feeling his abdomen then worked my way to his nose. He was breathing but his nose was warm and dry. He usually twitched in his sleep and changed positions frequently. Now he was just dead weight. I immediately hated myself for thinking of that phrase. He was breathing. That was the main thing.

"Hey, Fudge. Can you hear me?" I thought. No answer came. I tried the other occupant of the cavern. 'Hey, Ev. You awake?" I croaked out. He didn't answer me, either. I was awake in a place that was darker than night, thirsty as hell and yet had to pee. In a place with no bathroom, no privacy and definitely no toilet tissue. Well, I was apparently the only one awake so privacy wasn't so much of a concern but location was. I didn't want to do my business in a spot I'd be sure to walk in.

Recalling as much as I could from the night before, or whenever Marianna had fed and drugged us, I slipped away from Fudge and started crawling on my hands and knees toward what I thought was a corner, cautiously putting my hand out in front of myself before moving. After what seemed like an eternity, I touched a wall.

Just to be sure I'd be out of the traffic pattern, I moved farther along the wall four times the span of my arms. I tried to remember all the camping stuff I'd read about over the years (not that I'd actually done any of it before) and dug a shallow hole, using a little

160

energy to help move some of the hard-packed dirt. I was discovering that magic could come in handy. Hating myself for destroying one of my favorite silk blouses, I used my teeth to tear part of it off then squatted against the wall and relieved my bladder.

Once I felt better (in that regard), I retraced my crawl back to the cot. Fudge hadn't moved a muscle. I picked him up, sat down and cradled him in my arms. "If she's hurt you, Ev won't have a chance because I'll get to her first," I told him.

"*I will be fine. Allow me to sleep a little longer.*" His voice sounded far away. But I'd heard him! That helped.

My head was clearing, although I still *really* wanted about five gallons of water to drink. To distract myself from thirst, I recalled what I was thinking before I blacked out.

Like the ground back at the park on Lake Mille Lacs, the walls of our prison were mostly hard-packed dirt with some large rocks scattered here and there. The hole was about twenty feet up and about three feet from the closest wall. I wondered if I could somehow build us a rock ladder or staircase to the top with the surrounding dirt and rocks, while not collapsing everything on top of us in the process.

Not having anything else to do, I started feeling around with my witchy senses. The "roof" seemed to be concrete then dirt about six feet thick altogether. I found plant roots in the dirt. In addition to the hole where Marianna had dropped the tray, there was another one some five feet away that felt like a tunnel large enough, perhaps, for a big rat. That curved a couple of times before it, too, opened to the air. That must be the air source. The curves were why no light came in with the air.

As far as I could feel, there were no trees above us. So, we were in the middle of a field of some kind. I didn't know enough about plants to be able to identify what sort of roots I was feeling but the word 'grass' felt right. I shrugged my shoulders to myself. It didn't matter.

I continued extending my senses. I'm not sure how far I stretched but I finally found a few tree roots. Then, a little farther than that, more concrete. I felt along the cement, trying to gauge what it was. A basement?

I came back to myself, let go of the breath I was holding and gulped air. Even in the cool damp of our confines, I had broken into a sweat. This process was more difficult without Fudge's help. I'd only gone in one direction and was already as tired as if I'd run a marathon. I would have dropped to the ground if I wasn't already sitting. I continued breathing deeply and my heart finally calmed down.

I was mentally preparing myself for the effort of trying to feel in another direction when a groan and a snort came from over Ev's way. He'd apparently found his way back to his cot, too. "Amy, you still here?"

"And where else would I be?" I grunted.

"I thought maybe I had dreamed you up. Just wanted to make sure I hadn't," he croaked out. It sounded like he was as thirsty as me.

I snorted. "You? Dream about me? Is that a nice dream or a nightmare?"

"In this case, nice. I'm not alone in this godforsaken place and you didn't yell at me about work. How are you feeling?"

"Probably about like you. Hungover from whatever drug she gave us and thirsty as hell. She said something about breakfast. I wonder if and when that will be."

"No idea. I have no idea what time it is, much less what day. I just eat, drink, pee and sleep. What are you doing?"

"Oh, come *on* Ev. I'm in a dark hole. What do you think I'm doing? I'm sitting on my cot, holding Fudge and trying to think of a way out of here."

I heard joints popping. He was moving around. "Is your cat okay? He ate and drank the same stuff we did."

"He's not entirely okay but says he will be. He's breathing but his nose is warm and dry."

I heard an intake of breath. "He *says* he'll be okay? Your cat talks?"

I sighed. "It's that witch stuff again. As I told you, Fudge is my familiar. He's apparently old enough to have mastered the art of talking to me – in my mind. So yes, he talks. In a way."

"What else can he – and you – do?"

"I'm just learning all this, remember? I know I can feel the earth around me and to some extent, move it. While you've been sleeping, I've been checking out our surroundings as best I can. I'm pretty sure we're in the middle of a field somewhere and about six feet down. Beyond that, I'm not sure of anything. I've been waiting for Fudge to feel better and wake up to see if he's got any bright ideas. He's the one with all the centuries of knowledge."

"I'd kill for a drink of water right now," came the exasperated reply. "Can you find water?"

"There's water in the dirt surrounding us but I haven't a clue how to draw it out. Or get enough to drink. Water isn't my element. I'm as thirsty as you are. Try not to think about it. Especially don't talk about it or *I'll* keep thinking about it. What else should we discuss?"

Ev was silent for a few minutes then said, "Um, can I offer your job back? Officially, I mean. I know you rehired yourself but I want you to know I'd like you back when we get out of here."

I grinned into the darkness. "Even though I'm a witch? I thought you couldn't work with a witch."

"I've had time to think about it. A lot of time. At least I think it's a lot of time. She must have cut back on whatever drug she's been giving me because this is the most awake I've felt since I've been here. Anyways, as long as you don't turn any employees or clients into toads or burn them to ashes, I think things ought to go back to the way they were. We work well together, don't we? I mean, you taking care of the details and me doing the people stuff?"

I kept my mouth shut. I wanted to hear him grovel some more. While I waited, I stroked Fudge. His tail twitched against my arm. That was a good sign – he was starting to wake.

"Oh, come on Amy. If you felt strongly enough about the company to go back in when you found out I was missing, you must want to go back to it permanently. Don't you? Say something, please?"

"I'm thinking," I said. "I only went back because I didn't like the thought of what I'd worked hard on going down the toilet while you were gone. But I have options. I'm considering them."

"What do you want? A raise? A big bonus? I'll buy your apartment building from James and put it in your name if that'll make you happy. Or I'll buy you a house of your own. What will it take?"

He was being very uncharacteristic. He didn't usually grovel and the few times he had, he didn't do it nearly this well. I let him stew a little longer, wondering if he'd agree to my just-thought-of condition. Finally, I said, "Okay, I'll come back permanently. But Sally and Gregory get their jobs back, too, with no repercussions."

"That's a no-brainer. I didn't fire them, they quit because of you. So, what do I have to pay *you*?"

"It goes without saying you're dumping Marianna. The authorities will get her for filing false charges against Gregory and I'll be sure to add kidnapping into the mix. But your taste in women sucks. Although Marianna's the worst, don't you remember the human woman who stalked you from party to office to club and back for three months after you broke up? It took her parents committing her to an institution for that to stop. Or the one who took your ATM card out of your wallet while you were sleeping and went on a spending spree? No, um, fourth date with anyone unless I've done the same background check on the woman that we do on our employees."

"*You want to control my love life?*" he yelled.

I cringed and covered my ears again. "Lower your voice, dammit. No, I don't want to control your love life. I just want to make sure you don't fall for someone unstable again. And since you seem to fall quickly, something to slow you down a little wouldn't be such a bad thing."

"No," he cried. "No. I won't have you meddling in my personal affairs."

"Fine," I shot back. "I won't come back to work and if you get mixed up with a crazy lady again, I'm not going to bail you out by coming into the office in your absence."

Ogres can sigh really loudly if they want to. Must be the enlarged lung capacity. The entire cavern echoed with it. "You win," he whispered. "If I decide to continue dating someone, I'll let you check her out. But I get the final say as to what's bad and what's not."

That was more than I thought I'd get. Gregory and I had talked over the years about Ev's poor choices when it came to companions. With him counting dates, I'd be able to keep Ev from the worst of them.

"Good. I have no idea what we'll have to straighten out when we get back but let me tell you what I've done so far." I spent the next hour or more telling him of the decisions I'd made in his absence, arguing about some of them, and getting a virtual pat on the back for others. Time had no meaning but at least it kept me occupied until Fudge came to.

The sound of the wood cover scraped and startled both of us. "Hello, darling. And witch. I'm sorry I wasn't here earlier but the office has been so busy, I've just now been able to get away."

Light spilled into the darkness, blinding me. I squinted into the bright beam and saw the tray once again being lowered. Through my half-closed eyes, I saw Ev stumbling his way over to the tray, hands over his eyes, as well.

"Woman, what are you doing? You'll destroy all I've worked hard to build."

"Oh, no darling. I'd *never* do that! It's surprisingly easy to match guards with clients, although I certainly don't agree with some of the witch's matches. I've taken steps to correct her errors. Here's your food. Eat and drink quickly. I have more phone calls to return."

"Do not eat the food. It is tainted. She uses herbs to disguise the flavor of the narcotic. Drink water only," Fudge's voice still sounded distant but not quite as far as the last time. I whispered his instructions to Ev, who quietly groaned.

"But I'm starving," he murmured back.

"Your choice," I answered. "Starving and awake, or full and asleep. I'd like to get out of here and can't do that when I'm knocked out. So, I'm going to scrape the food off my plate into a hole in the floor. If you're asleep, I can't help you."

For a few minutes, we both moved our forks around the plate, trying to make it sound like we were eating, relishing the fact that we could *see*. As I scraped metal against porcelain, I surveyed what I could see in between swigs of water. I saw Ev doing the same.

We were definitely in a place made by man. Three concrete pillars held up our prison's concrete roof. By the slight crumbling on the pillars, it looked to be at least a couple of decades old, if not more. My senses told me there was metal inside not only the pillars but the roof as well so it had been reinforced.

"Hey, Marianna," I yelled. "Since we're not getting out of here, mind telling me where we are?"

"I will tell you nothing, witch," I could hear the derision in her voice, making me wonder what a witch or wizard had done to *her*. What was it with ogres and magical folks?

I sighed. Loudly enough so she'd hear it. "Fine. But can we keep the water? And how about the light and blankets I asked about?"

"Between the marvelous party last night and getting into the office early this morning, I didn't have time to go shopping for you. Be thankful I brought food. I guess you can keep the water jugs. You can't do anything with them because they're plastic. If you're cold, I suggest you snuggle together. I know Ev has a hot body." She snickered at this last.

Ev and I looked at each other. We both made a face. The thought of snuggling with not only a normally smelly ogre, but an unwashed one at that made me very glad I'd put no food in my stomach. Why he thought cuddling with *me* was such a bad idea, I'll probably never know but there you have it.

Unspoken words had me throwing some energy toward the floor near his cot, digging a hole deep enough to dump the contents of our plates. I walked over and wordlessly handed him my plate, which he silently scraped off. After we'd buried the probably-poisoned food, Ev walked the plates back to the tray.

"Marianna," Ev's voice was reasonable this time, "let us out of here. I'm sure we can come to some satisfactory arrangement."

"Oh, darling," she cooed, "I know you're not ready to behave yet. Just a little while longer on vacation and I'm sure you'll be thrilled to be my docile, compliant husband."

I snorted. She apparently hadn't met many of her own species. Although I'd not met many, no ogre I knew would ever be "docile and compliant". No matter how long she kept Ev prisoner, I could almost guarantee he'd be "pissed off and rampaging" when she let him out.

"In the meantime, darling, I suggest you get some sleep. There's not much for you to do. I'm taking good care of your company." The lid slid over the hole, the padlock snicked shut and we were plunged into complete darkness once again.

I heard Ev moving around in the black then the creak of his cot as he sat down. I'd ensured I was back on my cot with Fudge in my lap before Marianna closed us in so I didn't have to do any crawling around. I'd already skinned my knees finding my way to the bathroom corner.

"Now what?" Ev's voice came at me out of the darkness.

"I'm thinking," I replied.

"About?"

"How to get us out of here without killing us in the process. I can move dirt but I'm afraid I'd collapse this whole thing on top of us."

"Help is on the way." Fudge was awake! I hugged him even closer.

"Loosen your hold. I cannot breathe." I complied. I'm sure to his sensitive nose I smelled almost as bad as Ev did on a regular basis.

No shower facilities coupled with the sweat I'd worked up earlier made for a not-nice perfume.

"I'm glad you're feeling better. What's this about help on its way?" I asked.

"*I can mind-speak with the Familiar Council, you nitwit, and I did so yesterday. It was just a question of them passing my location onto the Witches' Council and then getting some two-legged help to wherever we are. Someone should be here within a few hours.*"

I told Ev the good news.

"When I get out of here…" he snarled.

"You're going to let the authorities take care of her," I finished his sentence for him. "You can press charges in the mundane courts if you want but I'd let Gregory have his say in magical court, first. It could be fun to see what happens there."

"What are they going to do to her? Anything magical won't work."

"Wrong. Remember, you got kidnapped and tied up with magic. Gregory and the Council now know those spells and I'm sure there are others."

He growled. "My life has gotten so fucked up. First, that damned dwarf tries to ransom then kill me. Now, just a couple of weeks later, crazy lady is trying to take over my company. What did I ever do to deserve all this?"

"*Trouble always comes in threes. There is more on the horizon.*"

"You *know* something else is going to happen?" I asked.

"*I am not prescient. But problems always seem to happen in threes and your ogre is a problem in and of himself. It does not take a Tarot deck to predict he is going to get himself into some sort of trouble again.*"

I really didn't need to know this. I would now be spending time looking over my shoulder, wondering when the next shoe would drop. Ev was already so worked up I didn't have the heart to tell him what Fudge had said. Instead I murmured something meaningless in an attempt at consoling him.

Knowing we *were* going to get out of there without me doing anything actually made the waiting worse. In an attempt at distracting myself, I tried to imagine what I'd do if I knew the cavalry wasn't coming.

My one thought was for both of us to stand at one end of the cavern and pull down the cement and dirt at the other. Essentially, a targeted earthquake. Fudge put the kibosh on that idea immediately.

"There is metal inside the concrete. It would bend and twist before breaking, making very sharp edges that could harm you. You also do not yet have fine enough control to collapse only a small portion of what is above, leaving the rest intact. Not to mention the dust you would raise would choke you. No, wait for help."

"But I can dig a small hole. Isn't that fine enough control for you?"

Fudge paused his never-ending bath. *"Moving small amounts of dirt below you is very different than moving large amounts of dirt above you. The laws of gravity do figure into what you are doing, you know."*

I sighed. I knew he was right. But, "So, what would you do, oh wise and old familiar?"

"Exactly what I have done and am doing. Send out a signal for help and wait." He resumed licking himself, occasionally flicking his tongue over the hand that rested on his back. Rough it may have been but it was also strangely comforting. It also made me pine for a long, hot shower with water from Mr. Owens' boiler that was spelled to never run cold, no matter how many residents were using it at the same time.

I knew one thing for certain: as soon as I got out of there, I would be disposing of yet another suit. I'd just finished replacing all the clothing the vampire had destroyed when he went on a rampage in my apartment and here I was, ready to get rid of one that would probably be serviceable with cleaning but I knew I'd never want to wear again.

Chapter 20

Without a functioning watch and light to see it by, I had no idea how much time had passed. Fudge had long since fallen asleep but since he always did that, I couldn't tell time by his habits. I knew Ev had also fallen asleep. The snores coming from his corner sounded like foghorns. I was almost beginning to wish I'd eaten some of the tainted food so I, too, would sleep. I wasn't accustomed to having absolutely nothing to do but think and eventually I ran out of things to think about.

I was about to get up and start pacing, just for something to do, when I heard noise coming from above. The tingle of magic made its way to me and I knew the cavalry had finally arrived. The wooden lid slid aside and I heard an unfamiliar voice yell, "Yo! Anyone down there?"

"We're here," I eagerly answered. "Ev, wake up. We're being rescued."

The standard snorts and growls accompanied "Wha? Oh, fantastic!"

A flashlight beam swept the room, paused at Ev's supine form then finally swung around until it was shining directly into my face, blinding me. When I raised my hand to cover my eyes, the beam moved slightly to my left.

"Sorry," said the faceless person in the shadows. "We're bringing a longer ladder. Hang on a few more minutes."

The light disappeared above ground and I yelled. "Can we have a little illumination down here, please? It's awfully dark."

"Oops. Sorry again. Here." The flashlight dropped to the ground and immediately went out. Another light shone down, wandering this way and that until it settled on the now-dead source of illumination.

Ev lumbered over, picked up the light and slapped it on his palm a couple of times. "You shouldn't have dropped it. It's broken, you idiot," he called up.

"Sorry. I'll just shine mine down there, shall I?" A beam of light hit the floor directly below the hole and stayed still.

Within just a couple of minutes, I heard more voices and the area above the hole got much brighter, as if someone had lit a camping lantern. The scrape, squeal and then clang of an aluminum extension ladder hitting the ground let me know we would indeed be getting out.

"Ladies first," the voice called down. I cradled Fudge in one arm and started the climb to freedom. Two steps up, I kicked off my shoes. High heels and ladders did not agree with each other and if I slipped, it was a long way down.

I really needn't have worried. Ev was immediately behind me and if I'd fallen and taken him with me, it would have been a soft landing. Not that I looked down to see. I could smell his proximity and feel his breath on my legs. I chose to not breathe for the last eight rungs until my head cleared the hole. Three more steps and I felt an arm guide me to the side, while someone else wrapped me in a warm blanket. I was standing on grass, breathing deeply and looking at wide open spaces for the first time in two days.

I marveled at the sight. It was not too long after sunset, as the horizon still held a faint glow. Stars were just beginning to twinkle above. I bit back a few tears.

"Are you two okay?" I could finally put a face to the voice behind the flashlight. He looked like a Green Beret or Navy Seal. So did the other three men, one of whom had a bright ball of fire in his palm. They were all athletic-looking with closely-cropped hair and dressed in black uniforms of some kind, with a torch stitched in white on the left breast.

I looked at Ev who was also wrapped in a blanket and then answered for both of us. "All things considered, not bad. Food would be good. We haven't eaten today and I'm not sure when the time before that was. Coffee would be heaven and I'd kill for an hour-long hot shower."

One of the guys handed me a thermos. "It's coffee. Sorry I don't have any cups and I hope you like sugar."

I normally drank my coffee black but I wasn't going to argue with any adulteration of caffeine at this point. Another man handed a similar thermos to Ev. Both of us enjoyed the warm steam that came out of the top when we took the caps off before sipping. Even Fudge moved his nose toward the steam and he didn't usually want anything to do with my elixir.

"We need to get you back to headquarters," Flashlight Man said.

"What the hell happened, how did you find us and what the hell can I do about all this?" Ev was beginning to revive.

"Sorry, sir. Your questions will be answered at HQ. We were just to find, release and transport you. Please, follow me."

Ball-of-Fire Man led the way. It took about five minutes and I was beginning to regret kicking off my shoes. The ground was hard and cold. We finally skirted around what appeared to be an abandoned barn and my already-sore feet hit gravel. I minced the rest of the way to the open door of a large, black SUV and gratefully climbed in while Ev pushed his bulk through the other door and crowded me in the back seat. Fudge abandoned my arms for the seat on the opposite side of me from Ev. I didn't blame him and did my best to breathe shallowly.

Flashlight Man leaned into the car and placed something toasty warm across my feet. The smell of lavender drifted up to my nose and partially obscured Ev's aroma. "This should help you." The door shut. He and another of our saviors climbed into the front seat and we were on our way to wherever it was we were going, which I was certain wasn't going to be home for either of us.

Ten minutes later, we were on a freeway. Flashlight Man turned around in his seat, looked at both of us and said, "My apologies. You are not allowed to see where we are going so I am going to temporarily obscure your vision. I will remove the spell when we are at headquarters." He waved his hand first at Ev, who stiffened.

With an even more apologetic look at me, he waved his hand again and my vision went black. After two days of not being able to see, the feeling was extremely disconcerting. I'm sure Ev felt it even more keenly. But I was resolved to keep calm about *everything* so just kept "I will remove the spell" going round and round in my head.

Our speed slowed, telling me we had left the freeway. A stop then a few turns both left and right. Based on the interstate signs I'd seen before my vision was obscured, I knew we were somewhere near or in downtown Minneapolis. The SUV's wheels bumped on the edge of a driveway then the city sounds faded a little. A parking garage, then.

When the SUV came to a stop, my vision returned. I had guessed our relative location correctly but there were no other vehicles in sight. All I saw was concrete floor, concrete pillars and concrete walls. And an elevator door. Flashlight Man squeezed into the European-sized compartment with me and Ev while the other guy probably waited for the car to return. There simply wasn't enough room for two good-sized men, a petite woman plus an ogre. Fudge hopped into my arms and sneezed.

"I hope headquarters is not on the top floor or that this is an express. Your ogre **stinks***."*

I privately agreed but there was no help for it. My ears popped as the car rapidly rose, then popped again as it slowed its ascent, finally coming to a bone-jarring stop. The floor indicator pinged and the door slid quietly open.

The sniveling countenance of Mr. Blatherton greeted us. "Welcome back. Please accompany me." What the hell was Gregory's attorney doing here?

We followed, Flashlight Man parting company with us at a door. I paused long enough to thank him. Before he could open his mouth, Mr. Blatherton said, "He was doing his job." Flashlight Man nodded, grinned and gave a small salute before closing the door behind him.

The four of us (including Fudge, who was now trotting at my side on plush carpet), continued down a long hall until we reached two oaken double doors at the end. These Blatherton opened to reveal what appeared to be a conference room. A large, mahogany table was surrounded by fourteen plush chairs. Six of them were occupied: one man and three women dressed in business-casual clothing, one man who looked just like our rescue team in a black uniform and *Gregory*. I rushed over to give him a hug.

His eyes twinkled as he hugged me back and said quietly, "You had better sit down or you will interrupt their schedule. We will speak later."

Ev lumbered over and shook Gregory's hand before he, too, was told to take a seat.

"I understand you've been through an ordeal but we have questions before you can fully relax," stated a woman with her blond hair severely pulled back into a bun. I knew she was a high magical muckety-muck as I'd met her at Cassandra and Tommy's handfasting but couldn't for the life of me remember her name.

Ev's stomach growled loud enough for the entire room to hear. He ducked his head and apologized.

"No need for apologies. We'll get you something to eat shortly. We need to confirm. Are you indeed Evander Thorson Angelich?"

Ev cleared his throat. "I am."

Another man who looked somewhat like my elderly wizard friend, Adamo, peered at him. "And did you voluntarily agree to be sequestered?"

I thought Ev was going to roar and break everyone's eardrums. He turned almost purple with rage. "I most certainly did not. That woman …"

"Thank you," the older man cut him off. Turning to me, he asked, "Did *you* voluntarily agree to be sequestered?"

"Absolutely not," I kept my answer short, as I assumed they wanted me to. I could feel Fudge's purr of approval in my lap.

"Thank you," the woman with the bun said. "We naturally still have plenty of questions for you but I believe you'd like to clean up a bit and eat. We have suites prepared for you. Please return here promptly in an hour so we can resume our debriefing. Mr. Tremayne can show you the way."

We were summarily dismissed. The five I didn't know pulled their chairs closer together and started talking in low voices.

"Come," Gregory said. "Your suites are next to mine." He rose and made his way toward the doors. The rest of us got up and followed.

Once we were in the hallway with the doors closed behind us, Blatherton told Gregory he'd be in touch and walked down the hall toward the elevator we'd ridden. Gregory turned to his right and we trailed after him down a similarly-rich looking hall. I felt the wards long before Gregory muttered something under his breath and still felt a tingle as we passed through an archway. He muttered again and the wards went back to full strength. Not that I was all that experienced in this whole witchy business but what I'd felt made me grateful I wasn't the one behind them all the time.

Gregory paused and opened a door. "Ev, you're in here. Amy, you're next door. Sorry for locking you in, as it were, but these are the only places that have showers. I got clothes for both of you. Once you've cleaned up, step near the bedside table and say out loud whatever you're hungry for. It's like hotel room service but your meal will appear on the table once it's prepared. I will come for you in an hour."

He closed the door on Ev, moved a few steps and turned the knob on another door to an identical room. I opened my mouth but before I could speak, he gave me a little shove and said, "Later. We only have an hour. The kitchen has cat food for Fudge."

He closed the door behind himself and I made a beeline for the bathroom. Oh, it was *civilization!* Flushing commodes, toilet paper, and running *hot* water. On the counter was a pile of my clothing: slacks, a favorite turtleneck and…underwear. He'd better not have been going through my drawers! I'd ask about that later. The only thing I wanted to do was stand under the shower for as long as I could.

Thirty minutes later I looked like a prune but a clean one. There was no hair dryer so my back was cold and damp where my hair lay against it but at least it was clean. My stomach reminded me I really needed to eat and time was growing short. Although I felt a little foolish, I stood by the bedside table and said out loud, "Cheeseburger with everything but onions, French fries, water, both bottled and in a bowl, and cat food." I really wanted onions on my burger and onion rings on the side but given that I knew I'd be talking to strangers, I held back. The lamp blinked off and on once. I guessed that was the acknowledgement and sat on the edge of the bed to wait. Fudge was already curled up on one of the pillows, fast asleep.

He perked right up a few minutes later when a tray twinkled its way into existence on the table. A covered plate held my food, a bottle of water lay on its side and two plastic containers with lids held water and food for Fudge. Whoever sent it was much smoother than Gregory with their transportation spell as the cover on the plate wasn't the slightest bit askew. I put Fudge's stuff on the floor and dug into my own food.

As soon as I wiped the last smidge of ketchup off my mouth, there was a knock and then my door opened. "Ready?" Gregory said as he held the door, obvious in his intent that I follow him. Fudge took one swipe at his whiskers with his paw and trotted on ahead.

Pausing long enough to pick up Ev (who grumbled because he hadn't finished with the food on his serving platter), we trailed after Gregory once again, through the wards and back down to the conference room.

Chapter 21

The same five people were sitting at the table but this time another chair was occupied – by a Rottweiler. Fudge stopped in his tracks and lowered his head. I looked from the dog to my cat and back again before I felt a small shove at the base of my back.

"Head of Familiar Council. Sit," Gregory whispered. I did as I was told, continuing to look back and forth between the animals until the witch with the bun cleared her throat.

"Please be seated. I hope your accommodations were satisfactory? Good. As you might expect, we have plenty of questions for you."

Although I wanted to answer that everything was nice but I sure could have used a hair dryer, she didn't allow us to get a word in edgewise. Fudge finally hopped into my lap but instead of curling up as usual, he sat at attention.

"Please allow me to introduce the table to you," she continued. "My name is Althea Fitzsimmons and I am the current head of the Witches' Council Midwestern United States Region. To my left is Janice Kokurrun, my assistant. To her left is Delilah Emerson, our recording secretary. To my right is Howard Sharretts, my counterpart on the Wizards' Council. To his right is Edward Bartz, my head of security. To his right is Waldo, the head of the Familiar Council here in the United States.

"Now, Miss McCollum, I understand this is your first experience with Elders but I'm told you have read our rules." (I could hear the capital "E" in her voice.) I nodded.

She continued. "Mr. Angelich, because the ogres have no ruling council, will you agree to abide by our findings?"

Ev shifted in his chair. "It depends." I kicked him under the table. He glared at me. "I want that woman to pay for what she's done. If you can punish her well and good, I'll agree to it. At the very least, she should be locked up in a loony bin. But if you don't, I'll do it my way."

Ms. (Miss? Mrs.?) Fitzsimmons cleared her throat again. "If all your answers are truthful and we find in your favor, I believe we can satisfy your need for vengeance. However, if not, we have no jurisdiction over an argument between ogres and you will be free to do whatever you wish." She paused and fixed Ev with her ice blue eyes. "So long as you do no harm in the magical community. Do I make myself clear?"

"Yes, Ma'am." Ev was polite! I almost fell out of my chair.

"Good. Shall we begin? Mr. Angelich, please tell us what happened to you on or about the night of April the fourth, continuing to the present. You may tell it in your own words but please leave out any profanity."

The lady who was the recording secretary closed her eyes. "She has an eidetic memory," Gregory whispered. "She will remember everything verbatim and make a transcript available later." I nodded.

Ev began, "I was having a lovely candlelit dinner with Marianna Johannsen, the lady I was seeing…"

His side of the story didn't take long because he had no idea how long he'd been confined due to the drugs. All he knew was that he'd eat food off that tray, sleep, take care of bodily functions as best he could and repeat. When they told him it had been at least fifteen days, he gasped then growled out a string of expletives.

Ms. Fitzsimmons made a face. Ev apologized. She turned to me. "Miss McCollum, I will ask you the same thing. In your own words, please."

I took much longer because so much more had happened to me and they interrupted a lot with questions, asking me to clarify things, or to describe something in more detail. At some point my voice became a little hoarse. Mr. Sharretts apologized to the table and a bottle of water appeared in front of each person, along with a bowl of water in front of me – presumably for Fudge who was still in my lap, and a larger one in front of the Rottweiler.

Once I'd finished my side of the story, I heard a baritone voice growl, "*Are you certain of your description of the wizard who sent the sleeping spell?*"

Ev's eyes widened to saucer-level. Why? No one's mouth had moved. The voice was in our heads – Ev's apparently included. I could commiserate. Having a voice in your head was quite startling until you got used to it.

"She is accurate in her description," Fudge said in a strong voice. This time Ev didn't move a muscle. Apparently, he couldn't hear Fudge. I'd have to ask about that – later.

"Do you know him, Waldo?" inquired Mr. Sharretts – out loud. Ev's eyes widened again as he looked at the Rottweiler, something akin to awe on his face.

"If he is as described then yes, I know him. He has a familiar – currently in chameleon form. I will have his location tracked and give it to you, should it be needed."

"I didn't see any lizard," I piped up. No one bothered to acknowledge my statement.

"I do not go with you everywhere, either. At least I did not until just recently and that is for a very specific purpose," Fudge chided me.

"Ed, please call in the team leader," Ms. Fitzsimmons requested.

Flashlight Man came into the room at his boss' bidding and proceeded to describe the scene they found. Apparently, it took them a little longer to find us than originally anticipated because someone had put a masking spell on the area. Although the familiar of one team member knew they were in the right area, they had a difficult time locating the hole in the ground. But I finally got my answer as to where we were.

"The prisoners were being held in an old air raid shelter built in 1942 by the then-owners of the property, who are apparently related to Miss Johannsen. According to tax records, the property has been abandoned long enough to be considered undeveloped. The cousin who pays the tax bill each year is currently being interviewed and I will report back with those results once we have them."

"Thank you. You may go," Mr. Bartz informed him.

"Miss McCollum, Mr. Angelich, Mr. Tremayne and Fudge, you are free to leave. We apologize for your distress. As soon as we have the complete results of our investigation, you will be informed of our decision. Mr. Bartz' team will convey you to your homes." I had all kinds of questions but Ms. Fitzsimmons' pronouncement brooked no "buts". The security guy opened the conference room doors for us. Flashlight Man and his buddy were waiting in the hall.

As the door closed, I heard a growled, *"While you were too slow in recognizing a threat, you acted quickly in contacting me as soon as you awoke. Well done, youngling,"* in my head. Youngling? Fudge? How old *was* Waldo, anyways?

"Much, much older than I am. If rumors are to be believed, he lived in Babylonia as a youngster."

"Much, much older than I am. If rumors are to be believed, he lived in Babylonia as a youngster."

Back down the elevator, back into the same SUV (still carrying a faint aroma of unwashed ogre along with the smell of citrus – someone had made an attempt at deodorizing), back to being crushed in the back seat because Gregory climbed in with me and Ev, and back to not being able to see a damned thing. Flashlight Man apologized once again. "Security," he said with a shrug.

When my eyesight cleared, I saw my apartment building with every single neighbor standing on the steps. I stepped out of the car to cries of "Welcome home!" and "Are you all right?" The two human men gave me grandfatherly hugs, the dwarf neighbor pinched my waist, and Elinda and Marge clucked over me like biddy hens.

"I will come over about noon and we can talk about everything, okay?" Gregory's voice cut through the neighbors' chatter.

That startled me. "You're still staying next door?" I asked.

"For two or three more days, at least. Ev is probably going to sleep that long. You will probably still be asleep when I knock on the door so go hit the sack." He gave me a little pat on the shoulder and with a "let the girl find her own bed" to everyone else, turned toward his own building.

I finally extricated myself from the small crowd and made my way down the steps to my own apartment. Once inside the closed and locked door, I allowed myself to cry. The last few days had been stressful, to say the least, and I was completely exhausted. I cried even harder when I finally saw a clock. It was after two in the morning. No wonder I was ready to fall asleep on my feet!

Pulling myself together as best I could, I stayed awake long enough to wash three-day old coffee from the pot and then put everything together fresh for whenever I woke up. Disdaining the thought of making an effort to put my clothes into the laundry hamper, I left them in a pile on the floor and crawled into my soft, warm, homey-smelling bed. Fudge wasted no time in making his nest in my hair. I don't think I felt him curl up.

True to his word, Gregory banged on my door promptly at noon the next day. As always, I'd woken with the sun but managed to go back to sleep after pulling the pillow out from underneath Fudge and over my head. I was only on my first cup of coffee. At least I'd thought to put on a bathrobe instead of wandering around the house in just my jammies.

"You look like hell warmed over," he said as I handed him a steaming mug.

"Gee, thanks. Good morning to you, too," I retorted. "What do you expect me to look like after the last couple of days?"

He grinned. "No different. So, you managed to not cause any earthquakes?"

I puffed up at that. Yes, I'd kept my temper under control. Truthfully? Not because I was concerned about hurting the Earth or anything. It was really because I was afraid of burying myself under a ton of rubble.

"The point being you *did*, without Fudge's help," Gregory smiled. "From your testimony last night, it sounds as if you're really getting the hang of things, and I am proud of you. You've known about your abilities for less than a month and you are already able to spin energy into a string. Now, I know you have hundreds of questions. Ask."

Where to begin? I tried to organize my thoughts into at least a semblance of an outline so I wouldn't be jumping from one subject to the next without exhausting the first one. I refilled our mugs and started a fresh pot while I was thinking. Gregory sat patiently waiting.

Once organized, I had a question in capital letters. "What will happen now?"

"The investigation isn't quite complete and I really can't speak for the Tribunal but I suspect they will find that no magical laws were broken." He held up his hand to forestall my objections.

"That is not to say that Marianna will go unpunished. The transcript from last night, along with some other evidence they collected will be turned over to the mundane authorities. Two counts of kidnapping plus attempted extortion and fraud will ensure she is taken out of society. Whether their psychiatric examination will show the mental instability necessary for her to be institutionalized, I don't know."

My mouth opened and he held up his hand again. "Believe it or not, the magical and mundane law enforcement arms work quite well together when the situation warrants. In this case, the trial has already been held and the beings you saw last night were her jury. Everything will be presented to a human judge who is aware of our procedures. He will sign all the mundane legal papers and she will quietly be sent to prison, if not a mental health facility. You and Ev will probably have to sign statements and that should happen today, if not tomorrow."

"What about you?" I asked.

He grinned. "I knew Ev was alive. After Atlanta, I devised a twenty-four-seven beacon charm for him. Before you ask, it's in a tattoo on his shoulder. I spelled the ink. That's probably why Marianna targeted me. Because I was behind wards before I had a chance to follow it, I could do nothing but sit and wait. Oh, and pay a barrister to represent my interests, just as one would do in a mundane case. As soon as Fudge contacted Waldo, I was released but kept old Blatherton around just in case something went wrong. I stayed at headquarters to keep an eye on what they were doing and to be there when you were brought in. It's all good."

"How can you be so calm about all this? I'd be freaking out if anyone accused me of murder and then once released, I'd be out for blood."

"I've seen *a lot* in my years. This isn't the first time I've had dealings with the Councils and probably won't be the last. Shit happens in our world, Amy, more so than the mundane world and if the television news is to be believed, that has its own share of bizarre happenings. You learn to go with the flow. Next question?"

I moved down to the next topic on my outline. "Why were all of the Councils involved?"

"Just as in the mundane world, this case was multi-jurisdictional. I'm a wizard, you're a witch and Fudge is a familiar. Fudge was just as kidnapped as you." He tilted his head, asking for my next question.

"Why did Marianna report you to the Witches' Council? Shouldn't she have gone to the Wizards' Council?"

"Yes, she should have but I don't think she's bright enough to have thought of that. Plus, Althea is located here in the Twin Cities whereas Howard lives in Chicago. But because it was Ev, you work for him and he rents office space from a witch, Althea kept hold of everything to protect your interests. Then when you went missing, it was definitely under the Witches' purview."

He sighed. "Howard, while a powerful wizard who plays politics well, is something of a namby-pamby when it comes to emergencies. Had Marianna gone to him in the first place, he probably would have dithered long enough for me to actually find Ev and disprove Marianna's accusations. Althea tends to get right to the heart of a problem and get whatever it is dealt with so she can move on.

"I may not have liked confinement but I knew with Althea and Ed on the case, it would get resolved quickly. I do not have the same confidence in Howard."

That jived with my initial impressions of both of them. Ms. Fitzsimmons acted like the decision-making executive she was. Mr. Sharretts, on the other hand, let her lead the questioning. On to the next topic.

"Waldo?"

"Ah, the old man," Gregory smiled. "As far as I know, Waldo is the oldest magical being on Earth. He not only heads the US Familiar Council but the international one, as well. His age and experience make him the most powerful familiar known. That's probably why he is capable of mind speech with anyone. I know it disconcerted Ev. That was fun."

"Who's familiar is he?"

"Althea's. If I understand correctly, he chooses his own witch or wizard, making that person quite special. It also means he heads the area council wherever he happens to be. Three hundred years ago or so, he was a rabbit with a wizard somewhere in the Ottoman Empire. Or so I'm told."

Interesting. A rabbit, then a Rottweiler. When Fudge woke up and was ready to be interrogated, I had some questions for him, too.

"How come you know about this headquarters place but Ev and I had to be magically blindfolded? And how come you could disable the wards?"

"Ev? Think about it. Would you want an ogre with a temper knowing where you worked? As for you, you're still young. And inquisitive. They don't need you snooping around where you don't belong. Think of it as one of those super-secret places the CIA has. Only those who need to know, do.

"I've also done some work for the Witches' Council in the past that necessitated my knowing where Althea's office is. Once my name was cleared, I was given back their trust and a password to let me through the ward guarding their holding cells. I'm sure if I worked at it, I could have completely disabled Ed's ward but why? That would just have angered them further."

He got up and refilled his coffee. He was just as caffeine-addicted as I was. "Ed's a strong wizard and the wards change, depending on who they have back there. I will remind you that those rooms are only the equivalent of a holding cell, not full-blown prison. *That* you never want to see."

I had a million more questions floating around my brain but couldn't seem to formulate a coherent thought. Even with the caffeine flowing through my veins, I was still tired. I also had to check email and respond to what I assumed would be multiple messages from my editor. And had to call Sally to let her know Ev and I were okay and ask what had happened at the office from her end. But one last query surfaced:

"What did she use to drug us? Do you know?"

This time instead of giving me one of his small smiles, he grimaced. "Opium. The team found where you had buried your food. There was enough in the scrambled eggs to knock Ev out so you would have gotten a snootful, too. Based on what Ev said, his meals always included a sauce or something liquid the opium could have been dissolved in and the taste disguised with strong seasoning.

"Your metabolism helped dispel a dose large enough to have killed a non-witch. But Ev doesn't have that kind of metabolism and had been dosed long enough that he will go through withdrawal. Healers are at his house and will help him through the worst of it. He should be well enough to work by Tuesday but he will not be a happy camper for probably a week."

Gregory downed the rest of his coffee and politely put his mug in the dishwasher. "I'm going to let you enjoy the rest of your Sunday. Wait for me to call before going into the office tomorrow. Although I think Ed will have everything wrapped up today, Marianna may still be there and I want to ensure she's gone before you go back. We will resume your lessons next Saturday."

I shut the door behind him and groaned. I had a week's respite then would be back to the schedule I *didn't* want … office work, writing *and* school. In the meantime, I knew my email inbox would be packed. I padded over to my desk and fired up the computer. While I waited, I thought I'd call Sally. It took me a few minutes of looking around before I realized my cell phone was probably still in my purse, which was probably still on the floor under my office desk. I looked on the bright side: it would be a quiet afternoon!

Chapter 22

Three hours later, I'd read and answered the bulk of my emails, eaten the rest of the food in my refrigerator and showered. Fudge hadn't moved a muscle since I'd risen shortly before noon and was still asleep on the bed. I thought he had a good idea so curled up on the couch to nap during the afternoon baseball game.

The next thing I knew, the sun was shining through the living room window and Fudge was a ball of warmth next to my stomach. Given that the sun set on the opposite side of the building, I knew it had to be morning. I'd slept about fourteen hours – on the couch – and my neck was confirming what the clock said. Normally, I'd be running a little late since I usually woke around five-thirty but since I was supposed to wait for Gregory's call before going into the office…

More likely Gregory's knocking at the door since any call would go to voice mail on an undoubtedly dead phone. I heaved a huge sigh as I made my way into the kitchen, attempting to work out the cricks in my neck. I hated waiting for coffee and if I didn't put it together and turn on the timer the night before, there was no immediate caffeine infusion.

Not knowing when that knock/call would come, I went through my morning routine as quickly as I could. By seven-thirty, I was dressed and ready to go but there was still no word from Gregory and I knew there would be hell to pay if I walked over to the office without his okay. I decided to use the time to my advantage.

"So Fudge, are you always a cat?"

"*No. I have been many animals in my lifetime.*"

"How do you decide what you're going to be? Do you push aside the animal's awareness? How does being a familiar work?"

I heard a sigh. "*I know you well enough to understand you will not let this go. The Council determines what animal will be appropriate for the witch or*

183

wizard it is going to be assigned to. A pregnant mother appropriate to the species is found and we inhabit the body before birth, just as the fetus or embryo would gain awareness. Therefore, we wake with the knowledge and habits inherent in that species. Circumstances are **arranged** *so the witch or wizard finds us. My current mother was a feral cat living behind a nearby restaurant and I picked a fight with the tom you chased away, arranging it so I would end up in your apartment.*

"As you have guessed, we have magical abilities of our own but we are limited in what we can do. It has something to do with the bond between us and our human. The stronger the human, the stronger our abilities. We also act as guardian and something of an encyclopedia for our human to reference. **That** *my human, is all I will say."*

"What happened to you when you ate the food? I know you were knocked out like I was but despite the fact that a cat would have died, you didn't. And how did you know it was the food and not the water?"

"As I said, we have magical abilities of our own and a familiar will not die unless its human does. I caused the poison in my system to become inert then I had to repair the damage it caused my respiratory system. It took some time and effort to do so. I knew it had to be in the food because the water tasted fine. Will you cease questioning, now?"

I didn't have a chance to ask anything more because there was a knock at my door. I admitted Gregory, who also was dressed for work in slacks rather than jeans. "Is it safe to go to the office?" I asked as I filled my travel mug.

"I tried calling but only got your voice mail. Why didn't you answer your phone?" Answering a question with a question was not a good way to start the day.

I explained about my phone and sarcastically added, "If I had my phone on me, don't you think I would have tried to use it sometime in those couple of days?"

"Point. Although you may not have had a signal that far down. Let's walk over to the office and see what a mess there might be."

"Is Marianna taken care of?" I really didn't want to confront the bitch again. My temper might not hold and Cassandra would kill me if I damaged the building.

"She was picked up at her home by the sheriff, with Ed's help, a couple of hours ago. Ed said she did not go quietly."

I closed and locked the door, and the three of us trooped up my stairs. "How's Ev?"

"Still sleeping, I believe. I spoke with George, the healer on duty, an hour ago. They are keeping him under as long as possible so he doesn't feel the worst effects of opium withdrawal. Not to mention avoiding his temper when he wakes up to find Marianna has not been zapped to the ether for what she has done."

I mused on that. Ev probably didn't want her evaporated (or whatever the ultimate punishment was for a magical person). Beating her to a bloody pulp, waiting for her to heal and then pummeling her again would be more his style. Ev had a vicious side to him that, thankfully, didn't show up very often.

Him still asleep was a good thing, too. I hated to think what the office was going to be like. Marianna had had two days to really muck things up. His temper would rear its ugly head unless I had a chance to sort things out. It was going to be a long day.

As we approached the office, Cassandra flew out of the deli and enveloped me in her bony embrace. "Are you okay? I'm so glad you're back. That Marianna is a real bitch. You'd better call Sally. She's been on the horn to me several times a day and is beside herself with worry, although I finally got her to calm down yesterday when I relayed the good news from Mom. Come on in. Let me get your usual latte. Gregory, hi. I'll get you a cup of coffee, too. Oh, and Fudge! I've got a special treat ready for you."

She finally came up for air and let me go. I laughed. It was good to have people worried about me. "I'm fine," I said as we followed her into the deli. "Well, as fine as I can be worrying about what kind of mess I'm going to walk into upstairs." The deli smells were so comforting…coffee, fresh-baked bread and pastries coupled with the tang of whatever stew Cassandra had on the stove. The deli was technically closed on Mondays but she usually had something cooking, either for the next day or a catering job.

After promising to call that evening to give her all the gory details, I headed upstairs with Fudge climbing next to me and Gregory bringing up the rear. I took a deep breath before trying to open the door. It was locked and my keys were in the same place as my phone.

"Allow me." Gregory handed me his coffee. He rummaged in his pocket, pulled out a key ring and inserted his copy into the lock. Nothing happened. "The bitch even changed the locks!" He grumbled. "No matter." A small strand of sparkling red energy threaded its way into the keyhole. I heard a "click" and Gregory turned the knob to open the door with a smile on his face.

I wanted to ask how he did that so effortlessly when Fudge and I had exhausted ourselves but what I saw nearly made me drop both cups of coffee. Not only had she changed the lock but she'd also very quickly redecorated. Gone was the serviceable furniture and Sally's old secretarial desk in the reception area. She'd replaced it all with Louis XIV-style stuff that was so ugly I almost choked. Sally's "desk" looked more like a boudoir table. No ogre would be able to sit on the chairs. Not only would they not be able to get their butts between the arms down to the seat but I was willing to bet the legs would break like twigs under their weight. I felt the tingle of magic permeating the room.

An "oh" escaped my lips. I walked with hesitation to my office and then let out a huge sigh. Marianna hadn't gotten around to that room, yet, and all *my* stuff was still there.

I heard Gregory say, "Holy shit" and raced out of my office into Ev's. Once again, the plain but comfortable furniture was gone and in its place was more of the same frou-frou crap, ogre-sized this time. "He *cannot* see this," Gregory growled.

"How did she do this so fast? It was only a couple of days," I moaned.

"Her wizard, probably. Go do what you need to do. I can take care of this but it will take a bit of time. It's just a transformation spell but a good one. I wonder how much she paid him? No man in his right mind would have done this." He started muttering as I walked back into the comfort of my office populated by cheap, mahogany-veneered fiberboard furniture. I'd just sat down and reached for my phone to plug it into the charger when the office phone rang. My day was starting.

"Good Morning, Angelich Security," I answered, attempting to make my voice bright and cheerful.

"Thank goodness you're all right," Sally yelled into my ear.

"Hey, don't yell," I answered. "I'm fine but unless Gregory works quickly, you won't be when you get here." I told her about the redecorating.

"She turned a security office into the front room of a bordello? I knew she was off her rocker but damn that's a bit much! Now that you're back, do I have a job again?"

When I gave her a virtual thumbs-up, she told me she'd be there shortly and hung up. I turned my attention to the voice mail and was puzzled when there were only three messages, all of them from over the weekend. I knew Marianna didn't have the password and the telephone company wouldn't have given her the time of day without tons of legal paperwork. It should have been overflowing. So what happened?

I encountered the same thing when I checked the main email inbox. Just the standard reports and a couple of queries. Nothing unusual. And despite Marianna's statement that she'd rearranged assignments, everything was as I'd left it. I was at a loss…until I checked my personal inbox.

It was filled with quick notes from clients and employees alike, all saying pretty much the same thing: "Got Sally's message and will comply. Please contact me with an explanation ASAP."

I couldn't wait for Sally to get in and tell me what she'd done. Whatever it was, she'd circumvented everything Marianna had planned – except for the décor, that is. Knowing I wasn't going to have to untangle a huge web of deceit, I happily settled into a normal morning of reading reports and making notes.

I'd just finished with the weekend reports and was about to turn my attention to bookkeeping when Sally walked in. I heard an expletive escape her mouth before she walked into my office and, tossing her purse on the floor, sat in my guest chair.

"That is *hideous*. With the computer monitor, there's no room to work on that damned desk. So I'm sharing yours until Gregory finishes."

I eyed her. "What did you do? I've got a boatload of emails in my inbox that say they got your message and everything seems to be status quo."

She grinned. "Marianna is apparently deficient in the technology department. When I got here on Thursday she told me you'd quit and I was fired. Since I knew she was lying, I left and called your cell from downstairs. When you didn't answer, I asked Cassandra where you were and she didn't know. So, I borrowed her computer, logged on up here and sent an email to both the client and employee distribution lists saying that Ev's girlfriend had gone crazy and to ignore *anything* coming from the company until they got word from either you or Ev personally.

"Then I went home and paced until Cassandra finally called me yesterday afternoon. I think you have a bunch of emails to answer off your personal address."

I went around the desk and hugged her. "Thank you for that. And how did you think of it? I never would have!"

"Well, how else do you mass-communicate nowadays? I didn't want her screwing anything up and the only way to prevent that was to have everyone ignore her." The phone rang and before I could get it, Sally reached over my desk and answered.

"It's for you." She handed me the phone and as I brought it to my ear, I heard her ask Gregory how much longer it was going to take him – she needed a proper desk.

"Amy, it's John. Is everything okay?" the voice on the other end said. "I got Sally's email on Thursday and then Marianna showed up at my party Friday night, claiming she was the new head of Angelich Security. What the hell happened?"

John Minton, agent-to-the-stars, was a long-time business associate of Ev's, and a vampire. He was old enough, I knew, to be awake most of the day and operated out of an office in his basement. Without going into too much detail, I described Marianna's behavior, then told him she'd kidnapped both of us but that we were free and she was in custody.

"Damn, that ogre gets himself into more trouble, doesn't he?" John chuckled. "He really does have poor taste in women."

John didn't know the half of it. No one outside a close circle knew about the prior kidnapping and it was going to stay that way. I let John think *all* Ev's problems stemmed from his love life. Assuring him that we were fine and that I expected Ev in the office the next day, I hung up.

Only to be told there was another call waiting for me on line two. This one was Omar, an ogre who was a friend of Ev's and a former guard who, although officially retired, helped out every now and again when scheduling got messed up.

I gave him essentially the same spiel as John, only this time telling him of the opium problem and the fact that Ev was recovering at home. What he said next floored me.

"Expect him in the office this afternoon. The healers can't really do much for him because they're magic and he's not. I'll bet you a shiny new nickel he's awake, feeling like crap but thinking it's a hangover and will be calling Gregory to come get him shortly. He won't remember that he hasn't had any booze in almost three weeks."

Just then, I heard the introductory notes of "Danse Macabre". That was Gregory's ringtone for Ev.

"You're right! I can tell he's calling Gregory right now. How did you know?"

Omar barked out a laugh. "Known him for over a hundred years. Stubborn doesn't even begin to describe him. Plus, he's been out of the office for over two weeks, is going to want every single detail of what's happened in his absence and then will go back to doing what he does best – talk to people. That'll be the best medicine for him anyways. It'll keep him distracted and not thinking about the broad. You're sure she's locked up?"

"Gregory says she is and I believe him. He knows more about all this legal stuff than I do."

"Gregory's a good man and well-connected. If he says you're good to go, you are. Tell Ev to call me when he gets a chance." Omar hung up.

"Ev wants to come into the office," Gregory said as he poked his head in my door. "I tried to talk him out of it but he insists. So I'm on my way to get him. I got *his* office looking normal but only Sally's desk. He's going to have a fit when he sees the chairs and coffee table."

I walked out into the reception area. Sally's desk was back to normal (which meant a duplicate of mine) but she was sitting in one of those flimsy arm chairs. She grimaced at Gregory. "Can't you do my chair before you leave? It's a real pain when I can't just turn from the desk over to the computer."

Gregory sighed. "He knows exactly how long it takes me to get there. We've made the trip often enough. But I believe once he sees the rest of it, he will forgive the extra few minutes. Get up."

Sally rose and moved over to stand by me. It was a pleasure to watch a master work – for me, at any rate. I watched as Gregory enveloped her chair in a web of his energy. It revealed another web underneath it in shades of gray and pale yellow. Rather sickly looking, actually. As I watched, Gregory's red energy systematically unwove the other spell, sort of like taking knitting apart. It took a couple of minutes but when the sparkles faded, Sally's normal office chair replaced the Louis XIV chair.

"That is so cool. Teach me?" I gushed while Sally said a heartfelt "thank you" and sat back down.

"It's not a spell you will be able to do for awhile but yes, when you're ready, I will show it to you. Now, I *have* to go. I will see you two in a bit."

Sally and I spent the rest of the morning on the phone – her answering and forwarding worried calls to me. It seemed never-ending. I said as little as possible but apparently, just the fact that they'd called the office and were talking to *me* was enough to assuage most fears. I knew once Ev got in and was able to talk to folks himself that things would quickly get back to normal.

Cassandra, the sweetheart that she is, brought up beef stew and homemade bread for both of our lunches, along with some minced raw beef for Fudge. "You're eating what was supposed to be my dinner but since I know things are hectic up here, I'll eat leftovers tonight," she told me with a grin. "I do expect that phone call after dinner. I want to hear everything, including today. Ev's reaction to the furnishings is going to be interesting."

"You'll probably hear it downstairs," I said around mouthfuls. "It's really too bad he couldn't wait until tomorrow to come in. Gregory would've had it put back to rights by then."

"Do you want me to call Tommy? He can probably finish what Gregory started."

Nice though it was, I declined the offer. "They'll be here shortly so I doubt Tommy would be able to finish it off in time. Besides, I'm kind of looking forward to it. We had a talk about his taste in women. I want him to see the collateral damage."

She grinned. "In that case, I'm off. Just like you, I have paperwork to do. Talk to you tonight."

I looked down at my cat, who was just finishing off his lunch. "You're being awfully quiet. Is everything okay?"

"*Of course it is. I was just contemplating whether I should continue shadowing you. You seem to have everything under control. Although, what Cassandra gives me is much tastier than the commercial food you buy. Can we have pizza tonight?*"

He was right. I was doing very well at controlling my temper, if I did say so myself. On the other hand, I rather liked having him in the office. It seemed more…comfortable. On the *other* hand, Ev probably wouldn't like it. An office mascot wasn't his style. On the *other* hand…

I heard a roar and then "What the hell is this crap?" from the reception area, followed by Sally's laugh and Gregory's explanation.

"Get this shit back to normal, will ya?" I knew Ev was talking to Gregory. "Amy, my office, now!"

Oh yes. Things were back to normal. But working for an ogre, I knew normality would probably be short-lived.

About the Author

A semi-retired accountant, Master Herbalist, author and witch, Deborah J. "DJ" Martin is the author of non-fiction books about herbs as well as the Ogre's Assistant series.

She abandoned frozen Minnesota many moons ago and now lives in the woods of the southern Appalachian Mountains with her husband, four cats and numerous woodland creatures. If you can't find DJ in the garden or visiting her grandchildren, check Twitter @authordjmartin, Facebook www.facebook.com/authordjmartin, or her website www.authordjmartin.com